THE PROF CROFT SERIES

PREQUELS
Book of Souls

Siren Call

MAIN SERIES
Demon Moon

Blood Deal

Purge City

Death Mage

Black Luck

Power Game

Druid Bond

MORE COMING!

DEATH MAGE

A Prof Croft Novel

by

Brad Magnarella

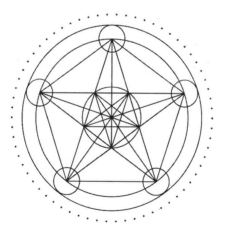

Death Mage

A Prof Croft Novel

ISBN-13: 978-154699-788-7
ISBN-10: 1-546-99788-1

Cover art by Damon Freeman
www.damonza.com

First Edition

Printed in the U.S.A.

For my parents

1

I staggered, my breaths coming in ragged gasps. The trees on all sides looked the same, their trunks mottled with black mushrooms. I had been in this dank forest before. I couldn't remember when, but it was familiar enough that I knew no matter where I ran, I would only end up more lost.

A chill wracked my five-year-old body as I stopped and tilted my head back. The gray sky through the branches was dimming with the coming night. When darkness fell, the creatures would emerge.

Horrid creatures.

I broke into another blind sprint. "Mom!" I shouted.

I had no memory of my mother. I knew her only as a framed photograph in the living room of Grandpa and Nana's house: a young woman looking out a large window, half her face in light, the other in shadow, one hand resting over the pregnant swell of her stomach. Even so, I sensed in my gut that she was the only one who could help me out of this place.

"Mom!" I called again.

Someone, or something, answered, a whisper that slithered from the trees to my right: *"Everson."*

The alien voice was familiar to me in the same way the forest was. The voice would chase me and eventually catch me. I veered away from it, heart slamming. The voice echoed from all sides now.

"Everson ... verson ... son."

I pumped my arms and legs as hard as I could. Around me the forest darkened. The mushrooms on the trees clotted into thick, dripping tumors. When I tried to shout for help, the spores that swept through the air closed my throat. Only a gasping whine squeezed out.

"Everson," the voice whispered again, seeming to reach for me. *"Join us."*

I arched my back, breaking through fresh whirlwinds of spores and into a deepening gloom. The air stunk of rot. Wet leaves squished underfoot. Sinister shadows moved among the trees.

"Everson ... verson ... son."

"Stay away," I gasped, batting through the crowding branches.

The forest pressed in until I had to slow down to pick my way through. I climbed between a pair of trees, the toadstools on their trunks bursting like pustules, and became stuck. I grunted and squirmed, but the space between the trees narrowed further, holding me fast.

No! I thought desperately.

But this was what always happened, wasn't it?

"Join us," the voice whispered behind me. *"Join the cluster."*

I peeked back. The forest shimmered in an insane dance of colors. Below, something wet was climbing my legs, but the colors around me, dazzling shades of pink, orange, and emerald, were too intense. I couldn't stop looking at them. In hungry squelches, the wetness inched up my stomach. When it reached my shoulders, I could see it in my peripheral vision: a gelatinous black fungus. I went to wipe it away, but I couldn't move my arms.

"Join the cluster, Everson," the voice whispered. *"Become one."*

The fungus squelched up my neck and spread over my jaw like a beard.

In revulsion, I tore my gaze from the shimmering colors. "Mother!" I shouted.

The word tapped into an undercurrent of power. Crackling energy broke from the sound, radiating out in all directions. The fungus blew from my body. The trees that held me parted.

I stumbled backward and fell into a quiet clearing.

"Everson," someone said—but not the whispering voice this time.

I turned and rose. At the center of the clearing stood my mother. A sob of relief hiccuped from my chest, and I ran toward her. Except for her lean stomach, she looked identical to the woman in the picture: half in shadow, hair brushed over one shoulder. But she wasn't smiling in the same faint way. Not like in the framed photo. Not like in the other...

Dreams, I thought suddenly. *I'm inside a recurring dream.*

I peered around, expecting the dreamscape to dissolve away, but the clearing only became more vivid. A scattering of stately trees creaked and rustled in a light breeze. Birds chirped in their branches. I looked back at my mother, a sea of emotions roiling inside me. I'd never known her, and yet she'd become a powerful force in my imagination.

By the time I arrived in front of her, I was a grown man—which had never happened before. No, the dream-child me would typically hug her leg and tell her I was lost. She would say that she'd found me, that she would always find me. She would then point the way from the forest, but tell me I had to make the journey on my own. She always said this with a smile.

Now, concern lines creased her young face. Before I could ask what was wrong, she embraced me firmly and stood back.

"Everson, there isn't much time. The Whisperer is coming through."

"The Whisperer," I echoed, remembering what Chicory had told me. An ancient entity older than the First Saints and Demons, the Whisperer had corrupted the youngest of Saint Michael's nine children. It had turned Lich against his siblings. In a one-man rebellion, Lich had nearly overthrown the Order. He was eventually defeated, the fissure to the Whisperer sealed. But centuries later, Marlow, a man the Order believed to be my father, discovered Lich's book. He replicated the spells, reopening the fissure to the ancient being.

"How do we stop it?" I asked.

My mother's eyes hardened as she looked past me. "Run," she said, but not in answer to my question.

I turned and realized we were no longer in a clearing, but a large stone room, the trees becoming pillars. Familiar-looking figures in black robes strode toward us, all chanting a single word.

"Traitor ... traitor ... traitor."

Backing in front of my mother, I groped for my cane, my amulet, my revolver, but I wasn't carrying any of them. I had witnessed this scene before, in Lady Bastet's scrying globe: the scene of my mother's execution.

"Leave her alone!" I shouted.

My mother spoke near my ear. "Don't let him know about you."

"Who?" I asked.

"Did you really think you could keep up this shameful duplicity without me finding out?" A tall figure emerged through the others, the face beneath his hood an ornate gold mask. The mouth frowned in judgment while the dark, vacant eyeholes seemed to stare through me.

Marlow.

"I did nothing," my mother told him.

Marlow stopped in front of us. "Nothing? You joined the Front as a sworn rebel against tyranny. You pledged your allegiance, your *life*. Only for us to learn that you're a plant for the Order."

"That's a lie," she said.

The mage drew a wand that smelled of elderwood. "Then you shouldn't have a problem submitting to a mind flaying."

"I will submit to nothing," my mother said.

I lunged for Marlow's wand, but my hands passed through it. He seemed not to notice me.

"Then you are admitting guilt," he said.

"If that's what you want to believe," she replied.

"*Vigore!*" I shouted, thrusting my palms toward him. The energy of the force blast rippled through the dreamscape. When it subsided, everything wavered still again, and Marlow remained in front of us.

"It's the truth, traitor," he said, raising his wand. "And you know the penalty."

"Do your worst."

"No!" I shouted.

The force from the mage's wand threw my mother against a stone pillar. She grunted in pain. Marlow spoke another Word, and vines writhed up through cracks in the floor, binding my mother to the pillar. An especially thick tendril wrapped her throat, making her gag.

"It didn't have to end this way, Eve," he said before turning to the others. "Behold the penalty for treachery. Death by fire."

Yes, I had witnessed this scene before, from inside my mother's memory. I had felt her fear, her pain. I raced back to her, intent on pulling the vines away. But when I reached for the thick tendril encircling her throat, my hands passed through it, as they'd done with the wand. Sadness filled my mother's eyes as they met mine.

"What can I do?" I pled. "How can I help you?"

A whisper strained from her lips.

"What?" I asked, leaning closer.

I love you, Everson, she mouthed.

"*Fuoco!*" Marlow shouted behind me.

Flames exploded from the floor, engulfing my mother and throwing me backward. I pulled off my shirt and ran at the fire to beat it out. But the fire became a reflection in a gold mask, and I was standing in front of Marlow, staring up at him, and he was suddenly huge.

Run, my mother had said. *Don't let him know about you.*

The rest of the room darkened as the mage's face canted down. Beyond the eyeholes, a pair of lights burned in recognition. His hand shot out and seized my wrist. A cold, aching power emanated from his grip. I strained against him, but I was a small child again.

"You've come to join us," he whispered.

I shook my head, unable to make a sound.

"To join the cluster." He lifted me from my feet.

When our faces were even, Marlow reached for his mask, which continued to glisten with the fire that consumed my mother. Terror paralyzed me as he began to pull the mask away. I didn't want to see his face ... but a part of me had to, had to know if this person was my father.

"To become one," he whispered.

Metal separated from skin in a wet squelching.

"Everson ... verson ... son."

2

A pair of ochre-green eyes stared at me through the dark. I snort-gasped and tried to flail back. Tendrils were wrapping my arms, my torso. I heaved with my legs. The top of my head hit something solid.

A snort sounded. "Nice to see you, too."

"Tabitha?" I shook my arms from the sheets and slid a hand between the headboard and my aching crown. I fought to get my bearings. I'd been in a dream, Marlow about to remove his gold mask. My cat calling my name must have awakened me. I looked around. Except for a crescent moon high in the window, the room was dark. "What time is it?"

Her eyes blinked slowly. "Apparently, time for you to moan in your sleep again."

I set my legs over the side of the bed and sat up, the horror of the dream still prickling through me. "Sorry about that."

"I told you to lay off the magic before bed."

"Oh, should I have eaten my weight in rib eye instead?"

Tabitha narrowed her eyes at me, then thudded down from the end table and sauntered back to her ottoman beneath the window. It wasn't as comfortable as her divan at home—a fact she reminded me of daily—but we weren't at home. The week before, Chicory had loaded us into his Volkswagen Rabbit and driven us to a safe house in New Jersey, an unassuming blue affair across the Hudson River. "To train you for your mission," he'd explained. Though all he'd done so far was fuss inside his lab, shooing me away anytime I asked what he was up to. Even now, I could hear his muttering voice down the hallway.

"I'm not the one having nightmares," Tabitha said as she arranged herself into a large mound. "The fifth in five nights?"

"Yeah ... except this one was different." I coughed to clear my sleep-clogged throat. "I was lost in a forest again, calling for my mother. She found me, but this time she didn't have any answers. Couldn't tell me how to get out. She just told me to run and hide."

"Run from what?" Tabitha asked.

"From whom," I said, remembering the way the flames had danced in the gold mask. "The Death Mage."

"He *is* all you've been talking about for the last week. No wonder you're having nightmares." She yawned and smacked her lips. "Waking everyone up," she added in a mutter, eyelids sliding closed.

"Everyone meaning you?" I asked testily. "Look, I don't know if it's occurred to you, but I'm shipping out soon, and there's a chance—hell, maybe a good chance—I won't be coming back."

The thought lanced through me. As punishment for willingly giving my blood to Lady Bastet, which was then stolen by Marlow, the Order was mandating that I infiltrate Marlow's hideout and destroy Lich's book. It was a daunting mission. Magic-users more powerful than me had tried and failed, my mother among them. Hence Marlow's title as Death Mage.

"I *will* miss you darling," Tabitha said sleepily.

"Gee, thanks for the vote of confidence."

"But you'll come back."

I looked at my cat, her words catching me by surprise. As a succubus, Tabitha had no divine powers, but hope flickered inside me anyway. "Oh yeah?" I asked cautiously.

"You always do."

She had a point. Whether it was facing demon lords or ancient vampires, I had a knack for pulling something out of my hat at the last moment. Part of that went with being a magic-user. We carried a "luck quotient," as Chicory called it. More accurately, we lived in a symbiotic relationship with magic, a force keen on being moved and manipulated. That relationship often led to sudden insights and synchronicities, especially in times of acute stress.

But this challenge felt different—probably because I would be going up against another wizard, one much more powerful than I was. Not only would his luck quotient cancel mine, it would likely exceed it.

"We'll see," I said.

Instead of answering, Tabitha began to snore. Shaking my

head, I stood and paced the crowded guest bedroom. While Chicory had spent the last week shut up in his lab, I'd been devoting my time to reading from a selection of books he'd picked out as well as performing exercises to enable me to channel more energy. I did feel stronger, more focused, but would it be enough?

I stopped at the window and released a shaky breath. The dream, my mother's warning to run...

The Order wouldn't be sending you if they thought you would fail, I reminded myself. Granted, they were a mysterious, often confounding, organization whose directives didn't make a ton of sense sometimes—all right, *most* times—and yet they had been around for several millennia, suggesting they possessed more than an inkling of what they were doing.

You're going to have to trust their judgment.

I looked toward the door as a burst of expletives sounded from down the hallway.

I would also have to trust that Chicory knew what the hell he was doing.

I emerged from my room the next morning and shouted in alarm. Across the dining room table, my cane was in a state of complete disassembly. I ran up to examine the carnage. The blade was without a hilt. The white opal stone, usually embedded in the staff, sat on the table's very edge. And a set of copper metal bands I hadn't even known belonged to the cane were scattered everywhere.

"My sword and staff!"

"Crotchety old thing," Chicory said, as though in agreement. My round little mentor appeared from the kitchen, blowing the steam from the mouth of a coffee mug. His mop of gray hair looked messier than usual, telling me he probably hadn't slept. Is this what he'd been doing all night?

"It—it's in pieces," I said, still not believing what I was seeing. Thin wood shavings covered the round table in what appeared to have been a failed attempt to inscribe runes into the staff. The result was chicken scratch.

Chicory took a loud slurp of coffee as he arrived beside me. "I've been trying to give her a needed upgrade, but she's not having it. Had to get a little rough with her, I'm afraid."

"You're going to put it back together, right?"

"Eventually," he replied, scratching his stubbly chin. "I'll let her sit like this for another day, see if that doesn't temper her spirits. Rest assured, once I complete the upgrade, she'll be better than new. And *you'll* be better prepared. I never intentionally send a wizard to his death. Well, unless so ordered."

"I appreciate that," I muttered, my gaze drifting over the scattered parts again. After ten years, the sword and staff had become extensions of me. I couldn't imagine life without them.

"There's extra coffee, if you'd like some," my mentor said.

Dragging a hand through my bed head, I gave a begrudging nod and shuffled into the kitchen. "Speaking of preparations," I called as I poured myself a mug of the strong-smelling brew. "When are we going to get into serious training? I mean, I appreciate the exercises and extra reading, but it's not the same as having spells slung at you. Blood spells, in particular."

The coffee shook slightly in the mug as I lifted it to my lips.

The blood Marlow had stolen could be used to cast any number of spells, including a death spell. Though such spells *did* take time to prepare, that time was getting shorter.

"Yes, yes, we'll get to that," Chicory replied irritably. "More important now is outfitting you."

I returned to the dining room, where my mentor was frowning over the cane parts, his bushy gray eyebrows nearly touching in the center. *Did* he know how to reassemble it? I pulled out a chair and sat.

"Do you mind going over what that will entail?" I asked.

"Outfitting you?" He lifted the tail of his corduroy sports jacket and hopped onto the chair across from me. I didn't have to look to know his feet weren't touching the floor. "Well, the first step is establishing a link to Marlow's hideout and getting you inside. No sense teaching you magic you won't be in a position to use. To that end, I've been tinkering with your blood."

"My blood?"

He took another loud slurp of coffee. We'd only been living together for a week, and already his habits were starting to annoy me. Besides the slurping, there was his singing in a loud baritone in the bathroom as well as his tendency to leave dirty dishes everywhere. A small plate with a half-eaten slice of toast and curdled eggs from two days before sat precariously on a window sill. Were it not for the magic surrounding the old house, flies would be everywhere.

"I drew a small sample from your neck the other night while you were asleep," Chicory said. "I didn't think you'd mind."

"Not at all," I replied thinly.

"Now, if Marlow *is* your father, about half of your magic came

13

from him. The other half from your mother, of course. Fortunately, the qualities of the two are different enough that I've been able to set up a process that will distill out your mother's portion. Once that process is complete, I'll add an enhancer and re-infuse the blood back into you. For a time, your magical aura will be a dead ringer for Marlow's."

"He won't be able to sense me?" I asked, thinking about the hunting spell I'd cast a couple of weeks before. A hunting spell Marlow had detected and counterspelled, possessing Tabitha in the process. With three fingers, I traced the healed claw marks along my right cheek.

"No," Chicory confirmed. "You'll be able to penetrate whatever defenses he's employed and enter his domain unscathed." He hesitated for a beat. "Again, assuming he's your father."

"And once I'm inside?"

"Well, ah…" He coughed into his fist. "We'll have a plan, of course."

"Which is?"

Chicory grumbled for a moment before his eyes seemed to sparkle with an idea. "You said you wanted to get on with your training? Advance to something a little more challenging?"

"Yeah…" I answered carefully.

"Well, I think I have just the thing."

He bustled away from the table and returned a moment later with a badly refolded map. He spread it over the table, knocking some of the cane parts onto the floor. My molars ground together as I stood and came around. The map showed a grid of Manhattan, circa 1930.

"A bit outdated," I remarked.

"Here," he said, tapping a brown square just north of Central Park.

I read the label. "Grace Cathedral?"

"They have a robe on exhibit believed to have been worn by John the Baptist. In fact, it belonged to a Franciscan monk who came along some centuries later, but the point here is that the robe is special. You see, this monk was a descendant of Saint Michael's, but never told. An oversight by the Order, no doubt. In any case, he was an ascetic who took a vow of silence early in his career. For more than half a century, he walked softly and said not a word. It got to the point that his fellow monks were barely even aware he existed."

"And those qualities became instilled in the robe," I said, guessing the rest.

"Exactly, and can be bestowed upon the wearer." He looked pointedly at me.

"Wait, you're asking me to *steal* the robe from the church?"

"Borrow it," Chicory countered. "We'll put a duplicate in its place so as not to alarm anyone. When you complete your mission, we'll return the original."

"*If* I complete my mission. But what happened to all of your highbrow talk about following the rules? Acting responsibly? Not taking stupid risks? Doesn't this sort of fly in the face of that?"

"Acting responsibly as a *wizard*," Chicory said. "You're not being asked to summon or perform dark magic. To the contrary, you're obtaining an item in the service of *opposing* such magic. An item that belongs just as much to the Order as to the Church, after all."

I considered that for a moment. "And if I'm caught?"

"Well, that's sort of the point of the exercise, isn't it? To not let that happen."

I sighed. I had just gotten back into the good graces of the city and press, not to mention Detective Vega. And now Chicory was suggesting I return to Manhattan and commit grand larceny. "Do I even need the robe?" I asked. "Why can't I just mix a stealth potion?"

Chicory's eyebrows seemed to bristle as he glared up at me. "Because stealth potions wear off, and then mentors have to get involved." I remembered him rescuing me from the band of angry druids in north Central Park the year before. "Not true for magical artifacts," he finished.

"I don't have my sword and staff." I looked dismally at the scattered parts.

"I'll give you a wand that's ready for use. Less obtrusive and it won't set off the metal detectors."

The wand was among several magical items that had come into the vampire Arnaud's possession. Following the vampire's demise, I acquired the items from the NYPD and gave them to Chicory for cleaning and redistributing. I still hadn't mentioned Arnaud's story about Grandpa stealing artifacts from fellow magic-users during the war against the Inquisition. I didn't fully believe the story and wanted to check it out for myself—assuming the Death Mage didn't kill me first. My more immediate concern, though, was staying out of jail.

"Well, what about the church threshold?" I said lamely. "It's not going to care for my, you know, companion."

"Who?"

"Thelonious, my incubus."

"Hmm, then you better get an invite," Chicory replied, refolding the map. The ungainly way he went about the job, ripping several of the seams, didn't give me much hope for my cane.

"How?" I asked.

"That's for you to figure out. Again, part of the point of the exercise."

"Great," I muttered.

3

When Detective Vega raised her eyes from the scatter of files across her desk, the sharp concentration lines that converged in the center of her brow let out slightly. "Croft," she said. "What's up?"

I showed her a plain cup of coffee I'd bought from a street vendor and placed it on the corner of her desk. "Gourmet roast."

She smiled wryly. "Thanks."

"Am I catching you at a bad time?"

"Other than between a stabbing in Spanish Harlem and a double murder in Chelsea?" Fatigue weighed on her face when she shrugged. "At least we know it's not ghouls. Do you have something for me besides coffee?"

I noticed that several files on the right side of her desk were for the Lady Bastet murder investigation. Officially, the mystic's murder remained an open case. I had promised to keep Vega in the loop on my end of things, which was the least I could do after the help she'd given me that summer. At some point she and I had stopped being adversaries and become allies. She had even introduced me to her son the last time I'd seen her.

"Well, sort of part update, part request," I said.

She frowned as she smoothed back her black hair and refastened her ponytail. "Why do I get the feeling I'm not going to like this?"

"Which do you want first?" I asked, closing the door to the din of the Homicide unit. I took a seat in one of the folding metal chairs that faced her desk.

"Update," she said.

"The suspect's name is Marlow Stokes."

Vega jotted it down. "Contact info?"

"That I don't know."

She raised her eyes, pen poised above the file.

"He's not exactly ... in this world," I said.

"I'm listening."

I took a deep breath, reminding myself that Vega's openness to the supernatural had come a long way in the last year. "Are you familiar with the Greenbrier Bunker?" I asked.

"That place in West Virginia? Yeah, it was a relocation center for the U.S. Congress when we thought the nukes were gonna fly. The reps would survive while the rest of us got radiated."

"Look at you," I said. "Miss U.S. History. Well, once upon a time, the magical order to which I belong faced a similar existential threat. They also built a bunker, but in a parallel world—a thought pocket."

"A thought what?"

"An imagined place made real, if that makes any sense. The thought pocket was called the Refuge. From the way my mentor describes it, the Refuge was modeled on a Grecian palace. Elevated, fortified, easy to defend. Anyway, the Order got through the crisis, but the Refuge sort of hung out in this parallel space."

"And that's where Marlow is?"

I nodded. "He accessed the Refuge decades ago and turned its powerful defenses to his own purposes. The Elders—the ones who created the thought pocket—can't even access it."

"I'll take your word for it," Vega said. "So he's beyond our reach?"

"Maybe not. I told you that he murdered my mother, right? What I didn't know at the time was that he might also be my father."

Vega's eyes widened. "Are you serious?"

"Yeah, as if I needed a Freudian complex on top of everything else," I muttered. "To make a long story short, because of my similarity to Marlow's makeup, I might be able to slip inside the Refuge."

"And then what?"

"Well, I'm going to try to destroy an arcane book from which he gets his power. Once that's done, he'll be defenseless. My order will apprehend him and put him to death." I nodded at the file for Lady Bastet. "If it helps you close the case, I'll be willing to testify on the match between the residue found at the murder scene and Marlow's brand of magic."

"You don't sound very hopeful," she said.

"No? After the vampire situation, the DA's office seems a lot more open to—"

"Not about the case," Vega interrupted. "The whole thing."

"What do you mean?"

She set her pen down. "I'm getting to know you, Croft. When you believe in something, you get this intense, almost manic, look in your eyes. And when you don't, your eyes just sort of go dead."

I wasn't aware of that about myself, but now that she mentioned it, I felt a weight in the backs of my eyes, like they were trying to retreat into my skull. "Just a lot of unknowns right now, I guess. Whether or not he's my father, Marlow is a powerful mage. And I'm, well, a wizard with about a decade of practice under my belt—pre-puberty in magical terms."

"Isn't your order helping you?"

"There is someone training me, yeah," I said, picturing Chicory frowning down at the hopeless mess of my cane across the table. "But that sort of brings me to the request part."

"You mean the part I'm not going to like?"

"Probably not."

She sighed and circled a hand for me to continue.

"All right, on the *off* chance I'm arrested tonight..." I rubbed the back of my neck. "...can I count on you to intervene?"

She lowered her voice to a harsh whisper. "Arrested for what?"

I told her about the magical robe and how it could offer me extra protection inside the Refuge. "It'll only be for a few days," I assured her. "And there will be a replica up in the meantime."

"Stealing is stealing, Croft. But stealing from a *church*?"

"Believe me, I know how sketchy that sounds. Especially since it's my denomination. But with Marlow trying to call forth an evil being, I don't think the Church would disapprove. I mean, one of the reasons churches came into being was to act as a bastion against this very thing."

"Then why not just ask them for the robe?"

"I do have an in with the Bishop of New York," I said, thinking about the official I'd rescued from the demon Sathanus the year before, "but the request would still have to go up the chain. We're talking weeks or months, and with no guarantee they'd agree to the request."

"And you don't have weeks or months." Vega lifted the coffee from the corner of her desk, cracked the plastic tab from the lid, and took a sip. She grimaced and set the cup back down. "All right."

I blinked. "Really?"

But I didn't need to ask. I could tell by her expression that my reasoning had gotten through. Though the law remained important to Vega, she had seen enough to know the law had to be weighed against larger threats—ones the mundane world wouldn't necessarily understand.

I smiled in appreciation.

"Just do me a favor," she said.

"Sure. Anything."

"Don't get caught."

4

I stood on the edge of a knot of tourists, several of them snapping photos of Grace Cathedral's hand-carved front doors. "...modeled on the doors from its sister cathedral in Florence," our guide was saying. I had signed up for the final church tour of the day, a one-hour in and out, though I wasn't planning on coming out. Not with this group, anyway.

I made a small adjustment to my fake beard—a precaution so no one would recognize me as the "star" of the mayor's recent eradication campaign—and listened as the guide finished her explanation of the doors.

"Now, if you'll follow me, we're going to go inside and look at the famous mural above the doorway."

I followed the group as far as the threshold. A curtain of energy hummed and pushed against me. I felt Thelonious shift uncomfortably, a dark spirit shying from the divine light.

"Are you coming?" the guide asked impatiently.

She was standing just beyond the threshold, the tour group filing through a metal detector behind her.

"Oh, can I come in?" I asked.

"You paid for the tour, right?"

I showed her my wrist band. "So that means I can...?" I gestured toward the door.

Her eyes widened as though to ask, *What are you, some kind of idiot?*

Just give me a goddamned invite, lady, I thought.

"Yes?" I prompted, gesturing at the door again.

"Um, *yeah.*"

That was all it took. With the personal invitation, the threshold relented. Though the ley energy here wasn't as powerful as at St. Martin's, I felt a portion of my wizarding power fall away as I stepped through the doorway and into the church's cool interior. Fortunately, I was only planning on casting a few minor invocations.

"All right," the guide said when we had reassembled beyond security. "If you'll look straight overhead, you'll see..."

I tuned her out as I got my bearings. We were standing at one end of the massive nave. At the other end, past a series of statues, stained-glass windows, and iron gates that led onto side chapels, was the main altar. According to Chicory, the robe was on display near the altar, in the baptistery.

It took almost the full hour to arrive at the baptistery, a small, circular room with a child-sized baptism pool on a raised dais at its center. The water gurgled quietly as we moved past the stone basin.

"If you'll direct your attention up here," the guide said, "we have a very special piece on exhibit."

I stopped looking for a pump in the basin and raised my eyes to the far wall. About halfway up, between a pair of colorful saints images and encased in glass, was a tattered brown cassock, sleeves spread.

"The robe belonged to John the Baptist and was worn during his later years," the guide continued. "For centuries, it was believed to bestow divine protection on the wearer."

Let's hope you're right about that second bit, I thought.

As the tourists moved in to snap photos, I peered around. The security appeared basic. Iron gate over the entranceway, one security camera, probably an alarm on the glass case. I imagined that a guard or two patrolled at night, but the acoustics of the cathedral would make them easy to keep track of. Underneath my shirt, tucked into the back of my pants, was the ringer.

The tour ended back in the nave with an invitation for us to look around on our own for the final few minutes. Stepping into a shadowy archway, I pulled the wand from my inside coat pocket and whispered, *"Oscurare."* Even though the church threshold had sheared off a chunk of my power, the wand had no trouble absorbing the immediate light, deepening the shadows around me.

I proceeded through the archway and into an empty corridor.

Before long, I found an unlocked office that looked as though it was being used for storage. I slipped inside, hunkered into a corner behind a stack of chairs, and waited for nightfall.

From my hiding place, I listened to the cathedral being secured, the echoes of doors closing, locks snapping home. I waited another hour for a wandering set of footsteps to taper off before I emerged with one of the chairs. The patrolling guard had taken up a post beside the front door. Music with an electronic beat issued from a phone whose screen outlined his face in white light.

Thank God for youth culture, I thought.

I eased across the nave and into the entrance to the baptistery, beyond the guard's view. A padlock secured the iron gate. One of these days I was going to have to learn how to pick these things. I inserted the wand into the padlock's shackle and whispered, *"Vigore."*

The expansion of energy was enough to crack a shaft. I waited to ensure the guard hadn't been alerted to the sound before removing the lock and opening the well-oiled gate. Beyond a short entranceway stood the stone pool, the robe mounted on the wall beyond. I expanded my wizard's aura until something crackled inside the security camera above me. Then, calling light to the wand, I rounded the pool and placed the chair beneath the mounted robe.

"Still can't believe Chicory is having me do this," I muttered.

As I climbed onto the chair, a series of bubbles glugged from the pool behind me. I looked back, causing the chair to teeter. Nothing there. Swearing, I retrained my focus on the glass box.

A simple plunger lock with a lever arm held the box closed. Yeah, definitely alarmed. I swelled out my wizard's aura again. Behind the backing against which the robe was mounted, something popped and sent up a drift of smoke. I just had to hope it was the final piece of security. I had already worked out an escape plan for if things went sideways. And if sideways veered south, Vega was monitoring a police scanner, ready to intervene.

But Chicory was right. If I was going to have a chance against Marlow, I needed the robe.

Aiming the wand at the plunger lock, I whispered a force invocation. With a scrape, the lever slid out and the door opened. A hay-like odor of old fabric seeped out.

Easy enough.

I listened to ensure no one was coming before pulling out a series of slender pins that mounted the robe to the backing. How long would it take for someone to notice the camera was out of commission and come to investigate? I didn't know, nor did I intend to find out.

A minute later I slung the robe over a shoulder and began pinning up the ringer. It was my bathrobe, actually. Chicory had cast a powerful veiling spell over it to mimic the robe of John the Baptist, down to the frayed threads. As long as no one touched it, the ringer would pass muster.

I was leaning back to examine my work, when something tapped my right shoulder. I jerked my head around, but there was no one there. Another tap, this one on my left shoulder. Then on the crown of my head. When I touched the spot, my fingers came away moist.

What the...?

Droplets pattered the floor around me. I craned my neck back and nearly shouted in alarm. Wavering above me was a giant snake's head, saliva dripping from its jaw. No, not saliva—baptism water. The entire creature was composed of it, its slender neck ending at the pool from which it had quietly risen.

A water elemental? I thought dumbly. *In a church?*

I dropped from the chair. With a sputtering hiss, the elemental drew back its head to strike.

I aimed the wand at it and whispered, *"Vigore!"*

The creature curled deftly around the brunt of the blast and dove down. Seizing the chair, I heaved it up like a shield. The impact of the elemental's head cracked the chair's wooden seat and knocked me to the ground. Water sprayed everywhere.

I scrambled to my feet, slipping and sliding toward the pool's other side. The elemental curled around and headed me off. It undulated from side to side in a menacing dance.

With my wand poised at ear level, I held out the fractured chair like a lion tamer and backed from the elemental. The moisture on the floor was already compromising my magic. If the elemental got a hold of me and dragged me into the pool, I was a dead man.

Even so, the analytical part of my mind was still trying to determine what it was doing here. Elementals made excellent guards, sure, and this one was taking its duties as seriously as cancer, but they also required powerful magic to manifest. I highly doubted the church kept a wizard on staff, given the institution's suspicious stance toward the arcane.

The elemental started into another sputtering hiss.

"Vigore!" I whispered harshly, this time directing the force at the pool.

The water erupted in a large spout, pulling the elemental with it. When the water collided into the ornate dome high above, the snake burst apart and rained down in a sudden cloudburst. I hoisted the chair overhead like an umbrella, sparing myself a drenching.

An elemental separated from its source was a doomed elemental, and this one was no exception—regardless of how it had come to be. I splashed through the water and retrieved the robe of John the Baptist from the floor. I then climbed onto the broken chair and closed the glass box. Channeling a force strong enough to swing the lever arm closed took more time, thanks to the moisture, but within moments, it was done. Exhaling, I stepped off the chair.

Wasn't pretty, I thought, *but mission accomplished.*

My gaze dropped to my feet. In the second it took me to realize the floor was no longer soaked, the elemental coiled around my upper body, crushing my arms to my sides and the air from my lungs. Magic had reconstituted the damned thing. The elemental made two more swift passes around me and jerked me into the air, its face hissing inches from mine.

"Respingere!" I grunted, not caring who heard me now.

Energy sputtered through my mental prism but expired before it could manifest from the wand I held in a death grip.

Shit.

The elemental upended me. I kicked my legs as the room swooped. In the next moment, I was being plunged headfirst into the pool. I tried to twist and break free, but the elemental held me fast, the top of my head grinding against stone.

Think, think, think!

If the elemental hadn't come from the church, what did that leave? The robe of John the Baptist possessed magical properties, but the origin story—a monk and a vow of silence—didn't jibe with a guardian creature. Not as Chicory had told it, anyway, though my mentor's disorganized nature hardly inspired confidence. I remembered looking skeptically at the wand he'd given me that morning, despite his insistence that he'd wiped it of any lingering magic. "As much of it as I could, anyway," he'd added before tossing it to me. Hadn't he said it once belonged to a seafaring wizard? A light went off in my head.

Oh, I don't frigging believe this.

I tightened my right fist to make sure the wand was still in my grip. I then worked my left hand over and grasped the casting end. As black spots began to crowd the edges of my vision, I bowed the wand away from my body. I grunted with the effort, forearms trembling—

Snap!

My inverted body dropped, and I fell from the pool. I landed on the floor of the baptistery on my back with a hard splash. I remained there for several moments, gasping and stunned. The culprit came to a rest in two pieces beside my head: the damned wand. Its nearness to water and a magical item, in this case the robe, had triggered the wand to call up a guardian elemental, something the seafaring wizard had no doubt trained it to do.

"Wiped it of any lingering magic, my ass," I muttered, pushing myself to my feet.

Chicory was going to get an earful when I got back. Right now, though, footsteps were approaching from the nave. I retrieved the pieces of wand, jammed them into my back pocket, and lifted the dripping robe. A light swam around the entranceway. A moment later, the guard appeared, his flashlight performing a sweep across the room.

I stiffened, having just pulled the robe on, hoping to hell it was as good as advertised.

I watched the guard unclasp the holster holding his firearm. He lifted his walkie-talkie to his mouth. "I need everyone down here," he said. "Something's going on in the baptistery."

Well, wonderful.

But when the guard's light reached me, it kept moving, hesitating on the pool before flashing back to the toppled chair. "The lock on the gate's busted," he went on, "and there's a chair in here."

"Security cam's out, too," a voice squawked back. *"Exhibit still there?"*

The guard's light shone on the ringer. "Still here," he confirmed.

"All right, we're calling the NYPD. Let them handle it."

"Fine by me," the guard said.

He gave the baptistery a final pass with his flashlight, the beam hitting me once more, before leaving. I followed him to the front of the church. The guard hadn't the faintest idea I was on his heels. When he opened the door ten minutes later to let the police in—Officers Dempsey and Dipinski, it turned out—I slipped out behind them and pattered down the cathedral steps to the street.

I waited until I was a few blocks from the cathedral before I removed the robe and stuffed it into the back of my pants under my shirt. The heist had been a success, but my confidence was in the crapper. A mission that should have been a cinch had nearly gotten me killed.

With a wave and sharp whistle, I flagged down a cab.

Time to give Chicory that earful.

5

"How did it go?" Chicory called as I slammed the front door behind me.

Around the corner from the entranceway, I found my mentor in the living room in a plush chair, stocking feet poking out from beneath Tabitha's bulk. He was stroking my cat's purring head while taking contented puffs from his pipe. An orange-tinted liqueur sat in a snifter on the end table. The thought that he had been relaxing while I was being dunked in a baptistery pool by a water serpent raised my hackles even more.

"How did it go?" I asked. "Other than nearly *drowning?*"

"Drowning?" Chicory's brow furrowed. "What are you talking about?"

I pulled the wand from my pocket and tossed the two pieces onto the coffee table. "This thing that you assured me was ready for use had enough frigging magic in it to call up a water elemental."

He frowned down at the broken instrument. "But you retrieved the robe?"

Sighing, I pulled it from the back of my pants and dropped it beside the wand pieces.

His face brightened. "Well, there you go! All's well that ends well, as I like to say."

"No, Chicory, you're not hearing me. You gave me a magical item that nearly killed me."

"And you said you wanted a test."

I glared at him. "Are you telling me you did that intentionally?"

He took another puff from his pipe, seeming to consider the question. "Well, no, actually," he said after a moment. "I must have missed some enchantment or other—but that's beside the point. The point is that I can't prepare you for every eventuality. If you're to have any chance, you'll need to improvise on the fly. Tonight was good practice. You encountered an unexpected challenge and you overcame it. Well done. Though I do wish you wouldn't have snapped it in half. Wands of that caliber are incredibly hard to come by."

"Look," I said, deciding to let the wand comment go, "it's one thing for the unexpected to come from your opponent, but it's a hell of another for it to come from your own corner man."

"I'm not following, I'm afraid."

I pressed my lips together. "Any day now I'm going to be sent to the Refuge. Up until tonight I was afraid that I wouldn't be prepared, that it would be a one-way trip. But now I'm terrified the preparations are going to kill me before the Death Mage ever gets a crack. I mean, you send me off with a cursed wand, my staff and sword are in pieces, and the blood you're distilling ... I'm seriously starting to wonder if I should let you inject me with it."

Chicory chuckled.

"What the hell's so funny?"

He set his pipe down beside the snifter, lifted Tabitha with both hands, resettled her on the ottoman, and stood and waved for me to follow.

"Where are we going?" I asked in annoyance.

"Just come along."

Muttering, I followed him to a door beneath the staircase to the attic. For the past week, I'd assumed it led onto a closet, but when Chicory opened it, I could see the top of a wooden staircase descending into darkness. The thought of going underground stretched the skin over my chest like a drum and thinned my breaths.

"I'm not going down there."

"Believe me," he said, "you'll want to."

Chicory waved his wand, manifesting a bobbing orb of white light. Chicory gave the wand another flick, and the orb began to descend the stairwell, illuminating the way. Chicory followed it down. I fell in behind him despite my anger, his words just vague enough to entice me.

After a steep descent of several sharp turns, the stairwell deposited us onto the dirt floor of a basement. Chicory flicked the wand again, and the orb rose to a set of rafters fifteen feet above us, suffusing the entire basement with light. The space was surprisingly large and must have extended beyond the house to the borders of the property.

"I believe that belongs to you," Chicory said.

I looked at where he nodded. About twenty feet ahead of us lay Grandpa's cane.

"It's in one piece," I observed.

"Aye."

But does it still work? I thought dubiously.

I arrived at the cane, almost afraid to touch it. I lifted it from the ground and tested the white opal with a finger. It was re-embedded in the wood, as secure as ever. Runes lined the staff. Not the chicken scratch I'd seen that morning, but ornate letters, each one seeming to hum with power. I drew a breath and pulled the sword from the staff. The blade released easily. I made a few thrusts and cuts, half expecting the blade to feel loose or clunky—or even fall off—but it was as light and sturdy as I remembered, and even seemed to zing.

"I'll be damned," I muttered. "You actually fixed it."

And hadn't he said something about an enhancement?

"En garde!" Chicory shouted.

I wheeled just as a fireball ripped from his wand and sped toward my head. With no time to invoke a shield, I threw the staff up into its path. As the fireball collided into it, I squinted my eyes closed to the flames that would inevitably break past it and burn my face. But the fireball just ... stopped. It was as though the staff had sucked it right out of the air.

I was bringing the staff around to examine it when two more fireballs flew from Chicory's wand. More confident now, I slashed the staff high and low, batting them out of existence.

When I saw Chicory preparing to cast again, I ran at him. *"Protezione,"* I called.

Light swelled from the staff's opal. Enhanced by the runes, the light crackled into a formidable shield around me. A succession of fireballs broke against it, each one vanishing into harmless wisps of smoke. When I was mere feet from Chicory, he unleashed a firestorm.

I waited patiently for the flames gushing around me to expire, then touched the tip of my blade to his paunch.

"Got you," I said.

Chicory cocked a bushy eyebrow. "Oh?"

A low moan sounded behind me. I wheeled to find a pair of earth elementals pushing themselves up from the ground using fists the size of wrecking balls. Powerful magic wavered around them.

"Oh, c'mon," I complained.

"No shields this time," Chicory said, snatching my staff away.

"Wha—?" When I turned to reclaim the staff, Chicory was already gone.

Oh, no he didn't.

But he had, and I was on my own. The ground shook as the elementals, fully formed, plodded toward me.

"Vigore!" I shouted, aiming my sword at the nearer one.

The force that erupted from the blade broke around the elemental's protection, barely slowing it. Its partner came around my other side, blocking the stairwell as an escape route. I backed away, sword held out. I considered invoking a stronger force blast, but it would only deplete my power. I feinted right and attempted to dart left, but they herded me into a corner. Next, I tried to split them, but the closer elemental planted a leg in front of me. The other one raised a giant fist.

"Chicory?" I called shakily. "A little help?"

This was part of my training, I got it. But without my staff, and these guys encased in powerful defensive magic, I couldn't do a blasted thing. I expected Chicory to suspend the session, show me what I'd done wrong, and then run it again so I could apply what he'd taught me.

Instead, the elemental's arm descended like a falling tree.

"Whoa!" I shouted, raising my sword in an attempt to parry the heavy blow.

I felt almost nothing as the blade cleaved the elemental's arm in two. The magic holding the creature together dispersed with a shudder, its decaying fist raining chunks of earth over me. The rest of its body collapsed into a mound. The other elemental looked at its fallen partner and backed away.

"Not so big and moany now, are you?" I said, advancing on it.

When the elemental turned to run, I launched the sword like a javelin. The blade pierced the center of its back. The elemental fell forward and, under its own momentum, scattered across the floor.

"Booya!" I shouted.

I looked around to make sure Chicory wasn't throwing anything else at me before kneeling to unearth the sword. When I stood again, my mentor was in front of me, handing me back my staff.

"Do you still doubt me?" he asked.

I held the sword and staff out at arm's length and examined them. "What in the hell did you do to these?"

"To the staff, I added an absorption charm. Like a sponge, it will soak up any offensive magic that hits it."

"*Any* magic?" I asked, examining the runes more closely now.

"Well, up to a point. But it's a powerful charm. Those weren't first-level fire balls I was slinging at you. Even better, the magic it absorbs will bolster the staff's defensive capabilities."

I remembered the strength of my shield and nodded. "What about the sword?"

"That was easier, actually." His eyes shifted with mine to the blade. "Your grandfather had imbued it with an enchantment that can cleave through magic. You'd just yet to channel enough of your energy through it to access it. The enchantment is very powerful, and it works just as well on magical defenses as on magical beings. Again, to a point."

I moved the sword and staff through the air, my anger at Chicory almost forgotten as I considered their enhanced power. Throw in the robe of John the Baptist, and I was beginning to feel like I had a chance.

"So if I get close enough to Marlow to strike..." I started.

"The blade could destroy him, yes," Chicory said. "But we'd rather you use it to destroy Lich's book."

I slotted the blade back into the staff. "Why?"

"Because the book is the source of Marlow's power, and it's safer."

I thought of the man who had set fire to my mother and then watched as the flames consumed her. I imagined him smiling behind the gold mask, reveling in the power he held over a woman he'd rendered defenseless, a woman who had birthed his child. The anger inside me rose up more fiercely than the remembered flames. I grunted as I imagined myself driving the blade through Marlow's chest, giving it a hard twist. *Surprise, you piece of—*

"Everson," Chicory said sharply, bringing me back. "You talked about your fear of being ill prepared? It's much worse to be fully prepared only to be subverted by revenge. Find and destroy the book. Depriving the mage of his power will be justice enough. We'll take care of the rest."

"And if he tries to stop me?" I said, my knuckles still white around the sword's hilt.

"Just don't go looking for a fight, is what I'm saying." Chicory's eyes seemed to waver.

"There's something you're not telling me."

"I'm getting there," he said irritably. "When you asked earlier, I said the blade *could* destroy him."

"What, now you're saying it can't?"

"Would you stop and listen? It could if he gives you a chance to use it against him. Whisperer magic is different from the magic you're accustomed to up here."

"Different how?"

"When Lich nearly overthrew his siblings, it wasn't a simple matter of being more powerful than the others. No, he tapped into a magic that bends minds, shapes thoughts. Whisperer magic. Lich made his siblings see what wasn't there. Believe what wasn't real. He turned them against one another, nearly driving them insane in the process. Were it not for the oldest Elder, who was able to resist the magic, Lich would have destroyed them all."

"What about the staff?" I asked.

"The staff will absorb common magic. However, if Marlow or his followers get inside your head, all bets are off."

"Oh," I said, my confidence flagging again.

"That's why we're telling you to focus on the book. With the distilled blood, you'll be able to access the Refuge and slip past any wards. With the robe of John the Baptist you'll evade detection. With the staff, you'll frustrate magical attacks. And with the sword, you'll destroy the book. You need never face Marlow."

"Just wish you would've told me about Whisperer magic sooner."

"Would you rather I had told you when you still believed the preparations for the mission would kill you?"

He had a point. "So how would I even know if I encountered Whisperer magic?"

A shadow seemed to pass over Chicory's face. "That's the thing, Everson. There's no good way to know."

"What do you mean?"

We had been walking back toward the staircase, and now he stopped and sat on one of the bottom steps. I stood facing him. The orb of light arrived above us and sputtered quietly. While waiting for Chicory to answer, I couldn't help but appreciate the power he wielded—summoning fireballs and elementals, all while maintaining an illumination orb, and with almost no effort. I'd given him less credit as a magic-user than he deserved.

"If you allow them inside your head," he said, "they'll invert reality, turning the ugliest lies into the most enchanting truths. No matter what you do, you won't be able to see your way out. Only the strongest magic can penetrate it. Elder magic."

"What's the point of them using magic?" I asked. "Why wouldn't they just kill me?"

"They'll first try to subvert you. How do you think Marlow built his army of resistance? Your mother was an exception, convincing

Marlow she'd joined the rebellion willingly. An intercepted communication tipped him off." He looked over at me with sober eyes. "I'm sorry to bring her up again, Everson. But your mother's sacrifice is the reason the Order was able to learn as much about Marlow and the Front as it did. Marlow took a huge risk emerging from his hiding to murder Lady Bastet in his attempt to keep the truth from you, from us."

I nodded, understanding that was why there had been no signs of resistance at the murder scene. Marlow had infiltrated the mystic's mind with Whisperer magic before cutting her throat and then ripping her cats' heads from their bodies to make the crime look like the work of werewolves. He'd then shape-shifted into a cat and fled the scene as I was arriving.

"Why didn't Marlow kill me too?" I asked. "He had a chance."

Chicory sighed. "We've been wondering the same. Perhaps he believed the murder would be enough to throw you off his scent." My mentor's voice turned darker. "Or maybe he has plans to use you down the road."

I remembered the chilling voice from the nightmare.

Join us, Everson. Join the cluster. Become one.

Everson ... verson ... son.

"And we must remember," Chicory said, "Marlow is controlled by the Whisperer, a being as old as the universe. If you think the Elders are hard to read, well…" His chuckle was without humor. "There's no telling that creature's plans."

"Hey, sorry for giving you crap upstairs. I just…"

"It's daunting, I know," he said. "But feeling better, are we?"

I considered the magical robe, the enhanced sword and staff, Chicory's warning about not confronting Marlow. "I am, yeah," I admitted. "When will the blood be ready?"

"Another week, I imagine," Chicory replied, pushing himself to his feet. "And now that we have you outfitted, we'll spend the remaining time in simulations, preparing you for the task ahead. How does that sound?"

"Best news I've heard today," I said.

6

A week later I was back in the basement, staring down at the casting circle Chicory had created. It wasn't large, but it was sophisticated, featuring several sigils I'd never seen before. Beneath the orb of light overhead, metal shavings glittered in the circle's earthen grooves.

"Let's have a look at you," Chicory said, turning me toward him.

His curmudgeon's lips curled and fussed as he looked me up and down. I'd dressed as he'd instructed: a dark shirt and pants with enough pockets to hold several spell items. I'd draped the tattered robe of John the Baptist over my right forearm. Around my waist was a belt to secure my sword cane. When Chicory's gaze fell to my running shoes, he gave a critical grunt but said nothing.

"How are you feeling?" he asked, eyes returning to mine.

"Honestly? Like I'm about to hurl all over the casting circle."

"Nerves, hm? Just remember what we practiced."

I nodded, going back over the last week of training, a week in which everything seemed to come together. The books Chicory had had me read, the exercises to grow my casting prism, the enhanced weapons. Combining these with my mentor's instructions, I'd been able to steal past complex defenses, elude or slay a variety of creatures, and dispel potent magic. Indeed, it seemed as though I'd grown more as a wizard during that time than in the ten years prior.

"This is going to sting a little."

Before I realized what he was doing, Chicory had my elbow in his grip and was sticking the needle of a copper syringe into the crook of my arm. I flinched at the bite. Chicory depressed the plunger, and the bluish blood in the glass tube disappeared inside me.

He removed the needle and held his thumb over the injection site. As he chanted softly, I felt the distilled blood diffusing through me, my father's essence displacing my mother's.

After a minute, he stepped back and nodded. "You're ready."

I took a steadying breath and stepped into the casting circle. This was it. When I turned to face Chicory, I noticed that Tabitha had come down, her green eyes swimming through the gloom outside the orb's light. She sauntered up and rubbed her body against Chicory's leg.

"Don't give him a hard time while I'm away," I said.

She snorted. "Compared to the drills you put me through, this is going to be a vacation."

I shook my head before addressing Chicory. "Thanks for looking after her."

"Not a problem." He checked his pocket watch. "It's almost dusk, though. We need to start the ritual while the barrier between our realms is thinnest." From a jacket pocket, he produced a black book and opened it. While he wet his thumb and leafed through the pages, I reviewed the plan in my mind, up to finding and destroying Lich's book. A frightening thought hit me.

"Wait!" I said. "How am I going to get back?"

"Ah, yes," Chicory said as though he'd forgotten something minor. He reached forward and mashed his thumb between my brows. A small bolt of energy pierced my forebrain and smoldered behind my eyes and deep in my ears. A bonding spell. "There," he said, stepping back again. "When you're ready to come home, concentrate as hard as you can, and I'll retrieve you."

"Great," I said, wondering what would have happened if I hadn't said anything.

"And if this works, if Marlow is your father, I *will* see you again. You're as reckless as a child sometimes, but you're more than capable. You've proven that this week."

"Thanks." And I meant it.

Aiming his wand at the circle, Chicory uttered a Word. The circle glowed white and closed around me. Beyond the hum of energy, his lips moved as he read from a book of the First Order.

Tabitha watched with bored eyes.

I smiled back at her even as a lump swelled in my throat. I had to remind myself that if Marlow was not my father, the blood that coursed inside me wouldn't allow me past his defenses. I would be repelled back here. Which meant the tide of emotions I was feeling at the prospect of never seeing Tabitha or Chicory again would be for nothing.

I was just beginning to settle into that thought when I realized I was no longer in the basement.

Except for a slight tingling, there had been no warning. One moment I was standing in Chicory's casting circle, the next, I was in a forest. A cold breeze carrying a stench of decay batted my hair and clacked the branches overhead. Beyond a low ceiling of ashen clouds, the sun was setting. Or rather *a* sun was setting. I wasn't in our world anymore. I was inside the Refuge.

Which means the Death Mage is my father.

The knowledge didn't bowl me over. Ever since Chicory had told me of the Order's suspicion, a part of me had begun to accept it as truth. Nana's story about my father being a hippie had never jibed, not in my child's mind and even less so when I discovered my magic as an adult. My grandparents were trying to protect me, God love them. This explained from what.

Stuffing down a swirl of emotions, I checked my belt and patted my various pockets. Everything had made the journey with me.

"Let's go ahead and put you on, then," I whispered, donning the robe of John the Baptist.

As had happened in the cathedral, a quiet descended over me and calmed my thumping heart. I peered around. The dark forest looked uniform in all directions, reminding me of my recurring dream. But I wasn't a powerless child and I didn't plan to wander aimlessly.

I had a target.

Kneeling, I wiped out a small circular area in the forest floor. The carpet of rotten leaves hid jelly-covered toadstools, which I wiped away, too. With my sword, I scratched my family's casting circle into the earth and filled the grooves with copper filings. I then produced a Ziploc bag from one of my pockets and upended it over the circle. A clump of cat hair landed in its center—hair which held Marlow's casting residue from when he'd murdered Lady Bastet.

A current of fear wormed through me. The last time I had cast through the hair, Marlow had sensed me. He'd attacked me. This time, Chicory assured me, he couldn't. The distilled blood that had delivered me to the Refuge would veil me from Marlow's detection.

Hope to hell Chicory's right.

"Cerrare," I said, closing the circle.

I incanted then, my staff aimed at the hair. The clump of hair shifted and rolled, sending up smoke, which the staff's orb inhaled. I braced for a counterattack, but none came. Within moments, the staff was tugging me from the circle, in a direction opposite from where the sun had set.

He's here.

Planting a foot against the tug, I returned what remained of the hair to the bag, pocketed it, and then broke the circle and covered it with debris. Veiled or not, I couldn't get careless. The cane pulled me past trees, toward the man who had killed my mother.

Not to confront him, I reminded myself as black anger smoldered inside me. *To find Lich's book.*

Before long, the forest thinned and opened onto a wide plain. A rocky hill rose from its center, an ancient palace at its plateaued pinnacle. Though impressive, the scene was hardly the stuff of postcards. The palace was made of black stone, the columned stories that stood atop one another unwieldy and wicked looking. Here and there firelight burned in windows.

Looks like someone's home.

I scanned the open plain around the palace for guards. Instead, I spotted the silhouettes of what looked like large, hunchbacked dogs. Wargs, I realized, vicious predators with keen senses of sight and smell. Marlow was using them as an outer ring of security.

I checked to ensure my robe was secure around me before stepping from the trees and toward the palace. I moved quickly and quietly, keeping track of the wargs as I went. There were at least two dozen of them patrolling the large plain. Every so often, one would stop and raise a ragged muzzle before resuming its patrol.

Realizing I was on a collision course with one of the wargs, I crouched, retreated several steps, and held still. The approaching patrol was the size of a small rhino, its hair dark and bristly. Harsh breaths huffed from its wet muzzle.

When it got to within twenty feet of me, the creature stopped and raised its head. I stiffened. A jelly-like substance dripped from the warg's face. Bald patches showed over its coat, where the same substance appeared to have corroded through. The warg's face waxed toward me, toadstools ringing its glowing eyes like blackheads. Could it sense me?

I tightened my grip on my sword, debating whether or not to strike before the warg could send up an alarm. With a final snuff, the warg lowered his head again and resumed patrolling.

Exhaling, I set my sights on a staircase that climbed to a wall surrounding the palace complex. I had considered circling the hill to search for a more concealed way up, but I didn't like how the warg had looked in my direction. And the way that stuff was eating into its face...

I grimaced and hurried my pace.

Near the staircase, I opened my wizard's senses. The approach looked clear, but a ward protected the staircase in a field of barbed energy. I followed a path up to it. The energy crackled and spit. My enhanced blade might cleave it, but without Marlow knowing? No, better to leave the ward intact and trust that the distillation of blood would fool it.

I was bracing myself to step through when something rammed into my side.

I stumbled into a backpedal from the largest warg I'd ever seen. It crouched onto its haunches, equally startled. The warg must have doubled back on its patrol.

Now, it came sniffing forward. When I stepped to one side, it pivoted toward me, a growl shaking the thick foam over its fangs. The damned thing could sense me. When I inhaled what smelled like spores, I imagined them communicating back to the toadstools and slimy fungi that covered the warg's face, their root-like threads penetrating its canine brain, whispering to it.

I took a quick look around. Two more wargs were approaching, eyes glowing a sickly green through the darkness. I gauged the distance to the staircase—about fifteen feet away—but the large warg had cut me off. With my sword held out, I slid the staff into my belt and dug into my pockets.

Where are you?

At last my fingers encountered the golf-ball sized rocks. Coughing grenades. I pulled one out and whispered, *"Attivare."* The rock tingled as the magic at its core came to life.

I turned and hurled the grenade as far from the palace as I could. With a bark, the large warg charged me. I pivoted and brought my sword around, twisting my grip so the flat of the blade caught it instead of the edge. Metal rang against the side of the warg's head. The beast stumbled past me and ate dirt.

I backed toward the staircase as the warg recovered and wheeled. The skin over one half of its face had shorn off, revealing plates of bone.

Fifty yards away, the grenade landed, releasing a burst of human coughing. The other two wargs that had been closing in on me turned and sprinted toward the fake sound. The large warg looked over its shoulder, then back in my direction. It took two stalking steps forward.

Go, dammit. Go with the others.

The warg moved its sniffing head from side to side, as though no longer sure where I was. Maybe the result of half the fungi being wiped from its face. I switched to an underhanded grip, ready to thrust the blade up into the warg's heart if it lunged again.

Its glowing gaze roamed all around me.

At last the creature released a snort and sprinted off to join the others.

I let out a trembling sigh and hurried past the defensive ward. A searing heat broke through me, but thanks to the blood match, my magic remained intact. I started up the steps. Very soon I realized that the palace complex wasn't composed of black stone, but covered in black mold.

On the dwindling plain below, the wargs resumed their patrols. I didn't slow until I reached a landing that ended at the defensive wall. My staff tugged me toward a large door that hummed with locking magic. My sword could cleave it, but would that send up an alarm?

I scanned the rampart high above. I couldn't see anyone—or anything—patrolling its length. The dome of protective energy that extended over the palace looked to be identical to the ward at the base of the hill. It would let me through.

Judging the wall to be about twenty feet high, I took several steps back, sword aimed down. With a running start, I whispered, *"Forza dura!"*

The energy from the sword erupted against the landing and launched me up. As the cold air rushed past my ears, I saw that I was short. Afraid of overshooting the wall, I'd gone too soft. At the height of my parabola, I stretched out an arm and managed to catch the lip of the rampart. My body banged against the wall, but I held on, working my fingers into a slimy groove in the stonework. I threw my sword arm over and heaved myself the rest of the way onto the rampart. As I fell, I broke through the second ward in another searing wave.

I bit back a grunt and lay panting. I was alone on the walkway and, by all appearances, still hidden. Above me, the columned palace teetered into the night sky. I stood and looked down. Far below, a courtyard led onto a lower level of the palace. But the hunting spell was tugging me in the direction of a guard tower farther along the rampart.

I entered the square tower through a low archway and descended a spiral staircase. Though torches burned in brackets in the wall, the shut-in air carried a stench of rot. After one flight, I left the stairs and crept down a covered walkway. It soon opened onto a large columned room, the hunting spell tugging me toward a doorway on its far side. Halfway across the room, I stopped cold.

I knew this place.

The large column to my right was black at its base, but not from mold. I knelt down to examine it more closely. The cracks in the floor that radiated from the column held bits of gray ash.

This is it, I thought in numb certainty. *The site of my mother's execution.*

I rested my head against the column's cold stone. Despite having experienced my mother's death in Lady Bastet's scrying globe, despite the event having been confirmed by Chicory, being here, now, in the same spot, made it real in a way those experiences hadn't. My heart broke as I remembered the way her cracked lips had shaped her final words.

I love you, Everson.

"I'm here to finish what you started," I whispered, blinking back tears.

A gargling voice made me turn. A pair of black-robed figures were entering through the far doorway. I rose slowly and, tamping down the hunting spell, gripped my sword and staff.

Were you among them? I asked silently of the two. *Among the ones who called my mother a traitor? Who hurt her? Who stood here and watched her execution?*

Anger tightened my grip until it hurt.

The book, a more rational part of my mind whispered urgently. *You're here to find and destroy the book. Do anything that raises an alarm, and you can kiss the mission goodbye.*

That seemed to work. Forcing down my anger, I moved behind the column as the robed figures came closer, continuing their gargling exchange. I was preparing to let them pass when, deep inside their hoods, torchlight glistened over large, inhuman eyes. Fish's eyes.

Revulsion turned to fresh rage.

You were there, I decided, lips trembling. *Both of you. And you watched her burn.*

With an anguished cry, I swung my blade at the nearer figure's head.

7

The blade flashed, ripped through fabric and flesh, and came out the other side on a gout of dark fluid. Something wet thudded to the stone floor and rolled over. I glanced down to find large, vacant eyes staring up at me from a scaly face covered in the same fungi I'd seen on the wargs.

The creature's companion let out a sputtering shriek and jumped back. Before it could get a fix on me, I drove the sword into its gut. The blade seemed to break through an exoskeleton. I lifted the hilt with both hands. The creature gargled, the hood falling back from its face. A pair of vile fish's eyes searched around in vain before seeming to settle on me.

"I can play judge and jury too," I grunted.

The blade broke through the creature's breastplate and cleaved its heart. I yanked the blade back, depositing the creature beside its headless companion. I then stared down at the two of them for several moments, panting in the horror and exhilaration of what I'd just done.

I dragged their bodies into a dark corner of the room and dusted the main floor with dragon sand. A whispered *"fuoco"* ignited the sand, evaporating the trails of fluid and hiding evidence of the slaughter. No other creatures had come to investigate, suggesting no alarms had been raised.

Need to keep my anger in check from now on, though, I thought as I cleaned my blade on the side of my pants. It had been the dual shock of standing in the same spot where my mother had been slain and then suddenly seeing the creatures who had participated in the act. Still, I didn't know how these things communicated with one another. If it was through the fungal growth that seemed to coat everyone and everything, word of the attack could reach others.

I restored the hunting spell. As it pulled me toward the far doorway, I wondered about the two I'd just slain. I had thought the Front was a splinter group of magic-users, of humans. But those fish eyes... Was that what decades of worshiping the Whisperer had done? Devolved them?

The hunting spell led me down a corridor and up several flights of stairs. More robed figures appeared, their cadence telling me news of their murdered companions had not reached them. I eased into shadows until they passed and their gargling voices receded away.

In another flight, my cane jerked me from the stairwell and

into a small courtyard on the top level of the palace. Cold wind blew around me. From a building opposite me, low chanting sounded. I stiffened as one voice climbed above the others. The forceful yanks of my cane notwithstanding, I knew the voice belonged to Marlow. The Death Mage.

My heart surged into a full sprint as I canceled the hunting spell, pulled my cane into sword and staff, and crept across the courtyard. The building was tall and narrow, moldy columns bracketing a doorway through which greenish firelight glowed. I edged along a shadow beside the doorway and peered inside, the robe of John the Baptist concealing me.

The altar-like room featured a rectangular pool of water at its center. Statues of what looked like gods and goddesses—the original saints, most likely—rose along the perimeter of the room to act as pillars. But the statues, along with the rest of the room, were covered in a gunk that dangled in thick ropes and dripped over the twenty or so robed figures chanting around the pool below.

My gaze followed the pool to the far end where a tall figure presided over the chanting, one arm raised. The green flames that rose from the pyres on either side of him glistened from a gold mask inside his hood. My stomach clenched into a nauseous fist.

It's him.

I picked up the chanting as I watched him. The words were nonsensical, but they evoked visceral sensations of death and decay. At the end of the verse, something stirred inside the pool's foul waters. Another elemental? I could just make out a viscous web-work of black energy that seemed to unite the chanters to whatever lurked below the waters.

The Whisperer, I realized. *This is the ritual that opens the portal.* It was work Lich had begun centuries before and that Marlow had resumed upon finding his book. The larger the portal, the more powerful Marlow and the Front would become, and the more likely they would be to defeat the Order.

Ultimately, the Whisperer itself would emerge.

My eyes fell back to the pool in time to see a tentacle lash up before disappearing into the depths again. Beyond the pool, Marlow dropped his hand momentarily before raising it and resuming the chant.

A charge shot through me. *A book. He just turned the page of a book.* I eased forward, squinting. Yes, it was hard to see, but it was there, his black robe almost camouflaging the tome he palmed at his chest, tendrils of dark magic twisting from its pages.

Okay, I thought, *deep breaths.*

I slid my staff into my belt and reached into a pocket until I encountered a vial. A light shake told me it was the dragon sand. With a trembling hand, I loosened the cap. I doubted Marlow kept the book on him twenty four-seven. I could hold out for a more opportune moment, but with a pair of corpses downstairs waiting to be discovered, the risk felt too great.

I had to strike now.

I gauged the distance to the book and aimed my sword at it. The tip of the blade wavered as I drew a breath.

"Vigore!" I shouted, drawing the sword sharply back.

The force invocation hooked the book and yanked it from Marlow's grasp. The book shot across the room, over the pool, between the chanters, and into the doorway, where it smacked into my raised hand like a fastball into a catcher's mitt. I ducked around the side of the doorway, already bringing the book down and flipping through the leather-bound tome.

"Someone's taken the codex," Marlow shouted. "Stop him!"

The chanting broke into a confusion of shouts, and I could hear more splashing from the pool.

This is the book. This is it!

Heart slamming, I dropped the book at my feet and pierced it with the blade. The magic swirling around it fractured and broke apart. The plan was actually working! Emptying the vial of dragon sand over the defenseless tome, I leaped back and shouted, *"Fuoco!"*

An explosion of flames burst from the book and gushed into the altar doorway. Voices and shrieks sounded from beyond. The pages of the incinerated tome floated up and disintegrated into ash.

Chicory! I called through our link as I backed away. *It's done! The book's destroyed!*

I chucked away the empty vial of dragon sand and drew the staff from my belt. I raised it just as a black bolt of energy shot past the flames. The enhanced staff drew the bolt inside, where the energy swirled. With shouts, two of the chanters broke through the flames.

"Rifleterre," I commanded, aiming the staff at them in turn.

The energy absorbed by the staff discharged twice, nailing the chanters and knocking them to the ground.

Did you catch that Chicory? I called again. *I'm ready to come home!*

More figures shifted beyond the flames. I jammed a hand into a pocket holding several lightning grenades and pulled two of them out. *"Attivare!"* I shouted, throwing them into the doorway. Lightning ripped from the heavens and slammed through beam and stone, collapsing the entranceway.

Ears ringing, I wheeled and sprinted across the courtyard toward the stairwell I'd arrived by. I was nearly there when a battalion of the fish-headed creatures came swarming up. Gargling at one another, they fanned around me, scimitars in hand. I enclosed myself in a crackling shield as the first wave moved in. Blades slashing, they set upon the shield.

"Respingere!" I called.

A potent white pulse detonated from the shield, sending the attackers tumbling over the courtyard and each other. Before they could fully recover, I hacked a path through them to the stairwell and descended, throwing a shield over the opening behind me to deny their pursuit.

Chicory? I tried again. *Now would be a really good time.*

I was beginning to worry that the link wasn't working, that he couldn't hear me, when the place on my forehead where he'd mashed his thumb began to tingle. The sensation spread over my body. Any moment I expected to find myself back in the basement. But as quickly as the sensation came, it began to fade. Chicory's voice echoed through my thoughts.

Go back to the place where you arrived.

The forest? I asked, still racing down the stairs. *Why not here?*

The barrier is thinner there.

But I destroyed the book—there shouldn't be a barrier!

His voice broke in and out, but I caught something about the dissolution process taking time. The tingling sensation disappeared from my forehead. A pressure remained behind my eyes and deep in my ears, but those had persisted since he'd first stamped me.

Chicory? I tried again.

No answer.

Great, so I was going to be escaping the palace and re-crossing the plain of wargs with the place on full alert. I grunted out a curse. The hunting spell had shown me the shortest route in; retracing my steps seemed the surest bet for getting back out. If I could remember the way.

I emerged from the staircase, raced down a corridor, and found myself in the pillared room where my mother had been executed and I had slain the two creatures. It still smelled of burned blood.

I was halfway across the room when a robed figure filled the doorway ahead of me. "Stop," he commanded.

Recognizing his voice, I skidded to a halt, heart pounding in my ears. A gold mask glistened from his hood as he strode forward and drew his wand. Marlow had escaped the altar room, evidently, but how in the hell had he beaten me down here?

The mask turned from one side to the other, searching for me.

"Vigore!" I shouted, thrusting my sword toward him.

A storm of energy burst from the blade. The Death Mage sliced his wand through the air, and the force broke to either side of him, shaking the walls. I dug in my pocket for the remaining lightning grenade as he continued his confident advance.

Let's see how you like a face full of electricity, pal.

"Attivare!" I called and winged it at him.

"Ghioccio," he answered, slicing his wand again. The magical grenade thudded to the ground at his feet, encased in a snowball.

I summoned a shield around me and began to search for another long-range weapon when I remembered that with the absorbing properties of the staff, the Death Mage couldn't hurt me. Conversely, with the magic cleaving properties of the sword, I could hurt him. Badly.

Still, Chicory's warnings about Whisperer magic stole through my thoughts. I couldn't just run at him headlong. I eased beside the charred pillar and adjusted my sweaty grip on the sword.

"Show yourself," Marlow demanded, coming nearer. "Who are you?" Though the mage could sense me, the robe was still cloaking my identity. His footsteps came closer and closer until they were almost beside me.

Someone who thinks you're a lowlife piece of shit, I thought, and stepped out. The sword glinted as I put everything into my swing. The blade disappeared into the neck of his gown and came out the other side. Only there had been no resistance. And the mage was still standing.

What the...?

"Ah!" he called triumphantly.

In a blink, he was several feet from where he'd been standing, black energy curling around the end of his wand. An illusionist? He snapped the wand toward me. The bolt slammed into my shield, knocking me backward. I recovered my footing and thrust the sword at his torso. Once more, the blade disappeared into his gown as though it were thin air.

Marlow was suddenly on my other side, fresh black bolts cracking from his wand. They slammed into my shield one after the other, the second bolt lifting me from my feet. I landed against a pillar with a grunt, sword and staff falling from my grasp. The shield shattered into sparks around me.

No, I thought, pawing for my weapons.

The skirt of the mage's black gown swished toward me. He spoke a Word. Vines broke through my mother's ashes in the floor cracks and climbed around me, binding me to the pillar. Before the cinching tendrils could crush the air from my lungs, I drew in a breath.

"Resping—"

A vine wrapped my neck, choking off the Word. The Death Mage stopped in front of me. I raised my eyes to that awful gold mask with the empty eyes and the mouth set in a frown. The mage was holding his wand at shoulder level, ready to cast again. I struggled, but the vines were like steel cables, growing thicker. I knew how this would end. Any second, flames were going to burst around me. In my peripheral vision, I could see other black-robed figures drifting into the room to witness my execution.

At least I destroyed your damned book, I thought. *And when the Order gets their hands on you...*

But the Death Mage seemed to hesitate, head tilted to one side.

The vines had torn the robe of John the Baptist apart, and I was visible to him now. He turned and said something to the others, his voice taking on the gargling quality from earlier. A pair of mages came forward, one lifting my sword from the ground, the other my staff.

Marlow turned back to me. "Everson Cro—"

A bright fireball exploded against his side, blasting him across the room. The other mages let out choking sounds as their robes began to strangle them. I cut my eyes toward the sound of footsteps. My mentor was running toward me, corduroy jacket flapping at his back.

Chicory!

"I decided it would be easier to just come myself," he said in a pant. "And with the book destroyed..." He waved his wand, and the vines around me withered. I broke my arms free from the pillar and tore the tendril from around my neck. I then began to kick my legs free.

Meanwhile, Marlow had recovered and gained his feet. Chicory turned and hurled another fireball at him. Marlow repelled it with a slice of his wand, but a third Chicory fireball knocked him back with a grunt, flames flashing off his gold mask. Marlow's magic might have been powerful, but it was fading, and Chicory was throwing haymakers.

I struggled to break the last of the vines from my legs so I could help him.

Marlow incanted quickly. Tendrils of dark magic writhed from his wand like tentacles and sprung out to encircle Chicory. The energy swallowed him, blacking out his light. Panic rose in my throat. But in a blinding flash of magic, Chicory blew the tentacles apart.

He and Marlow circled one another, wands raised.

"You won't defeat us," Marlow said.

"You've already lost," Chicory replied matter-of-factly.

Light and dark magic exploded from their wands in a savage exchange. The other magic-users were still struggling against their throttling robes. I spotted the one who had taken my sword. White hair spilled down either side of a moldy face. A woman? The sword had fallen beside her. As I scrambled toward it, the woman's robe released her neck, and she drew a ragged breath. Marlow must have broken the strangulation spell. I lunged for the sword, but the woman grabbed the handle first.

Crap.

She shouted something in her gargling tongue as she swung the blade toward me. I jumped away, but too slowly. A force blast numbed my right side and knocked me the length of the room. I landed on my back and skidded across the floor several more feet. When I came to a stop, I lifted my head. The woman was rushing Chicory from behind.

I stretched a hand toward her and shouted, *"Vigore!"*

But the energy that stormed through my prism died inside me, stolen by the magic-cleaving power of my own sword. The woman closed in on my mentor and drew back the blade.

"Chicory!" I cried.

But among the detonations of magic, he couldn't hear me. I recoiled as she drove the blade forward, my mind supplying the crunch of flesh and bone as the blade disappeared into his back.

That didn't just happen, I thought. *That* couldn't *have just happened.*

Chicory sagged, his wand clattering from his grasp. The blinding magic around him blinked out, and the room fell dim. The woman withdrew the sword, and I watched in horror as my mentor collapsed to the ground.

Chicory? I called through our rapport.

But the connection was severed, the pressure behind my eyes and inside my ears releasing like a dying breath. The Death Mage looked down at Chicory, then over at me. I imagined the smile behind his mask. The same smile he'd worn while watching my mother burn.

I stood slowly. "Think that's funny?"

The room wavered with odd colors, like the ones I'd seen in the dream of the forest. I took a drunken step forward. I would die too, but not before ripping the mask away and beating his grinning face to a pulp.

Marlow sent the Order her ashes in a trash bag, I remembered Chicory saying, referring to my mother.

"You think that's fucking funny?" I asked more loudly, breaking into a shambling run.

Marlow's frowning mask continued to watch me. The colors of the room grew more intense and discordant. They spiraled around, making my head pound. I was no longer aware of the other magic-users, couldn't even see them. The room seemed to have been reduced to a crazy, spiraling tunnel, Marlow at its far end, but growing larger, getting closer.

"I'll show you funny," I promised.

The pounding swelled in my head. I staggered and willed myself upright again. I was going to reach him, dammit ... was going to tear the mask away ... was going to pound his...

And then Marlow was right in front of me, uttering something I couldn't understand.

With a clawed hand, I stretched for his gold mask and collapsed into blackness.

8

I was in a dark forest, running for my life, but everywhere I turned, there were the black-robed creatures, their fish eyes staring, mouths opening and closing, scimitars slashing. Everything hurt. God, everything hurt, down to the marrow in my bones. But I had to keep running, had to find the place in the forest where Chicory would bring me back. Most of all, I had to escape the whispers.

Everson … erson … son.

Sweating and shaking, I doubled over and vomited up a green bile that seemed to come from a deep and evil pit inside me. I willed myself to stand and run, to push my way past the fungus-coated trees and festering pools where wretched things lived, past the jabbering, stabbing creatures, none of which seemed to end.

But every so often they *would* end, and I'd find myself in a clearing, and I would fall onto my back, succumbing to the pain and exhaustion. My mother would be speaking over me, wiping my face with a clean, cool cloth, while sun shone down through her hair, turning it a radiant white.

"Help me," I would mumble. "Help me to the place where I can go back."

She would only smile and continue to speak in what I realized was a chant as soft and melodic as a lullaby. But as the chant carried me into sleep, I would find myself back in the dark forest, running for my life, trying desperately to evade the evil creatures and the whispers.

Especially the whispers.

Everson...

I cracked open my swollen eyelids. I was on my back, tucked into a bed of white sheets. A light dew of sweat coated my body. When I swallowed, my stomach felt as tight as a stretched drum.

"Everson," the person repeated.

My head swam when I rotated it. A woman was rising from a chair to my left, the sunlight through a window behind her infusing her hair with hazy white light. Morning light. I fought to think back.

The forest, the vomiting...

No, that hadn't been real. I'd been dreaming. Or more accurately, nightmaring.

I strained to remember how I'd gotten here. The evil ceremony,

Lich's book in flames, my confrontation with the Dark Mage. The horrible image of a blade—*my* blade—crunching through Chicory's back. And then my effort to reach the mage, to rip the mask from his face, only to fail, to fall.

Had I died? Had the experience in the forest been some kind of purgatory? Was this my... I squinted at the woman. ...*mother?*

"You're awake," she said in a strong, maternal voice.

I peered around the small room. Walls of handsome stonework shone white up to a high ceiling. Colorful rugs covered the floor. *I'm not in the palace anymore, that's for damn sure.*

I looked back at the woman. "What is this place?" I croaked.

"It's an infirmary," she said.

"Infirmary?"

"We had to sedate you for several days while the poison was purged from your system."

Though fresh air breezed through the room's open windows, I picked up an undercurrent of illness. I remembered the vomiting from the dream—or whatever that had been. *Poison,* she'd said. All right, so maybe I wasn't dead. I struggled again to think back.

"What happened to the Death Mage? Those ... those creatures. How did you get me out of there?"

"We'll answer all of your questions, but first you need to eat."

I watched her as she stepped from the sunlight and walked around the bed. Without the backdrop of light, her face aged, her cheekbones becoming more stark. The whiteness of her hair had not been an effect of the sunlight, I saw. This woman was older than my mother would have been.

"Who are you?" I asked.

"My name is Arianna." Moving with strength and grace, she

arrived at a table on the other side of the bed and picked up a bowl with a spoon inside it. She was the woman I had seen in my feverish sleep. "I knew your mother," she said. "Can you sit?"

I pushed weakly with my arms and scooted up until I was sitting against the wooden headboard, dizzied by the effort and what the woman had just said. "Knew my mother? When?"

"Before you were born," she answered, handing me the bowl. Inside was a broth that held what looked like a suspension of grains and minced herbs. A rich scent drifted up when I stirred them, making my stomach quiver with hunger. "In fact, I helped deliver you."

I stopped stirring the broth. "What?"

"In this same room," she said. "More than thirty years ago."

I looked around as my mind crunched the numbers. If Marlow was my father and I was one year old when he killed my mother, I would have been born while my mother was infiltrating the...

"You're a member of the Front," I said coldly, setting the bowl back on the table.

Arianna's white hair shifted as she straightened. I gauged the length. It was the same hair as on the magic-user who had seized my sword and driven it through Chicory's back. I incanted quickly while pushing myself out the other side of the bed. An invisible field blocked me.

"Yes," Arianna admitted, "but the Front is not what you've been led to believe."

Her voice propagated through the air in calming waves. *Whisperer magic,* I thought, recalling what Chicory had told me. *Making one see what isn't there, believe what isn't real.* I was still in the palace, then, magic worming through my mind, my senses.

I stared around. The stone walls weren't really as clean and white as they appeared, but oozing with black gunk, the air swirling with poisonous spores. I inhaled sharply, trying to catch a whiff of them. And this Arianna was no woman, but a mold-covered creature, the killer of my mentor.

"Vigore!" I shouted, thrusting a hand toward her.

A surprising charge erupted from my fingers only to slam into a cocoon of energy around the bed. The transparent shield shuddered as it absorbed the blast. When the shield stilled, Arianna remained where she had been.

"I know this is confusing," she said, no hint of scorn or menace in her voice.

I hammered the shield several times until my arms tired and then tried to break through with another force invocation. The shield felt even stronger than the last time, powerful magic maintaining it. I sagged back against the bed, my body trembling, hair matted with sweat.

Arianna, who had looked on compassionately while I struggled, said, "We didn't expect you to understand. Not right away. Your confinement is only temporary. We're going to explain everything."

A soothing breeze blew through the windows and washed over me.

An illusion, I had to remind myself. *All one big goddamned illusion.*

"There's nothing to explain," I said. "You're a clan of sickos and murderers. But guess what? Your book's history. If Chicory got through, so can the Elders. It's just a matter of time."

"There are no more Elders," a man's voice said.

I turned toward the lean figure striding into the room. He looked to be late middle aged, strands of silver streaking through his dark, shoulder-length hair. He took a position beside Arianna. Intelligent gray eyes looked down from a handsome face etched with faint scars.

"There is no Order," he finished.

"Keep telling yourself that," I scoffed.

"Where are they, then?" he asked, looking around. "It's been almost five days since your battle with Marlow." Arianna whispered something to him, but he showed a staying hand, his gaze remaining fixed on mine. "Hmm?"

I incanted quietly, building up my prism, my capacity. I didn't know how long I'd been out, but my mind had clearly been screwed with. That's what the feverish dreams had been about—not detoxing, as Arianna claimed, but being poisoned by Whisperer magic.

"Rivelare," I whispered, attempting to disrupt the veil, to peer past it to the black rot and evil from earlier. But everything remained horrifyingly pristine. Through the open windows, birds tittered merrily.

"Ask yourself this," the man said. "Have you ever seen a representative of the Order?"

I stared at the ceiling. *Don't listen to him.*

"Sure, there was Lazlo, your first mentor," he said. "And Chicory. But other than those two? Well, how about a fellow magic-user, then? An organization that goes back several millennia, vast, branching lineages—it seems you would have been introduced to at least one or two others, no?"

"They're out there," I said defiantly.

"But the Order keeps everyone compartmentalized, is that it?"

"Connell, he needs to rest," Arianna said.

"Naturally," the man replied. "But I want to leave him with something to consider. Assume for a moment, Everson, that everything to this point in your wizard's life was an illusion and that *this* is the reality. Assume that we're not the enemy, but the ally. Assume that the Front isn't opposing the Order, but fighting in its memory. Assume that our goal was never to call the Whisperer into the world, but to strain with the last fibers of our magic to keep it out."

I remained staring at the ceiling, trying to bar his words from my mind.

"Assume for a moment that your mother was helping us," he said, "and was killed for doing so. See if that doesn't make more sense than what you've been led to believe."

I turned enough to glare at him. "Don't you dare mention my mother."

Connell watched me intently for another moment, then turned and strode from the room. Arianna remained standing over the bed, head tilted. She seemed to be struggling with what to say.

"Call out if you need anything," she said at last.

Then she too departed.

9

When Arianna's footsteps receded, I felt the cocoon-like shield around me expand to the walls of the room. My head swam as I threw my legs over the side of the bed. The expenditure of energy in my attempt to break through the shield earlier had left me weak. Being down for five days didn't help.

I sat for a moment, my gaze edging over to the bowl of broth on the bedside table. I lifted the bowl and brought it to my nose, its rich smell making my stomach quiver again. But I couldn't trust it.

It's something vile, I decided, setting the bowl back down.

When I pushed myself to my feet, the ends of a gown I was wearing fell to my knees. My shins looked thin and pale. I checked my chest, not surprised to find my coin pendant missing. My cane wasn't anywhere to be seen either. Ditto Grandpa's ring. I walked, using the wall for support—a wall of clean, solid stone—until I arrived at the window Arianna had been sitting beside earlier.

Squinting against the sun, I peered past the energy field and out into the world.

The courtyards inside the palace wall were handsome. The wind-blown plain below shimmered golden. The forest that ringed it appeared lush. I peered more closely at the plain. It was being patrolled, but not by wargs. The creatures looked like ... common mastiffs?

I grunted. The illusion was impressive, I'd give them that.

I completed a circuit around the room, which included a small corner bathroom. The room's other window as well as the door were covered by the shield—a defensive system I lacked the power to break through. I made my way back to the bed and sat, disturbed by how exhausted the short tour had left me. I leaned forward, hands dangling between my knees.

What was I doing alive? Why hadn't the Death Mage killed me?

Because the Whisperer wants to use you, I answered, remembering what Chicory had said. *And that's what this is—one big mind fuck to get you to believe that they're the good guys.*

I peered around, considering the magic at work. Just as powerful as my mentor had warned me it would be. But though the Front could make me see, hear, and smell whatever they wanted, I still had my beliefs. I would be damned if I was going to let them crack those open.

The first step to resisting them would be knowing the Front's strategy. I began cycling through Connell's suggestions. My original impulse had been to block them out, but I needed to analyze his words, get a better grasp on how the Front would try to influence me.

There are no more Elders, he'd said. *There is no Order.*

They were trying to chisel cracks in the foundation on which my concepts of wizarding and my role in it were based. They were trying to challenge my identity.

My thoughts turned to Connell's questions. Who had I encountered in the Order besides Lazlo and Chicory? The answer was no one, but so what? That was how the Order operated. Absent more often than they were present, taking forever to respond to correspondences—or ignoring them all together—giving confusing directives. It wasn't like I didn't have my marching orders, and I'd been reprimanded more times than I could count. If there was no Order, then who in the hell was doing the threatening and punishing?

Assume for a moment that everything to this point in your life was an illusion and that this *is the reality,* Connell had said. *Assume that we're not the enemy, but the ally. Assume that the Front isn't opposing the Order, but fighting in its memory.*

More attempts to undermine my identity, only now planting the seeds of a replacement identity, one that included the Front and whatever the Whisperer had them working toward.

And finally, the coup de grace:

Assume for a moment that your mother was helping us.

Bringing family into it, making it personal.

Taken together, the Front's strategy was to merge my identity with theirs. *Join us. Join the cluster. Become one.* I wouldn't let it happen. Would they resort to torture? A mind flaying?

Hopefully the cavalry would show up before then.

I caught myself listening for them, but all I could hear was bird song. My fingers began to fidget with the hem of my robe. It *was* strange no one from the Order had come. But knowing how absentminded Chicory could be, he might have neglected to tell them that I had crossed into the Refuge. I mean, the guy almost forgot to cast a bonding spell before sending me in.

"The Order knew he was preparing to send me," I said quietly, urgently. "I'm here at their mandate, after all. If it's been five days, they'll know he's fallen off the map. Will probably send someone to the safe house to check on him, someone who will talk to Tabitha, see the circle in the basement, put it all together." I stopped to listen again. "Help will be here soon."

Unless there is no Order, an insidious voice in my head whispered back.

"They'll come," I insisted, my fingers ditching the hem and digging at one another. "It's just a question of when."

Days? I wondered. *Weeks?* I could attempt to escape, but getting out of the room and palace weren't the issues. Getting out of the Refuge was, and that required advanced magic. Meaning I needed to figure out a way to send a message to the Order, something that would spur them to act *now*.

A grumble from my stomach interrupted my thoughts.

I eyed the bowl of broth again.

I didn't see Arianna or Connell for the rest of that day or the next. Instead, I was tended to by a pair of what appeared to be automatons. Young men and women who looked part mannequin, part robot. They were pleasant in appearance and manner, leaving me to guess at their true monstrous forms. Probably something similar to the two creatures I'd slain with my sword.

I ate the broth they brought up and drank the water. If I hoped to recover my strength, I had no choice, I'd decided. And after each meal, I *did* feel stronger—which bothered me more than anything Connell might have told me. Probably the point.

By late the second day, I was strong enough to pace the room without frequent rests. I thought as I paced, still concerned by the absence of the Order. It had been a week now.

My direct line to the Order is a flame, I thought. *That flame is held in a silver cup, fed by an oil crystal, and linked to the Order's ... switchboard, I guess you'd call it, through an incantation. So, material wise, I need a silver cup, an oil crystal, something to write on, and something to write with.*

The last two would be easy. I was given a cloth napkin with each meal, and blood pricked from my finger would make a passable ink. It would just be a matter of smearing out the message and then folding and waving the cloth over the flame. Producing that flame would be another matter, though. Oil crystals were hard enough to find in the city, and the cup I was being served water in was some sort of brass alloy, not even close to silver.

Would substitutes work?

From the way Chicory had explained it, the combination of silver and the incantation I'd been given were my connection to the Order. Anything else, and the message would end up in a different dimension, or more likely as a pile of ashes in this one. Back in my library, my shelves held several books on alchemy, but little good they did me here. I blew out a hard sigh.

"I'm sorry to interrupt," a man's voice said from behind me. "We've come to change your bedding."

I turned to find two of the automatons, a young man and woman, entering, sheets and fresh pillows in their arms.

"Oh, sure," I said absently. "Thanks."

They nodded and went about their work. I watched them strip the bed, reflecting on how I'd uttered the thanks on instinct. Assuming the two *were* automatons, they were hardly sentient. I could have told them to piss off and cracked my chair over their heads, and they would have simply left, not phased in the least. But everything from their blinking eyes, to their subtle gestures, to the way they stooped to their work was all so convincingly human that I couldn't divorce myself from the social norms that had compelled me to thank them. And to think that they were products of someone's thoughts.

I stopped. *Of course.*

I let out a choked laugh, prompting the automatons to glance over. Fresh energy surged through me. I hadn't been thinking. The Refuge, brought into being by the Elders a thousand years ago, was the product of thoughts. As an ideational realm, thoughts here had special manifesting powers.

I didn't possess Elder-level magic, no, but I wasn't talking about thinking a *world* into being. I only needed a cup and a crystal. Though I'd never manifested matter before, I had performed projection spells—taking something solid and projecting its likeness somewhere else.

I was betting that here the same process would work with thoughts.

I waited for the automatons to leave, then waited a little longer to ensure no one else was coming. As the sky darkened outside the windows, revealing the realm's two moons, I left the room's lamp off. I climbed into bed, rolled onto my side, and pulled the covers over my head.

"Oscurare," I whispered, deepening the darkness around me.

Certain I was as concealed as I could be, I pictured the silver cup from my apartment, rotating it into a three-dimensional model in my mental prism. *"Imitare,"* I chanted. *"Imitare."*

Energy coursed around the prism, seeming to harden the thought into something independent of my mind.

"Liberare," I said, and released the thought.

The energy around my prism rushed out of me, and the image of the cup disappeared. I was sure the attempt had failed, when a moment later something cold rolled against my forehead. I worked my hands up into the pocket in front of my face until I was holding a metal cup. I brought it to my nose and sniffed.

Silver.

Holy crap, it worked.

I repeated the ritual for the crystal, manifesting the thought and then releasing it. Something pinged into the cup. I reached inside and rolled the oil crystal between my fingers. *Okay,* I thought hiding the cup and crystal beneath a pillow, *now for the message.* I extended an arm and pawed for the cloth napkin on the bedside table, then stopped myself.

If I could manifest the other items, why not the message?

Gathering energy to my prism, I composed the message, as though giving dictation. I found myself using the formal system the Order required, a case of an old habit dying hard, but I was also worried that if I didn't defer to the Order's specifications, the message would be tossed.

To the Esteemed Order of Magi and Magical Beings,

Re: Imprisoned in the Refuge/Chicory Dead

Urgency: Ultrahigh

Pursuant to your mandate, Chicory sent me to the Refuge about one week ago tonight to find and destroy Lich's book. I succeeded in the task; however, in attempting to retrieve me, Chicory was slain. I am now a prisoner of Marlow and the Front, a group intent on subverting my will and magic to the Whisperer's malevolent ends. I urgently request your help.

Humbly Submitted,
Everson Croft

I repeated the ridiculous message in my mind, imagining it handwritten on a sheet of parchment paper in lampblack ink. When the thought hardened in my prism, I released it with another *"Liberare."*

The parchment settled in front of me. I took it and blew across the wet ink. Then, as casually as I could, I drew the sheets back, placed the cup with the crystal on the bedside table, and sat up.

"Fuoco," I whispered, my heart pounding through the Word. I was sure that any second, someone was going to come through the door, banish my creations, and prevent me from conjuring others.

The oil in the center of the crystal glowed, then jetted into a bright flame. It sputtered and smoked, as if on the verge of going out, before shifting into a familiar plum-colored column, where it steadied. I pumped a fist. My magic was almost spent, but the thought items were doing their jobs. I reread the message and folded the parchment into a six-sided disk.

"Consegnare," I said, waving the disk over the flame, my eyes cutting to the door and back. *"Consegnare."*

The report began to smoke. *C'mon, c'mon, c'mon,* I thought, then jerked back as a bright flash tore the report from my fingers. I leaned forward again slowly, riveted on the flame. It cycled through the color spectrum, becoming orange, before returning to its original plum color.

I let out my breath in a long, shuddering sigh.

The message had gone through.

10

"It looks like you've recovered."

When I raised my head, sleep seemed to run off it like thick water. Morning light filled the room. Connell was standing at the foot of my bed. I followed his gaze to the bedside table. Beside a fresh pitcher of water, the plum-colored flame continued to burn from the silver cup.

Fear shot through me. After sending the message last night, I'd closed my eyes, planning to rest just long enough to recharge my powers and manifest a weapon for protection. Instead, I'd fallen into a deep sleep, the manifestations having drained me much more than I'd thought.

Connell dragged the chair to the foot of the bed and sat so

he was facing me. He nodded toward the cup. "It's why the Front chose this place," he said. "Its responsiveness to thought magic. The defenses the Elders created were superior to anything we could have manifested on the material plane or by our own magic. Through collective thought, we've maintained the Refuge."

"Until now," I shot back.

He nodded grimly. "That was an Elder book you incinerated. And yes, it contained powerful symbols that cannot be replicated, symbols instrumental in countering Lich's efforts."

"Nice try, but I saw the book."

"You saw what someone wanted you to see."

"Give it a rest. Lich was destroyed centuries ago." I sat up on the side of the bed, emboldened by the knowledge that the Order had received the message, that they were on the way.

"I assure you," Connell said, "Lich is alive and well."

"Then where is he?"

"I'm going to tell you everything."

"Your version of everything?" I snorted. "Don't bother."

"You've been conditioned to distrust us, and I accept that." His gaze cut over to the plum-colored flame. "But what I'm going to tell you will explain why no one's coming to your rescue."

I shook my head even as a ganglion of fear formed in my gut.

"And when I finish—"

"Yeah, yeah," I interrupted, "I'm going to throw my arms around you and thank you for showing me the light."

"When I finish," he repeated patiently, "we'll release you."

I felt the sarcastic retort I'd been preparing fall away. "Come again?"

"Return you through the portal you entered by."

"And I'll be back in New York?"

"New Jersey, technically. But yes."

I stared at him. "Why?"

"Because we know the only way you'll accept the truth is by investigating it for yourself."

"Why is that so important to you?"

"If you'll let me begin..."

I looked around the room, searching for an anomaly, just one. I knew what I'd seen when I arrived at the Refuge, dammit. Mold-coated walls, fish-faced creatures, a summoning ceremony fit for the seventh circle of hell. My perceptions had only changed once the Front knocked me out for five days. And Chicory had warned me their mind-warping magic was potent. I mean, hell, it had turned the Elders against one another, almost toppled them. I had resisted thus far, but would listening to Connell's account endanger that?

"You'll send me back as soon as you're done?" I asked.

"We'll give you time to change into some clothes, of course."

I bristled at his attempted humor. "And if I don't investigate your claims you'll, what, pull me back here?"

"We don't have that kind of power, Everson. We can pull, but you would have to push. You'd have to be willing, in other words. But it's a moot point. You'll want to investigate."

I didn't like his self-assuredness. But for a chance to be sent back, especially if the Order was slow on the uptake... I snuck a peek at the plum-colored flame that didn't seem to concern Connell. I would keep an iron-clad hold on my skepticism, I decided. The second I felt my mind starting to bend, I would block out what he was saying and re-center myself.

"Fine. Tell me."

Connell nodded. "I received a similar training to yours. We all did. You know the story of the First Saints, Michael's nine children, how the Order came to be. That much of our history is true. You also heard the account of the rebellion in which Lich tried to overthrow his siblings."

Not wanting to give Connell a finger hold in my thoughts, I simply looked back at him.

"Lich made a pact with an ancient being called Dhuul. Chaos itself. In exchange for the power he felt he'd been denied, Lich sacrificed his soul to Dhuul and pledged to help him into our world. By his very nature, Dhuul reduces systems of order to darkness and madness."

Chicory hadn't told me that part of the story. *Because it's a lie,* I reminded myself.

"So, yes, Lich did die, but not at the hands of the Elders. He rose as an undead being, a demigod, in full possession of Whisperer magic. And with that magic, he slaughtered his eight siblings."

"Bullshit," I said, unable to help myself.

He ignored the remark. "No more Elders. No more Order."

"Then who in the hell have I been working under for the last ten years?"

"Lich," Connell said. "After destroying the Elders, he used the same magic to create the illusion that the First Order continued to exist. Then, assuming various guises, he murdered the representatives of the Second Order, those with direct access to the Elders. From there, the Elders existed in name and legend only, a legend Lich could manipulate to his, and Dhuul's, ends."

"So you're saying that all of the creatures I've captured and sent back were illusions?" I fingered the place where a nether creature had torn off a chunk of my right earlobe.

"No, Everson. The work of everyone who served under what we believed to be the Order was very real. Beings do exist in the nether realms, the lesser ones seeking sustenance in our world, the greater ones hungering for dominion. Much of the critical work of the Order actually continued."

"And that helps Lich how?" I asked skeptically.

"In two ways." Connell stood and began pacing the room, hands clasped behind his back. Something in the way he carried himself bothered me. "First, it acts as a distraction, keeping magic-users like us busy. We don't question what we're being told to do, nor by whom. That has given Lich freedom to devote himself to building the portal between our world and Dhuul's. Second, the practice and experience we obtain grow our power. And—"

"That doesn't make any goddamned sense," I interrupted. "Why would Lich want magic-users to become powerful enough to challenge him?"

"Oh, they never get to that point. He only lets them grow powerful enough to sacrifice them. The lion's share of their power goes to the portal while a quotient is entrapped in a glass pendant that sustains Lich himself."

I blew a raspberry with my lips. "Like other magic-users aren't going to know their colleagues are suddenly missing."

"Even under the policy of compartmentalization?" he asked, one eyebrow raised. "And let's not forget the zero-tolerance policy. Magic-users are hit with enough warnings and threats in their early years that were any of them to learn about the execution of a fellow magic-user—or told they were up for execution themselves—they would hardly be surprised. Terrified, yes, but not surprised."

I couldn't keep myself from revisiting the numerous warnings I'd received over the years. But that didn't explain Grandpa, an old and powerful mage. His death had been an accident, stepping into a street at the same moment a bee happened to sting an approaching driver. He hadn't been sacrificed or had his soul harvested.

I was going to say as much, then remembered something the vampire Arnaud had told me shortly before I blew him apart. *I kept close tabs on your grandfather since his arrival in Manhattan,* he'd said. *He was behaving quite curiously, performing work far beneath his station. A stage magician and insurance man?*

Almost as though Grandpa was trying to hide his abilities from someone. I broke off the thought when I realized Connell was watching me intently.

"Yeah, nice story so far," I said. "There's only one problem. If Lich the Great and Terrible created this perfect artifice, fooling everyone, how in the hell do you know about it?"

"Your grandfather," he said.

I stiffened. "What about him?"

"Asmus Croft was a scholar in Europe, a brilliant man."

"A scholar?" I'd never heard anything about that.

"Yes, of mythology. Interesting how you followed in his footsteps without ever knowing. In any case, in his early days as a wizard, Asmus took a great interest in the history of the Order. He learned everything he could about it, going back to the earliest records. That had been Lich's role in the First Order: penning its history and protocols, its first spell books. After overthrowing the

Order, Lich took many guises, but he kept up the history. He gave an account of the rebellion, and his own role in it, but reported that it ended in his death and the closing of the seam to Dhuul. The falsehood was not only to evade suspicion, but to enact harsher punishment for magic-users who committed any number of infractions. Lich set up wards to spy on them. Thus began the regime of warnings and executions."

That was actually consistent with what Chicory had told me about the Elders taking steps to ensure nothing like the rebellion would happen again. *Careful, Everson,* I warned myself. *Probably exactly how Whisperer magic works, grafting lies onto what one already accepts as truth.*

"But Asmus was exceptional in languages too," Connell continued. "He developed an expertise in what would later become the field of linguistics. Though Lich had altered his penmanship in composing the post-rebellion history, your grandfather saw similarities in the diction between that history and what had come before. He began to ask questions. Not aloud, no—he knew better. The questions he posed were to himself: What if the rebellion had succeeded? What if Lich had destroyed his siblings and not vice versa? What if this Dhuul was directing what everyone believed to be the Order? With those questions in mind, your grandfather simply observed. What was said, what was done, what was promulgated down the ranks. He did this for many years, continuing his work as a scholar and wizard, never letting on what he suspected but becoming more and more convinced of it. When the regional enforcers of the Inquisition grew bolder in their threats against European magic-users, he requested guidance from the Order, and this was where Lich slipped up."

I caught myself leaning forward slightly and sat back.

"The Order advised your grandfather to ally with the vampires to confront the threat," he said.

"What was wrong with that?"

"It went against the Order's entire reason for being," Connell replied. "Saint Michael sired children to combat the offspring of the Demon Lords, which included vampires. For hundreds of years, the Order had never wavered from that position."

"Yeah, but this was for survival."

"Saint Michael forbade his children from warring against humans. Again, it went against their reason for being. But now, just like that, two of the central tenets on which the Order was founded had been altered."

"How would that have been advantageous to Lich?"

"Your grandfather believed Lich saw war as the best chance for the long-term survival of magic-users. The longer they lived, the more powerful they grew, and the more of that power Lich could channel into his portal. Thus, the more powerful he would become."

"Then why did my grandfather fight?"

"He saw the fog of wartime as an opportunity to meet with other magic-users in secret. That was how he met Marlow. They compared stories on their experiences. Both of the mentors who had inducted them into the Order had been put to death for one violation or another. Other magic-users shared similar accounts concerning their own mentors. It was there, during the war against the Inquisition, that your grandfather, Marlow, and several others formed a rebellion to defeat Lich. It would take time and resources. Lich had been building his portal for centuries, after all. Several magic-users faked their deaths during the Inquisition, Marlow among them. They came here, to the Refuge, where they discovered Elder books and began the work of stalling Lich's progress. Following the Inquisition, your grandfather feigned a serious head wound and claimed he'd lost much of his own power. He requested and was granted a release from the Order. Lich had no more use for him. Keeping a low profile, your grandfather worked between worlds, gathering information and resources out there, supplying it to us here."

I thought about Arnaud's claim that Grandpa had stolen and stashed magical artifacts during the war. Connell's version of events seemed to fit that, but suspecting Whisperer magic, I pushed the thought away.

"His daughter eventually took over that role. Your mother."

"I don't want to hear anymore," I said, standing. His account was filling in too many gaps, and doing it too neatly. I could feel my mind beginning to bend to the logic, the magic.

"Are you sure?" Connell asked.

Two automatons entered the room, carrying the clothes I'd arrived in as well as towels and a basin of clean water. They set everything on the foot of my bed and departed silently.

"Tell me this," I said in challenge. "Since you know so much, how did I end up here?"

I stepped into my boxers and tossed away the gown.

"To answer that, I have to go back to your beginnings. You were born here, beyond Lich's and Dhuul's sight. Lich killed your mother without knowing who she was; your grandfather had seen to it that she never joined the Order. You were placed in your grandparents' care, and through veiling spells, they ensured Lich remained ignorant of your existence."

I pulled on my shirt. "I thought you said he was a god."

"A demigod," Connell corrected me. "And a distractible one, thankfully. Obsession with power does that to a mage. When you turned thirteen, you entered your grandfather's locked study."

I turned and looked at him. How did he know that?

"Asmus told us," he said, reading my expression. "And it concerned him greatly."

I remembered how Grandpa had pulled me from the closet that night and sliced my finger with the cane sword. I remembered the grave look that had come over his face when I told him how I'd entered, by uttering a Word of Power.

"In order to keep you from Lich's sight," Connell continued, "your grandfather suppressed your power with plans to train you in adulthood. That never happened, of course. When he died, there was nothing to hold back your power. It awakened and began to manifest once more. And it manifested of all places in Romania, in the domain of a Third Order magic-user."

Lazlo, I thought.

"He would have communicated with what he thought was the Order. From there, Lich would have probed your magic and determined who you were—not just the grandson of the late Asmus Croft, but the son of Eve and Marlow. It became his plan to turn you against Marlow, since you would have access to him. But he had to wait until you were powerful enough. The vampire Arnaud sped up that plan by telling you about his encounter with your grandfather regarding your mother."

They killed her, he'd claimed Grandpa had said. Had Grandpa been talking about Lich and Dhuul? *No,* I thought firmly. *He meant the members of the Front. Stop listening to this man.*

I sat to tie my shoes.

"You began looking into your mother's death, sending inquiries to the Order. Lich became concerned when you attempted to contact a gatekeeper. He would have followed you to the mystic, Lady Bastet, and then killed her to keep you from discovering a truth he couldn't manipulate. He then arranged the scene in a way that would compel you to investigate, to believe Marlow was responsible. By taking the vial of blood you'd given the mystic, Lich indebted you to the *Order*." Connell air-quoted the word with his fingers. "He set you up for a punishment that would mean being sent here. Are you beginning to understand how the regime of warnings and threats work? The residue he left on the cats—"

"Led me to Marlow," I cut in defiantly.

"—led you to wherever Lich wanted you to go," he finished. "It was Lich who spoke through your cat, pretending to be Marlow. Only when you arrived here did he have the spell actually lead you to Marlow."

How in the hell did Connell know so many details? Had he drawn them from me during the five days I'd been out? Was he in my head now?

"We know these things because of your demon," he said.

"Thelonious?" I blurted out.

"No, he's not with you enough. I was referring to your cat."

I shook my head. "There's no way Tabitha is working for you."

"Of course not," Connell said with a chuckle, as though he knew her as well as I did. "Not willingly, anyway. Tabitha inhabits a cat's body, but she also resides in a shallow demonic plane. A plane we've been able to tap into. Most of what she sees and hears in your presence, we can access and decipher."

"Then how come you didn't know I was coming?" I challenged.

"The energy around the safe house had a scrambling effect. We could no longer interpret what we were picking up on Tabitha's plane. We didn't know you were being sent so soon."

I found another hole in Connell's account. "If I was so important to Lich's plan, why has he allowed me to take on such dangerous work?"

"*Did* he allow it?" Connell asked. "Consider the times you were ordered to stand down or that someone intervened directly on your behalf."

I thought about Chicory showing up to save me from the druids in Central Park. It was the same night he'd ordered me off the demon cases.

"The rest of the time," Connell said, preempting my next challenge, "you were aided by Whisperer magic. Coming up with a solution, often a life saving one, at just the right moment."

"That's called a luck quotient. All wizard's have it."

"Is that what you were told?" Connell asked, the genuineness in his tone rankling me.

I rounded on him. "You're telling me there's no Order and that's why no one's come. That's the argument you're going with, right? Fine. I can use it too. There's no Lich. Want to know how I know? Because I destroyed your book, and look..." I peered over both shoulders. "...no Lich."

I crossed my arms smugly. *Checkmate.*

"He already came," Connell said calmly.

"When I was out?"

"No, before."

"Before?"

"Everson," he said, looking at me gravely, "Chicory is Lich. It's one of his guises."

I uncrossed my arms, unsure now what to do with them. For a disorienting moment I was sitting beside Chicory in his car after the druid encounter. *The Order can seem like an abstraction sometimes,* he was saying, *but when it comes to their mandates, they're rather black and white. Trust me. I've had to take care of two wayward wizards this month already.*

I recalled how dark and mercenary my mentor's eyes had looked.

"Forget it," I said, shaking off the memory. "You're never going to convince me of that."

"My job isn't to convince you," Connell said. "It's to give you enough information so you can investigate the claims for yourself. *You* need to decide whether what I'm telling you is true."

"I know what I saw."

"You saw what he wanted you to see."

I was barely aware of my fingers massaging the spot where Chicory had mashed his thumb. I felt a ghost of the pressure that had manifested behind my eyes and deep in my ears.

"If this crap you're telling me is true, why the hard sell?" I asked. "You killed him."

"Destroyed his form," he corrected me. "And only because he'd activated the powerful enchantment inside your blade. No, the being that is Lich can only be killed by destroying the glass pendant in which he stores his claimed souls. Naturally, he keeps the pendant hidden. His new body is forming beside it as we speak, coalescing from the magic within. He will be back soon."

An involuntary shudder passed through me. "Are you done?"

"For now, yes."

11

I followed Connell and Arianna down the steep steps of the palace to where the rocky hill flattened to the plain. Arianna had returned everything to me, including my sword and staff, claiming to have purified them of Whisperer magic. I carried both in my hands and kept a charge of energy around my prism. Neither of my escorts seemed to mind, which bothered me.

When we arrived on the plain, Connell whistled and one of the mastiffs hustled over, tongue lolling. I looked the dog over carefully as it sniffed me and then trotted beside us, escorting us toward the forest. It wasn't acting like a warg, but that could be illusory too, I reminded myself.

"To avoid additional holes in our realm," Connell said, "we're sending you back the way you came through."

Or are you taking me into the forest to sacrifice me? I thought.

But they'd already had plenty of opportunities, and that bothered me, too.

Soon, the trees took us in. Not the dark, fungus-riddled trees I'd arrived through, but a healthy growth of what looked like oak and spruce. After several more minutes we arrived at a small clearing.

"Here," Connell said, stopping.

As I arrived at the center of the clearing, he and Arianna stepped back.

"Do you have any more questions?" he asked.

"No."

"I'm sure you've been wondering about your father," Arianna said. "He visited your bedside while you slept. He is anxious to meet you and for you to meet him, but only when that is what you desire."

I *had* been wondering about him, of course, but I didn't let it show on my face. The man had killed my mother. I'd seen it, experienced it. The horror stuck like barbs around my heart. Even so, Connell had done his job. He'd managed to plant enough doubt in my head that I had no choice but to investigate his claims. Try to figure out what in the hell was going on.

"Are we going to get this party on, or what?" I asked impatiently.

"There is one more thing," Connell said. "Once Lich reconstitutes himself, he's going to come after you. Whether to seduce you anew or end you, I can't say. He got what he wanted by sending you here. The Elder book contained powerful magic to keep Dhuul from the world. Its destruction did not weaken our stronghold here so much as increase Dhuul's, and thus Lich's, power. Knowing you have spent time with us, Lich will see you as a threat."

"You have four days," Arianna said, "no more."

"And then, let me guess, I have to come back here, right?"

"If you want to live," Connell said bluntly. "You'll have no defenses against his magic out there."

"Why do you care?"

He looked at me for a moment. "Because you're one of us."

"So are all magic-users, if what you're saying is true. Why aren't you helping them?"

"We have no way to reach them," he said. "When Lich discovered us, he sealed us in. Though your arrival came with a cost, it also presents a new opportunity. We can't come and go, but *you* can."

Is that why they kept me alive? To use me as an agent against the Order?

"Just be open to whatever you find out there," Arianna said. "When you're ready, return to the portal on your side and we'll help transport you back here. Just remember. Four days."

"Don't hold your breath," I muttered.

She presented a small glass vial with a clear liquid inside. "Take this," she said. "The same magic that purged you is concentrated within. Should you find yourself beset, use it."

Sure, lady, I thought, but accepted it.

"Are you ready?" Connell asked me.

I gave a nod, and he and Arianna began an incantation. The mastiff, who had been sniffing around, dropped onto his haunches between them and gave a single, friendly bark.

A moment later, I was staring at complete blackness.

"Illuminare," I called in a panic.

The opal in my staff flickered and then cast an orb of white light. A dirt floor and empty space stretched out around me. Shadows shifted in the rafters overhead. I was back in the basement, standing in the casting circle Chicory had drawn days before. The Front had actually released me.

I stepped from the circle and found the staircase at the far end of the basement. Mounds of earth, where my mentor had manifested elementals during my training, stood on either side of me. I looked back, half expecting to see Chicory, but a hollowness in my gut told me I was alone. I ascended the stairs quickly, emerging through the door beneath the staircase to the attic.

"Hello?" I called. "Chicory? Tabitha?"

The inside of the house creaked and clicked in the stifling heat of high noon. I made a tour of all the rooms, starting in the kitchen. Everything appeared as I'd left it, down to the dirty plates Chicory had deposited around the house, only now black flies picked over them. With Chicory's death, the protective energies that once shielded the house were gone.

"Tabitha," I called again.

"In here..."

The weak voice had come from under the sink. When I opened the cabinet doors, a pair of green eyes squinted at me from behind pipes whose rusty joints glistened with moisture.

"Tabitha? What are you doing in there?" I reached a hand inside and, curling it beneath her stomach, hefted her out. She had lost a few pounds. I set her on the kitchen table and examined her.

"I thought you left me," she said in her hurt voice. She plopped onto her side as though her legs were too weak to support her.

"Yeah, I'm sorry about that."

"I couldn't get into the fridge and had to live off the spoiled crud Chicory left out. And then the water stopped running. After lapping up everything in the toilet, the only place I could find any water was on those disgusting pipes." She grimaced and smacked her mouth as though trying to rid it of the taste. "Where *were* you?"

I sat in a chair facing her. "Things didn't go exactly as planned."

She raised her head enough to look over a shoulder. "And Chicory?"

Chicory is Lich, I heard Connell telling me. "The night he went through the portal, did he say anything?" I asked.

"Oh, not now, darling. I'm starving and wretched."

"Please, just answer the question."

"He said he'd be back. Typical man."

"This is serious, Tabitha. I need you to think back. What were his *exact* words?"

"What do I look like, a stenographer?" My eyes must have looked as frighteningly intense as they felt because her own eyes cut to one side as though searching her memory. "He said you were in trouble and that he was going in to help. That he would come back with you soon."

"Anything else?"

"What happened down there, darling?"

"You and Chicory are close," I pressed. "Did anything about him ever strike you as, I don't know, funny?"

"Besides his green shoes?"

"No, anything he said? Anything he did?"

"Well, his sudden interest in you struck me as odd. I tried to tell him you were hopeless."

I thought about that. Aside from the brief visits here and there, usually to issue a warning, Chicory was absent for months, sometimes years. And all of a sudden he's committed to training me? That did seem odd.

And it had all begun the day I'd brought my mother's hair to Lady Bastet to divine from. In fact, it was only hours after the mystic's murder that I'd come home to find Chicory sitting in my apartment. All consistent with what Connell had told me. Chicory claimed to have been sent by the Order with information about my mother, but he'd damned sure been interested in the gatekeeper I'd summoned to learn about her death.

And what did the gatekeeper say? he'd wanted to know.

But that wasn't evidence of anything. If the Order had sent Chicory, the timing could have been incidental. And he would have been interested in *any* summoning, given that it was forbidden.

I looked back at Tabitha. Through her, the Front had access to my words, my actions.

"Here," I said, getting up quickly and opening the fridge. I pulled out a bottle of milk and some leftover food, fixed a meal for Tabitha, and set the plates and bowl on the floor. She hopped down from the table, wasting no time plunging her face into the fat and protein she'd been unable to get to.

While she ate, I returned to the bedroom Chicory had been

using as a laboratory. On one side, a table held different-sized beakers with dirty distillation tubes running between them. A disorganization of spell implements and spiral-bound notebooks lay in scattered piles. Inside the notebooks, I found scribblings on various spells, all of them benign as far as I could tell. Nothing to suggest Chicory was anything other than who he'd appeared to be.

I didn't sense any active magic either, but I spoke a reveal invocation anyway. Nothing new appeared. I glanced over a pile of newspaper clippings on the table, the topmost one about the robe of John the Baptist being on exhibit at Grace Cathedral. Chicory had once remarked that, in addition to his mentoring duties, he kept track of magical artifacts. The clippings two and three down, on similar exhibits around the country, seemed to confirm that.

I moved a chair—over the back of which he had draped a row of wool stockings—and picked up a pair of manila folders that must have slid off the seat and landed under the table.

On one of the folder's tabs, I read my name.

Heart thumping, I retrieved the files and opened mine. Was this where I would discover the truth? Inside was a thin stack of pages secured by a pair of metal brads. I read through the pages, which contained notes on Chicory's handful of visits, including the warnings he'd issued. A line at the bottom of his final entry read, "Shows significant promise but requires more guidance to get there."

Sounds like Chicory, I thought.

The other file, considerably thicker, was labeled "James Wesson." Another magic-user? I opened the file, but other than the name I could find no identifying features. Just a much longer scribbled list of infractions, ranging from dereliction of duty to substance abuse.

And here I thought I was the black sheep.

But more important than what the notes said about James was what it said about Chicory. Like the messy room I was standing in, the notes appeared consistent with an advanced, though absentminded, wizard.

A dead wizard, I thought, picking up a gold cup from the floor: Chicory's former communication system to the Order. An oil crystal clinked around its bottom, but no flame rose from it now.

My throat tightened with grief as I remembered his death. His murder.

Then why did no one from the Order come? a voice prodded inside my head.

That was what was nagging me more than anything. Chicory had gotten through, after all. If the mission had been as important as he'd claimed, if I'd been sent by the Order, why hadn't others followed? Why had no one responded to my message? Where were they now?

"Goddammit," I whispered, hating the growing tangle of doubt I felt.

I set the cup back atop the table and searched the rest of the house. In the attic, I found an open trunk with the various wands, weapons, and artifacts Arnaud had kept in his armory and that I had passed on to Chicory. By all appearances, Chicory had given them a quick cleaning, then dumped them here. I sealed the trunk with a locking spell and moved on, checking the walls and panels for loose boards, calling out reveal invocations at intervals. But nothing appeared or stood out as unusual, in the attic or the rest of the house.

I arrived back in the guest bedroom to find Tabitha conked out on her ottoman. I shook her awake.

"What?" she complained.

"We need to talk."

"Can't it wait?" She flopped onto her other side so she was facing away from me.

"Chicory is dead," I said.

She twisted her neck around and blinked twice. "Dead?"

Or undead, depending on who you talk to, I thought. But with the Front monitoring me, I didn't want to show the slightest wavering. Better to keep my doubts a secret, deny Connell and Arianna anything they could use to manipulate me. I didn't believe they were trapped in the Refuge as they'd claimed. If they could watch me, they could reach me.

"When Chicory came to bring me back," I told Tabitha, "he battled the Dark Mage. Chicory was winning, but one of the mage's minions snuck up and ran him through with my sword."

"Well then how did you make it back alive?" she asked, her voice bordering on accusing.

"They released me."

"Why?" she asked.

"To, ah, warn other magic-users not to mess with the Dark Mage," I lied.

I no longer saw Tabitha's eyes as eyes, but as peepholes. She narrowed them at me in suspicion. *Can they see me right now?* I wondered.

"Look," I said, "we just need to get out of here."

"Now?"

I stood and began gathering my clothes. "The house's defenses are down. We're not safe here anymore." *And whose house is it anyway?* a part of me wondered as I stuffed everything into the large duffel bag I'd brought.

"The defenses are down? You mean I could have just strolled out of here and fed on male souls?"

"I'll contact the Order when we get back to the apartment," I said, hurriedly throwing my books into the bag and mashing everything down to close the zipper. I was anxious to be behind my own defenses. "We can pick up some fresh goat's milk and tuna steaks on the way."

Tabitha stood and arched her back until several vertebra cracked.

"First sensible thing you've said since you returned."

12

Chicory had parked his compact car in the small garage attached to the house. Though I hadn't been able to find any keys in the house, a quick search of his cluttered glove compartment turned up a spare.

I opened the trunk to stow my duffel bag, but the space was too jammed with boxes. Several more rows filled his back seat, the files they held like the ones I'd found in Chicory's room. Names of whom I assumed were magic-users, along with scribbled notes. The files looked less like the work of a demigod than an overburdened social worker. But they might be a start.

I shoved my duffel bag atop the boxes in the back seat and opened the passenger side door for Tabitha. As she climbed in,

I took a final look at the door to the house. *When you're ready, return to the portal,* Arianna had said. I had scoffed, but *would* I be returning here?

"Can we go?" Tabitha said. "I haven't had any decent sleep in weeks."

The drive through the Lincoln Tunnel and down to the West Village was uneventful. I arrived at the apartment to find the door triple-bolted, the wards intact, and the inside of the unit as I'd left it. A quick scan revealed no signs of intrusion. Tabitha trotted past me and hopped onto her divan. She let out a contented sigh as she curled into her sleeping position.

I dropped my duffel bag and checked my voicemail. No messages.

Good.

According to Arianna, I had four days until Lich reconstituted his form. A narrow window, which might have been the point—to compel me to dive straight into the investigative work.

Instead, I climbed the ladder to my library/lab and glanced over my hologram of Manhattan. Though I'd been gone for two weeks, the hologram was dim. It had been Chicory's job to maintain the magic-detecting wards throughout the city. No Chicory probably meant no more wards, which meant no alarms. Another senior magic-user in the Order would have to restore them.

Assuming there are any left, the insidious voice inside my head whispered.

I pressed my lips together and turned to the plum-colored flame on the table. No new messages. At my desk, I sat and penned an update to the Order. I waved it over the flame, the orange flare telling me the message had been received.

But is anyone even home? the voice taunted.

"Shut it," I said.

With a Word, I revealed my books, then pulled down a tome on potions. I flipped until I found the most powerful one for dispelling magic that I could reasonably cook. It would take the rest of the day to prepare the potion, and I wasn't even sure it would work against Whisperer magic, but I needed to try. I wouldn't get anywhere if I couldn't trust my own thoughts.

I pulled out my burner and pots and got to work.

The next morning, with the bitter dispel potion cramping my stomach, I drove Chicory's car downtown. At the checkpoint at One Police Plaza, guards examined my ID and waved me through. Detectives Vega and Hoffman were waiting for me in the front of the building, Hoffman holding the handle of a large, four-wheeled dolly.

"Great. You again," he said when I got out.

I grinned. "Admit it, Hoffman. You missed me."

"Yeah, like a leaking appendix."

"Are those the files?" Vega asked, nodding toward the back seat.

"Yeah, and there are some more back here," I said, unlocking and raising the trunk door.

While the potion had been cooking, I had called Vega and filled her in on my trip to the Refuge. She had agreed to take the files as evidence in the Lady Bastet murder investigation. I had also called Caroline, my former colleague and now a fae princess.

At the very least, I'd wanted to find out what the fae knew about the Whisperer. But Caroline's old number was no longer in service and she hadn't been seen in the mayor's office in several days. Were the fae evacuating our world? I had considered going to the fae townhouse in the Upper East Side to find out, but I couldn't risk losing my magic again.

Vega gestured to Hoffman, who grumbled and began loading the boxes onto the dolly. She and I walked several paces away from the car until we were out of his earshot.

"Are you all right?" she asked, the skin between her eyebrows folding in.

"Yeah. I think so, anyway."

"So your father *didn't* kill your mother?"

"At this point, I honestly don't know. But either way, the same person who killed her killed Lady Bastet. That much I can say with confidence. The murderer wanted to suppress the truth. Whatever that truth is," I added in a mumble, feeling just as confused as before I gagged down the potion.

"And the perp might be the person whose files we're taking in? This Chicory?" She jotted down his license plate number.

"There's a small chance," I said, hating that I was even considering it. "I appreciate you doing this, by the way."

"What are we looking for exactly?"

"The files contain info about other magic-users like me, maybe. I just need you to find out what you can about them, who they are, where they live, whether they knew Chicory, when they last saw him."

"There must be hundreds," she said, eyeing the growing pile of boxes on the dolly.

"Which is why I need all the help I can get." I remembered something I wanted to ask her. "Hey, last month when you and I were on the outs, didn't you say something about consulting another magic-user in the city?"

She rolled her eyes. "Oh, *that* guy."

"Do you happen to remember his name?"

"James Wesson."

A charge went through me. His name had been on the other folder in Chicory's room.

"I should still have his info," Vega said, pulling a wallet from her back pocket and flipping through a batch of business cards. "Here it is." She separated out the card and handed it to me.

The card stated his name and phone number, nothing else. "I'll give him a call," I said. "See if I can't stop in and talk to him myself."

"Have fun," she said dryly.

"Why? What's wrong with him?"

"You'll see."

"Where did you find him?"

"Yellow pages. He's listed under both 'Sorcerer' and 'Supernatural Consultant.'"

That sounded odd for a member of the Order. I had always assumed those listings were posted by frauds. "Was he helpful?"

"You mean when he decided to do some actual work? Yeah, he came up with a few insights. Namely that the murder wasn't the work of werewolves, and magic had decapitated the cats."

I reread the card and put it away. "Sounds like he knows his stuff, anyway."

"Said he was going to run a test on the residue, but that was around the time you and I patched things up. I had the department cut him a check and tell him his services were no longer needed."

I thought about how that could be my in, telling this James that I had taken over the consulting gig and wanted to compare notes. I could then introduce questions about the Order, see how much he knew.

"So are you back for good?" Vega asked.

"Only until tonight. There's a trip I need to take."

"Where?"

"Romania."

"Romania? What's over there?"

"It's where my first mentor trained me, someone named Lazlo."

"Wouldn't a phone call be easier?"

"He doesn't own one—or at least he didn't ten years ago. And I have no other way of reaching him. Lives a pretty solitary lifestyle." I thought about the farm outside the village where he'd taken me to train that summer. The old house, the barn, the muddy fields.

"Can you trust him?" Vega asked.

"The Front implied he wasn't part of the conspiracy. So, either there really is an Order and he belongs to it, or there isn't an Order and he *thinks* he belongs to it. Either way, he should be able to help me sort out what they told me. He's really powerful, and he knew my grandfather."

Besides that, he's the only other member of the Order I *know,* I thought.

"Here," she said, reaching into her pocket. She pulled out the pager I had used while consulting for her and placed it in my hand. It still had the iron case that protected the electronics from my aura. "I'll call if anything important comes up. Let me know if you find anything on your end."

"Will do."

"Oh, and if you want your bathrobe back, I pulled it from evidence."

"Huh?" I squinted at her before remembering the robe of John the Baptist. My bath robe, which Chicory had imbued with a veiling spell, would have been laid bare when Chicory was slain. "Oh, crap."

"Yeah," she said, crossing her arms. "The papers had a field day."

"I'll be happy to take it off your hands," I said sheepishly.

"I already stuck it in a package and dropped it in the mail. It should be at your place later today."

"I owe you," I said.

"Just keep me in the loop."

"I will."

"And Croft," she said, her eyes as stern as ever, "take care of yourself."

13

I called James's number from a payphone and spoke to a young woman named Carla. He wasn't in, she said, not sounding especially happy about that fact. Probably why she volunteered the name of a bar where I could find him.

Twenty minutes later, I pulled up in front of the address, just beyond where the Upper East Side disintegrated into Spanish Harlem. I crossed the graffiti-tagged sidewalk, pulled the door open, and stepped into a drift of smoke. At first glance, the bar looked empty. I then realized everyone was gathered in a room off to the left, where I could hear the sharp clacking of billiard balls. As I entered the pool hall, I realized I should have asked Carla for a description.

In another moment, I realized I didn't need one.

Everyone was crowded around one table where a young black man in a battered bomber jacket and cowboy hat was cruising around the cushion, stroking in striped ball after striped ball, barely seeming to look at what he was doing. A membrane of silver magic moved around him.

"Eight ball, corner," he said, nodding at the far pocket.

Murmurs sounded from the audience of twenty or so. I rose onto my tiptoes and saw why. His opponent's solids were in the way. The shot was impossible. Lips barely moving, James slammed the cue ball into the edge of the eight ball, sending it in a spinning arc from the edge of the table, around the mass of solid balls, and into the pocket he'd indicated, dead center.

He just used an invocation, I thought in alarm.

Straightening, James adjusted his aviator sunglasses and grinned. "Game."

His opponent, a large man who had been watching with a constipated frown, removed a wad of bills from his pocket and slammed it on the table. As the loser stormed off, James coolly picked up his winnings and bounced it in his hand. Nodding as though he'd just calculated the dollar amount by its weight, he deposited the wad into a jacket pocket and looked around.

"Who's next?" he asked.

The other patrons peered at one another and gave dubious shakes of their heads.

"I'll up it to twenty to one," he said. "Five hundred dollar minimum. I win, I get the five. You win, you walk with ten G's." A rubber-banded fold of hundreds appeared in his right hand, and he waggled it back and forth.

The chatter around the table got louder, but still no takers.

"What about you, lanky?"

I didn't realize he was talking to me until heads turned. The crowd stepped apart, creating a smoky aisle between me and the table. James stood on the table's other side, cue over one shoulder.

He was younger than he'd looked at first glance, about my height but muscular and with the kind of carved face and lips women loved. Though he couldn't have been older than twenty-three, twenty-four, I still couldn't get over the audacity of the guy. A member of the Order using magic to hustle? Then again, his file was thick with infractions.

I cleared my throat. "You're James Wesson, right?"

"What's this look like?" he asked. "A meet and greet?"

The crowd laughed, making my face burn with embarrassment.

"I'm actually here on NYPD business," I said, affecting an official tone. "I have a few questions I'd like to ask."

"Tough tits, porky. I'm working."

More laughter broke from the crowd. James chalked his cue and gave it a casual puff.

"This is serious," I said. "A matter of highest *order*."

I emphasized the last word, but if James caught the meaning, he gave no sign. Instead, he looked around as though he'd lost interest in me, just someone taking up space in his world. The crowd shouldered me back.

"Forty to one," he offered now.

Whistles sounded at what the winner stood to gain.

"I'll take those odds."

A riotous cheer went up as the attention turned back to me and enthusiastic hands ushered me toward the pool table. The grin on James's lips hardened as he sized me up. I'd whispered an invocation before accepting his challenge, hiding my wizard's aura. I assumed a look of defiance now, someone who had just been humiliated and was determined to get even.

James recovered his grin. "Let's see the green."

I pulled out my wallet, which I'd just loaded with cash for my trip, and held it open. He nodded and rolled the cue ball to one end of the table as two guys fished balls from pockets and racked them at the other. I was reaching for one of the mounted pool sticks when James said, "Don't bother. This'll be quick."

I now understood Vega's eye roll. The guy was an arrogant ass.

I lowered my arm and watched him break. More specifically, I watched his lips. With the help of a whispered incantation, he sunk three solids. He strode around the table and lined up his shot. Magic fluttered across the green felt. The cue ball split two solids, knocking them into opposite side pockets. He used another force invocation for his next shot, hopping the cue ball over one of my stripes, and nudging his target into a corner pocket. With one solid remaining, he banged it off three cushions before dropping it into another corner pocket.

The jeers started from the crowd.

"NYPD fixing to get his ass *run!*" someone shouted.

James circled the table, eyeing the eight ball in relation to my scatter of untouched stripes. Passing on a direct shot into a side pocket, he indicated the far corner and crouched over his stick. Like the final shot in the last game, it was a challenging angle with way too much traffic. James wasn't just playing for money. He was playing for reputation.

I was going to enjoy this.

James snapped the cue ball into the eight, sending it on another arcing circuit toward the corner. Without a pool stick to hold, I had tucked my cane nonchalantly beneath one arm. Now, standing behind the corner pocket, I angled the cane's tip down and whispered, *"Protezione."*

The shield that spread over the pocket was too thin to be visible, but too thick to allow the eight ball passage. Instead of sinking, the ball rattled around the edge of the pocket and popped out.

A collective "oooh" pushed from the crowd.

James straightened slowly, staring at the missed shot in disbelief. I switched my aim to the cue ball, which was still rolling idly, and changed its trajectory by a few degrees. It clunked into a corner pocket. Stepping forward, I clapped James's shoulder and gave it a squeeze.

"Tough break," I said.

For another moment, the crowd around the table remained entranced in a questioning silence. Then, like waters breaking a dam, they shouted and clamored at once. "Holy crap, he scratched!" "James just blew twenty G's!" It was clear they were delighting more in his loss than in my win. Their voices coalesced into a chant of "Pay up! Pay up! Pay up!"

With a tight grin, James pulled out two of the rubber-banded billfolds from his pocket and pressed them into my hand like we were shaking around them. But instead of releasing them, he clenched and drew me up against him. I could feel the hard breaths from his nostrils.

"What the fuck was that?" he whispered.

"An unlucky shot, apparently."

"Who are you?"

"Someone who needs to talk. Now."

He clenched my hand harder. "You cheated me."

"Hey, man, I was only playing your game."

James didn't have an answer for that. The breaths cycling against my ear began to tremble in anger. I sensed him debating whether to hit me with an invocation, felt the charge building.

"Do it, and the gig's up," I warned. "Word will get out, I'll make sure of it. I'm guessing there are more than a few stiffs who will come looking for their money. Maybe even a few in this crowd."

The power around him ebbed. "I'm not telling you shit," he whispered.

"Tell you what, take a walk with me, and maybe you can earn back what you lost."

His breathing smoothed. His grip relaxed around my hand and his money. When we separated, he was grinning again. He shrugged at the crowd as though to say, *Win some, lose some.*

"Gonna take a little break." He tossed his pool cue to another player.

The crowd broke apart and started their own games at the other tables. James strode from the pool hall ahead of me, leaving me to follow in his path. When he reached the bar, the bartender had a bottle of beer waiting for him. James grasped it wordlessly and turned toward the exit, taking a pull from the bottle as he shoved the door open with a leather-booted foot.

We stepped out into the sun. James leaned against the building and took another pull, then let the bottle dangle at his side between a pair of hooked fingers. I couldn't see his eyes beyond his sunglasses..

"You some kind of magic-user?" he finally asked.

"Just like you," I said. "We belong to the same organization."

"Never seen you before."

"Seems to be how the Order likes it."

James tipped the bottle to his lips again, face aimed at a boarded-up building across the street.

"Do you mind telling me how it all started for you," I said.

"How all what started?"

"You know, discovering your abilities. Getting noticed by the Order. Your training. Your work."

He pulled in his lips in thought. Despite the heat, he made no move to remove his leather jacket. Underneath, he wore a plain undershirt. A silver cross hung over his chest. His jeans were stonewashed, shredded at the knees. I knew the type: too cool for school—and definitely too cool to answer to authority. But he was having to weigh that against the itch to get his money back. Blow me off, and he could kiss his twenty grand goodbye.

"I was in boarding school," he said at last. "St. Mary's, though we called it Catholic lock up."

"Your parents sent you?"

He shook his head. "Never had any."

Another magic user who'd grown up without a mom or dad. Orphan tales were a dime a dozen, apparently. *Either that,* the voice in my head whispered, *or Lich claimed them too.* James caught me looking at him. "I don't know their story, so don't bother asking."

"You were telling me about your boarding school?" I prompted.

"Yeah. Roomed with three other guys. We were sort of a pack." He gave a small snort of reverie. "Around the time we were in the eighth grade, Parker smuggled in a Ouija board. I didn't believe in that shit—I don't think any of us did—but to ruffle the priests' gowns, you know."

"Rebellion," I said.

"What can I say, we were little adrenaline junkies. You can only get caught smoking behind the chapel so many times before it's time to up the stakes."

I nodded as James took another swallow. He was beginning to loosen up.

"So, not really knowing what we were doing, we set up the board one night, lit some candles, put our fingers on that little plastic thingie."

"The planchette," I said.

"Yeah, whatever. At first we were just bullshitting. Will Mikey ever get laid?—crap like that. Then this feeling came over me, like I was being electrocuted. I went stiff, couldn't breathe. And then something talked through my mouth. 'Who's going to die next?' it asked. I remember the other guys laughing and tug-of-warring with the plastic thing, trying to spell out each other's names. But I couldn't move. I was suffocating. Felt like I was dying. All of a sudden, a force erupted through my fingers, and in three jerks, it spelled out a name: 'B-E-N.' And then I could breathe again. My buddies never noticed anything wrong. They were repeating the name to one another. Ben was this homely kid who lived down the hall. 'Bedwetting Ben' we called him, because, you know, he had that problem. The guys joked about him drowning in his own piss, but I was bothered, man. Had awful dreams that night, about leather belts and death. Next morning, the staff rousted us out of bed. We're going to an assembly, they said. As we filed out of the dormitory, I could see an ambulance and a pair of police cars. Didn't learn till that night they'd found Ben in the janitor's closet. He'd cinched a belt around his neck and hung himself from the pipes."

A chill went through me. "What happened to you sounds like demonic possession."

"Ya think?" James took another sip from his bottle. "The demon hung around for a while. Didn't take the Ouija board to call it up, either. For the next year, the feelings would just come out of the blue. I'd say something and it would happen. Always bad shit, though. Another suicide later that year. A fire in the administration wing."

"So you developed precognition?"

"That's what *I* thought. But then I started remembering the dreams more clearly. The one with the fire, for example. Word got around that whoever the arsonist was had set it with hymn books. When I heard that, I suddenly remembered dreaming that I'd stolen some hymn books from the chapel and was setting them around the inside of an office. Putting them under curtains and around wooden bookshelves—the things that would catch quickest. The dream was the same night of the fire. Freaked me out so bad, I told one of the teachers about being possessed. Thought I could trust him, but he got me to tell him about the dream, and from there, he and the administrators wheedled a confession out of me for the fire. Even though I still couldn't say for sure whether I'd actually set it."

"No exorcism?" I asked.

"Naw, they didn't believe in the possession part. Guess that's what I got for being a delinquent. They called the police, and I was taken out in cuffs. Tried and convicted in juvie and sent to a pen upstate."

"Jesus," I said.

"Yeah, thank God I didn't say anything about the suicides, 'cause I had dreams about them too." He sent down another swallow of beer. "Anyway, there was this gang in juvie, group of guys who trashed the new kid as a matter of course. I was there about a week when my turn came. We were out in the yard, and they bum-rushed me. Knocked me down, started stomping me. Then that cold feeling came over me, and I shouted a foreign word I'd never heard before."

"A Word of Power," I said.

"Felt like a stack of TNT had gone off inside me. Next thing I knew, the guys were scattered over the yard. Faces bloodied, bones broken, a couple of them throwing up. I didn't know what the hell had happened, but the story got around. Guys steered clear of me after that."

I thought about how my first experience had happened around the same age. I'd been thirteen when I entered Grandpa's study by repeating a Word I'd heard him utter. He'd suppressed my magic, though, and it wasn't until I called up Thelonious a decade later that the magic returned with a bang. James's latent magic must have been sparked by whatever took him over.

"About a month later, I was told I was being released into someone's care," he went on. "An older woman showed up, red hair, long white coat. Elsie was her name. She drove me to a Victorian house up in the Catskills. I just figured she was some strange broad who couldn't have kids of her own. I was looking forward to running roughshod over her, but that first night, she scared me straight. Hit me with a paralyzing bolt, then told me I was a magic born. She'd been sent to teach me how to use my gift. If I didn't do what she said, she would deplete my magic and send me back into the system. That's when I learned about the Order."

"How long did you stay with Elsie?"

"Till I was eighteen. So, five years."

"You got *five* years of training?" I'd only received a few months under Lazlo before returning to New York and being put under Chicory's mentorship—which hadn't amounted to much.

"Yeah, she taught me mental prisms, Words of Power, how to shape energy."

"What do you use as a conduit?" I asked out of curiosity.

James reached into his jacket and pulled out a metal wand. He twirled it over his first finger and thumb like a drummer before sticking it back in his pocket. "After that it was potions and spells, minor summonings. She took care of the demon, too."

An ember of envy burned in my gut. I'd had to learn those skills from books. And Thelonious was still bound to me.

"When I turned eighteen, she said I was ready. Set me up with a place in the city." He jerked his head. "Just north of here. Told me my new mentor would show up. After a couple of months I got tired of waiting, so I started putting what I'd learned into practice in pool halls and gambling houses. As you saw, the pay's decent."

"But someone showed up eventually," I said.

"Yeah, and said he wasn't happy about what I was doing."

"Chicory?" I asked.

James nodded. "He wanted me to focus on getting to amateur conjurers before the little creatures they called up could do any damage. He put me in charge of the Bronx, Queens, Brooklyn, Staten Island. Gave me a map that would light up when something popped into our world. The work was all right, but sort of dead in between. Magic or not, I was gonna live my life."

So, he'd been given the same job as me, but in New York's outer boroughs. More compartmentalization. "You and Chicory butted heads, I take it," I said, remembering the infractions in his file.

"You could say that."

"Weren't you worried?"

He looked over at me, his face blank. "About what?"

"Oh, I don't know. The *penalties*."

"Oh, you mean the Big One?" He drew a finger across his neck and gave a lazy laugh. "Yeah, Chicory tried holding that crap over my head, but after a while it got old. I just nodded and went back to whatever I was doing. The guy only showed up once in a blue moon, anyway."

I thought about the terror I'd felt upon being issued the same threats, the loss of appetite, the hives that would break out over my chest, the sleepless nights. And here James had tuned them out like they were background static. I felt like I was talking to a much cooler version of myself. But what did it mean that the Order had never followed up on the warnings?

"What happened to your first trainer—Elsie?"

James shrugged. "Never heard from her again."

"You never went back to visit?"

"Never thought to. It wasn't like we were friends."

"What about Chicory? Did he ever, I don't know, say what he was up to when he was away?"

"Checking up on other magic-users, best I could tell."

I nodded. That had always been my assumption.

"You consulted for the NYPD last month," I said, changing course.

"Yeah, was running out of people to hustle. Figured it was time to do something legitimate. Something the Order would be more agreeable to. So I hung out a shingle. Was sorta surprised when the NYPD called."

"You told them Lady Bastet was killed by magic. How did you know that?"

"A reveal spell. The magic was hidden but it was there."

Same thing I'd used. "You were going to run a test on the residue," I said, "the stuff found on the mutilated cats. Did you get anywhere?"

"The NYPD had me turn in my hours before I'd gotten started. And if they weren't gonna pay me for it..." He swirled his beer, and took a foamy swallow. He was getting to the bottom of the bottle.

Before I could ask him anything more about the case, a young woman sauntered up. She was curvy and coffee skinned with a midriff shirt and purple eye shadow. "There you are, baby," she said to James, planting a lascivious kiss on his mouth, which he seemed more than happy to return.

I shifted my weight, pretending to become interested in the bent fender of Chicory's car. When James's and the young woman's faces separated, she pressed herself to his side and turned toward me.

"I'm, ah, Everson," I said, extending a hand. "We spoke earlier."

She squinted back at me, not moving her arm.

"Carla, right?" I prompted.

"Carla?" The young woman jerked from James and planted her fists on her hips. *"Carla?"* she repeated, this time with even more venom. "You're still running with that skank?" Before James could answer, she slapped him across the face and stormed back the way she'd come.

James straightened his sunglasses and rubbed his jaw. "Thanks, man."

"Not Carla?" I said.

"What the hell is all this about, anyway?"

I sensed his impatience, but it was a good question. Everything he had told me could be consistent with either the official story, that there was an Order, or the alternate version, that Lich had created a shadow Order and was manipulating magic-users to feed his efforts.

"Did you ever meet anyone higher up in the Order?" I asked.

"The money first."

"Money?" Then I remembered I still had his twenty thousand in my pocket. I drew out one of the rubber-banded bill folds and handed it to him. "I'll give you the other one when we're done."

"If you want an answer, you'll give it to me now. I'm tired of talking."

"Even for ten thousand?" I asked, holding the other wad back.

"Keep it," he said and turned away.

I needed answers more than he needed the money, and he knew it, dammit.

"All right," I said, my jaw tensing.

James turned back, accepted the money, and pocketed it. Then he tilted his beer to his mouth, draining the last of it. He reared his arm back and heaved the bottle across the street. I watched it shatter against the side of the vacant building, wondering why he'd done that. I turned back in time to catch a close-up of his knuckles before they plowed into my chin.

More stunned than hurt, I staggered back and drew my cane, but not before James had drawn his wand.

14

Silver magic flashed from the end of James's wand and streaked toward me like lightning. I threw up my cane, forgetting that the magic-absorbing capacity of the staff had been cleaned. Voltage roared through me as the bolt struck and lifted me from my feet. I landed down the block, performing several backward somersaults before coming to a bruising rest.

I was surprised to find myself still holding the cane, the current apparently having locked my fingers around it.

"Protezione," I called as I staggered to my feet.

Energy coursed through my banged-up prism and emerged from the staff's orb, manifesting a shield. Sparks blew from it as another of James's bolts struck. The young wizard was pacing toward me, lips set in a determined line. The air around him glimmered with power.

"What the hell are you doing?" I shouted, drawing my sword.

He unleashed another attack, splitting the silver bolt in two. They arced around—much as he'd made the billiard balls do—and slammed into either side of my shield. My protection buckled. A clapping sound landed against my ears, as though they'd been hammered by a pair of open hands, the pain driving to the center of my head.

I stepped back, incanting to maintain my prism. My recent training with Chicory had increased my capacity to cast, but another couple of shots like that and I'd be toast. What was this about, though? The stupid pool game? Or was I dealing with something more sinister?

Need to put him on the defensive.

"Vigore!" I called, swiping my sword in a clumsy arc.

The force caught Chicory's car and heaved it toward James. With a Word, he manifested a silver light shield and used it to shove the car back into the street. Still backpedaling, I shouted another invocation, this time uprooting a section of chain-link fencing from an adjoining lot. With sharp clangs, the fence whipped around and encircled James.

"Respingere," he said.

His silver shield flashed, and the fence broke into pieces, his boots crunching over the broken links as he continued his advance. Thanks to his five years of training, the guy's magic was fundamentally sound. But I had experience on my side, not to mention a sword in which some of Grandpa's magic-cleaving enchantment still lingered. I'd have to employ the first to get close enough to use the second, though.

"Illuminare," I called.

The light that pulsed from my shield was meant to blind him, but James had anticipated the Word and countered with a Word of his own, one that intercepted the light with an orb of darkness. Damn. That was the problem with casting in the same language as your opponent.

Two more bolts slammed into my shield, rocking me backward. When I grunted, a smile formed across James's lips. His confidence was growing. He cast his next bolt from the hip.

As my shield shook and sparks blew across my face, I remembered how James had passed on the easy tap into the side pocket for the win against me earlier, electing instead for a trick shot. Something told me he'd do the same thing out here: go for the spectacular instead of the sure bet.

Deciding to test that theory, I turned and ran.

Behind me, James spoke four Words in rapid succession. Bolts ripped past my shielded body, leaving harsh ozone trails in their wakes. Several blocks ahead they wheeled in different directions, like jets at an air show, before storming back toward me en masse. I didn't have to look over my shoulder to know James had thinned his shield to feed the bolts.

I aimed my sword back between my legs. Using a force blast as a propellant, I released my grip and let the sword rip.

Behind me, James let out a scream. The bolts fizzled in midair.

I turned to find his shield shattered, James clutching his shoulder where the blade had gashed him. With another force invocation, I returned the sword to my grip and stalked toward him. His sunglasses had fallen off, and surprised blue eyes stared from his face. He jerked his wand at me several times, but no bolts would emerge. The blade's enchantment had broken his magic. I kicked the wand out of his hand and touched the blade to his throat.

"You're oh for two, pal. Care to explain why you attacked me?"

His eyes shifted, as though searching for an escape.

"You can try to get up, but this blade has cut through thicker necks than yours."

Muttering, he showed his hands.

"Better start talking," I said. "Fast."

"Can I at least grab another beer?"

I allowed James his beer, warning him that if he shouted for help or did anything funny, I would force blast him into next month. But he was already injured, his magic spent. I doubted he would test me.

We sat at the dark end of the empty bar, a couple of brown bottles sweating in front of us.

"All right," I said, the tip of my blade against James's side. "Mind telling me why you went homicidal on me out there?"

James sighed. "I was warned you might show up."

"Warned?" Coldness enveloped me. "By whom?"

"Chicory."

"Chicory? *Our* Chicory?"

"Yeah, he stopped in a couple weeks ago. Told me to be on the lookout for someone who'd come with a lot of questions. Said the person would be the agent of some evil wizard, a dude named Lich or Lech, and not to let him get away." James took a swig from his bottle. "And then here you come, driving Chicory's car. What the hell was I supposed to do?"

I took a sip from my own bottle and worked out the timing. Two weeks before would have been when Chicory was training me. He *had* ducked out a couple of times, though he'd never said for what. There was nothing about the visit in James's file, either.

"Were those his exact words?" I asked. "Agent of an evil wizard?"

"Best I can remember. I was sort of stoned when he dropped in."

I still couldn't believe this guy was a member of the Order.

"Did he say anything else?"

"Naw, that was pretty much it."

Had the warning to James been some sort of insurance in case the operation failed and the Front used Whisperer magic on me? Or had it been in case the Front told me the truth?

"To be honest, you don't strike me as an evil agent," James said.

"Would've been nice if you'd exercised that bit of judgment outside," I muttered.

By warning James, my former mentor had put me in a bind. No matter what I told him, James was now biased against me. *Just like Chicory biased you against the Front*, the voice whispered in my head. If the potion I'd drunk that morning had worked, I was hearing my own voice. If not, I could well be hearing the Whisperer's corrupting words. I squeezed my beer bottle in frustration. Never mind James trusting me—could I trust myself?

"Before you started firing bolts at me," I said, "you suggested you'd met someone higher up in the Order."

"Naw. I just wanted my money back." He froze with his bottle halfway to his mouth. "Shit. Does that mean you're gonna kill me now?"

"No," I said.

"Good." James took his swallow. "How about I ask you a few questions, then?"

I checked my watch. I still had a couple hours before I needed to be at the airport.

"Shoot," I told him.

"What do you really do?"

"Same thing as you," I said tiredly. "Stop amateur conjurers, blow up nether creatures, close holes to their worlds. Oh, and get threatened by the Order. I cover Manhattan. I helped the mayor's eradication campaign last month. You might have read about me in the papers?"

"Eradication who?"

"Don't follow the news, huh?"

He shook his head and took another swig. "So why does Chicory think you're working for an evil wizard?"

"It's a long story."

"I've got time. Not like I can hustle now."

I looked over at him. Something in his hunched posture spoke to sincerity. Maybe he'd been lonely for the company of another magic-user, someone he could talk to. I doubted he'd told his life story to anyone else—or at least anyone who wouldn't have laughed him out of the room. In any case, it wasn't as if I'd be giving away any secrets. I had nothing to lose.

"It's going to sound insane," I said.

"Hey, I dig insane."

"All right, but don't say I didn't warn you." In a lowered voice, I began. I told him about my mother's suspicious death, the silence from the Order, and how my consulting Lady Bastet had led to her murder.

"So *that's* why someone offed her," James said. "I'd wondered about that."

I nodded, going on to tell him about my own investigation, which had gotten me a warning from Marlow, or at least someone pretending to be him; my session in the scrying globe, where I experienced my mother's murder at the mage's hands; and then what Chicory had told me about Marlow taking up Lich's work to bring forth the Whisperer.

"No one ever told me about any Whisperer," James said.

"According to Chicory, that info isn't shared with novice practitioners." I wondered now if that info was shared with anyone, save in cases where a magic-user came too close to the truth.

"Always did feel like I was at the kid's table," he said.

"Don't take it personally. I was right there beside you, bib and all."

"So why were you told all this stuff?"

"Because Marlow's my father."

"No shit?" James said.

"Yeah." That much I knew to be true. Both Chicory and Connell had said so. I told James about being sent to the Refuge, allegedly to destroy Lich's book, and what had actually happened—from battling Marlow to being sent back here to investigate the Front's claims for myself.

James's sunglasses remained fixed on me as I spoke. When I finished, he said, "So ... Chicory's history?"

"That remains to be seen. Either he's dead, or he'll return in four days. Well, three days now."

"So you wait and see," James said. "That would settle that question, right?"

"If Connell is telling the truth, Chicory will be coming for me. I know too much now. Were I to alert the magic-using community, he'd be deprived of the power he needs to sustain himself and the portal to the Whisperer. Plus, he'd be looking at a much larger resistance." I thought of the hundreds of files I'd given to Vega. Convincing those magic-users would be another matter, of course.

"What if this dude Connell is lying?" James asked.

"That's what I have three days to find out."

James blew out his breath as though to say, *Sucks to be you, bro.*

"What do you think?" I asked pointedly.

"What do I think?" He set down his bottle and studied me for a moment. "I think if you're on the bad side of this, you don't know it."

"What makes you say that?"

"I play cards, five card stud mostly. There my magic only really helps when I'm the dealer, so I've had to learn to read people, pick out their tells. For the past hour, you haven't shown me a one. Which suggests that everything you've said either happened, or you believe it happened."

"So you understand my dilemma."

"Yeah, you're either looking at a bluff or a double bluff."

"What does that mean to us non-card-playing types?"

"It all goes back to the mystic's murder," he explained. "The perpetrator made it look like a wolf attack, right? With a simple bluff, he would've done that to hide his involvement—in which case the killer is Marlow. But with a double bluff, he'd have done that to make you *think* the second bluff about Marlow was the truth. In which case the killer is Chicory."

I nodded. I couldn't have put it more succinctly myself.

"The anti-hunting spell that earned you those claw marks from your cat," he said, "what you saw in the scrying globe ... Any advanced magic-user could have put those together."

I nodded some more, glad now I'd shared my story with James. I hadn't learned anything new, no, but the back and forth was helping to bring the essential questions into relief.

"Mind sharing your plan?" James asked. "I mean, besides shaking down guys like me?"

I rotated my bottle on the bar, wondering how far I could trust him. James had been warned I was coming. He'd been ordered to stop me. He had failed, but that didn't mean he wouldn't try again. The man was an admitted hustler. He claimed to believe me—and he'd brought up some great points—but he could also be playing me, setting me up for the next round.

And if Chicory had gotten into his head...

"I'd rather not," I said. "No offense."

James shrugged and signaled to the bartender he was ready for another round. We drank for the next few minutes in silence, billiard balls clacking in the next room. James was halfway through his new bottle when he said, "Before he left, Chicory did this strange thing he'd never done before. Sort of mashed his thumb between my eyes. Said it was supposed to protect me from mind magic or something. You ever heard of anything like that?"

I straightened. "Did you feel a pressure behind your eyes, in your ears?"

James shook his head. "Nothing like that. More like a tingling that just sort of went away."

I considered that. "What do I look like?" I asked suddenly.

"Huh?"

"Just describe me."

Connell had claimed Lich's magic had poisoned me, superimposing nightmare images over everything I'd observed in the Refuge. If James was seeing someone other than me, I would have my answer.

"Hell, I don't know," James said, "you look like you're about my height, dark hair. Could probably stand to gain a few pounds. You worry a lot too. Got these deep lines between your eyebrows. And I'm guessing by the episode outside you can't read women too well. Sort of awkward around them."

"Alright, alright," I said, my face growing warm. Yeah, he could see me, zits and all, which seemed to tip the scales toward Chicory's version of events. I checked my watch. "I need to get going," I said, pushing myself from my stool. "Thanks for talking to me."

"So, that's it?"

"I have your number. I'll let you know if I find out anything."

He rotated on the stool. "While you're out, doing whatever it is you're gonna do, is there something I could be doing?"

I stopped. "You said your first mentor was in the Catskills?"

"Yeah, about two, three hours upstate."

"Could you take a drive up there?" I asked. "Tell her what I told you? I sent a couple messages to the Order about my trip to the Refuge and Chicory's death, but I never heard back. I don't have a handle on what's going on yet, but certainly the more who know, the better."

He stood and tossed a twenty onto the bar. "I'm on it, boss. It's been sort of beat around here anyway. Hey, you got a number where I can reach you?"

I pulled out the pager Vega had given me. The number was taped to the back. "Do you have something to write with?"

"Here," James said, taking the pager. He turned it around and read the ten numbers aloud. Then he closed his eyes and repeated them before nodding and handing it back. "It's stored," he said.

"Offer you a ride?" I asked as we stepped outside.

"Naw, I'm just a few blocks north."

I gripped his elbow before he could turn away. "Listen, I'm not sure what I might be getting you into, so you need to tread carefully."

James's mouth leaned into a grin. "I'm not real good at that, boss."

I couldn't help but chuckle as I released him and we headed our separate ways.

Maybe I had an ally in James, after all.

15

The trip to Romania was long and sleepless. I wrestled with James's assessment the entire way: a bluff or a double bluff. Marlow or Lich/Chicory. I had good reasons to suspect both and not enough to clear either. I had to trust that finding Lazlo would tip the balance toward one or the other.

From the train station in Bacau, I hustled to the edge of town where I'd been told the final bus of the day would be departing for the villages in the foothills. Eleven years earlier, I'd arrived on a weekend day and had had to find a cart driver—who'd turned out to be Lazlo. After an exhausting twenty hours of travel, I hoped I was close to seeing him again.

A cold drizzle began to fall as I approached the end of an

asphalt road that turned into a rutted pair of tracks. I looked around in exasperation. No bus. Had I missed it? A car horn blew twice. I looked over at a livestock truck I had assumed abandoned. Its pale blue body was rusted, and it was leaning on one side of the road. When its lights flashed on and off, I spotted someone sitting in the driver's seat. The window cranked down as I hustled up.

"Has the bus to the villages left yet?" I asked in Romanian.

"That depends," a woman's voice replied in accented English.

From beneath the bill of a newsboy hat, a young woman with dark red hair and a mole over the left corner of her mouth peered back at me. Though she wore the grave face of so many in the countryside, her beauty startled me.

"Depends on what?" I stammered.

"If I have any riders."

It took me a moment to process what she was saying. "Wait, *this* is the bus?"

"What were you expecting?" she asked. "A double-decker?" Without waiting for a response, she said, "You can put pack in back and ride up front with me. The weather is not expected to improve."

I thanked her and did as she said, dropping my pack in the open truck bed. When I slammed the passenger door and settled in, cane between my knees, the young woman put the truck in gear and bumped forward, the rain already beginning to form brown puddles in the road ahead.

"I am Olga. Where are you going?"

"Hi, I'm Everson. There's a farm between here and the last village. The owner's name is Lazlo."

She stopped the truck. "There is no such farm."

I looked over at her, but her face remained fixed on the road ahead. "There is, actually," I said, trying to hide my irritation. "I stayed there for a summer, about ten years ago."

"The farm burned down five years ago," she said.

Horror prickled over me like a violent rash. "Burned down? What happened?"

"There was fire."

"Yeah, thanks, but does anyone know what started it?"

"No. Fire destroyed everything. House. Farm. Horses."

"And Lazlo?" I asked, my voice dry and husky.

"They think he was inside house. In cellar."

"What do you mean *think*?" I asked. "Did they recover his body or didn't they?"

"No one will go to farm now. Ghosts have been seen."

"Ghosts? What ghosts?"

"Do you want me to take you back to town?"

"No, I want you to take me to the farm," I answered stubbornly.

"I can take you in morning."

"There's no time," I said, which was true. If the Front could be believed, I had roughly two days until Lich's return—and one of those days would involve travel back to the States.

I expected Olga to object, but she released the brake, and the truck began to rumble forward again. We rode in silence. She twisted the headlights on shortly and rain sliced through the beams. The forests and fields darkened around us. Olga snapped on the radio, and a man singing a sad ballad crackled from the speakers. I refused to believe she had the right farm, refused to believe it had burned to the ground and that Lazlo was ... *missing? dead?*

No, I decided. *Once I show her where it is, she'll realize she was thinking of a different farm, a different person.* But I couldn't forget what Connell had told me about Lich eliminating the most powerful wizards, sacrificing them in his effort to bring the Whisperer into our world.

After thirty minutes that seemed longer than the flight over the Atlantic, a derelict chapel appeared among some trees. "The turnoff is up here on the right," I said, squinting past the headlight beams and pointing. "There. The farm is about a kilometer down that drive."

Olga pulled in front of the drive and idled. "This is as near as I will go."

I almost asked her why before remembering what she'd said about the ghosts earlier. This was the farm she'd been thinking of.

"Do you mind waiting for me?" I asked.

She looked at the bills I held toward her. "One hour," she said at last, accepting them. "Do you have light?"

I started to nod before realizing my staff wouldn't work as well in the rain, especially if it started coming down harder. Olga reached beneath her seat and handed me a brick-shaped flashlight. When I snapped it on, shadows sprung over Olga's face, making her appear sinister.

"Beware the ghosts," she said. "You will know them by their whispers."

Her words sent a bone-deep chill through me. Gripping the flashlight and my cane, I stepped out of the truck and into the Romanian night.

I made my way up the drive, rain pattering over a poncho I'd pulled from my pack and slid into. Though it had been more than a decade, I remembered every turn in the dirt drive and even some of the larger trees that bordered it. Toward the end of my training, Lazlo had challenged me to direct force invocations down the winding drive to a target without rustling the leaves. It was as hard as it sounds.

At the final turn, I stopped and looked out over an open yard that was almost unrecognizable.

No.

Olga was right. The place had been decimated by fire, and judging by the weeds growing up through the heaps of charred timber, it had happened a number of years ago. I stepped forward, shining the flashlight over the ruins of the main house and then the barn. The place where Lazlo had helped me to construct my mental prism, to strengthen and hone it, push energy through it … gone.

Even the fencing that had once penned his beloved horses, Mariana and Mihai, had burned to the ground. My heart thudded sickly in my chest.

I turned back to where the house had once stood. Though I could see nothing through my wizard's senses, dark energies seemed to pollute the atmosphere. Perhaps my own sense of foreboding. Far away in the mountains, wolf cries echoed.

They think he was inside house, Olga had said. *In cellar.*

I drew my sword and aimed it at the hill of ruins. *"Vigore!"* I shouted.

Energy pulsed bright from the blade, overcoming the dampness to slam into the ruins and plow it back in a wave. Chunks of charred timber rained down in the fields beyond. With a second force invocation, I cleared the remaining debris from the trapdoor that led down to Lazlo's cellar.

I stood over the door and listened. All I could hear was the rain tapping my poncho. The door broke away when I pulled the handle—the hinges had been baked black. I set the door aside and shone the flashlight down the steps. During my time with him, Lazlo had forbidden me from going down to his lab. That had been fine by me and my phobia then, but now I had no choice.

If Lazlo *had* been trapped, his remains might tell me something.

I set the flashlight down and, with a Word, summoned a glowing shield and descended. The steps groaned underfoot. At the bottom of the steps, I grew my light out. The brightness revealed a small room overgrown with black mushrooms and mold. Similar to what I'd seen in the Refuge, the wet growth swarmed over everything: stacks of old books, shelves holding vials and spell implements, even over the remnants of a casting circle that took up most of the floor.

In the circle's center lay a mound. No, a body.

Lazlo?

The body was on its side, facing away from me. As I approached, my light illuminated wisps of dark hair, a deflated wool sweater and trousers, the last tucked into a pair of battered rubber boots. Kneeling, I set my sword down, gripped the body's bony shoulder, and pulled it toward me. For a moment the body stuck to the ground before releasing with a wet rip.

"Jesus!" I cried, and jumped back.

My heart thundered in my chest as I looked at my former mentor. Or what remained of him.

The eyes staring up at me were large toadstool-filled sockets. Dark, wet growth had erupted over the rest of his face, reminding me of the wargs. I eased forward again, staff held up. Black mold glistened in the light, making it appear as though the growth was crawling over him.

"What in the hell happened to you?" I whispered.

The casting circle around Lazlo was for protection. He'd been trying to defend himself. But against what? Something stronger than him, evidently—and Lazlo had been a Third Order mage. My gaze moved back to his body. Bared teeth showed through Lazlo's decayed lips.

If only he could talk, I thought, then stopped.

Lazlo had had a barn cat, a tough gray tom named, well, Tom. During my final month here, I'd found Tom in a corner of the barn one day, his mouth open, tongue out. When I nudged him with my shoe, his body was as stiff as a board. I told Lazlo the bad news. He simply nodded and wrapped Tom in a towel that I assumed he would bury him in. The next day, though, while I was loading hay from the barn, a thick, purring body swiped my legs. I looked down and there was Tom: dusty gray coat, cloven right ear, and one hundred percent alive.

I sprinted inside and told Lazlo.

"It was not his time," my mentor said.

"Not his time?" I wasn't sure I'd heard him right. "Tom wasn't sick yesterday, Lazlo. He was dead."

"Yes, but that was my fault. Not his."

"Wait ... you *resurrected* him?"

"I shouldn't have put the rat poison where he could get to it."

"How?" I pressed.

The magic we'd practiced to that point had involved basic invocations. But resurrection?

Lazlo's lips tensed in what was the closest he ever came to smiling. "One day, Everson." Which was his way of saying it was an advanced spell for which I didn't have the necessary experience.

"Well, that day's today," I whispered now, grimacing at the idea.

I still lacked the experience, to be honest, but I'd read enough books in the decade since to understand how resurrection worked. For someone as long gone as Lazlo, I couldn't hope for much, maybe a few seconds of life, but if it was enough for him to tell me who had killed him, I would be closer to understanding what was happening, who I could trust. And if Lazlo had resurrected Tom, he would have the necessary spell ingredients.

I wheeled toward his shelves and began unstoppering old vials and sniffing their contents. *Fennel ... yarrow ...* I was looking for moschatus, a rare oil. On the top shelf, I found it. I re-stoppered the vial and began looking through his moldy collection of books until I found a familiar tome that focused on the dead. I had the same tome in my own collection. I flipped to the section on resurrection.

The next half hour involved reconfiguring the casting circle and preparing Lazlo's body with the moschatus oil.

At last, I stood outside the circle.

"Cerrare," I said. Energy coursed through my sword and closed the circle. Consulting the book, I began incanting in an ancient

tongue. Cold energies swirled throughout the room. I trembled from them as well as from a deeper dread around what I was doing. Restoring a decayed form to life, however briefly, felt wrong on so many levels. Also, except for in exceptional circumstances—and with prior approval—the Order forbade resurrections.

What if the rule is to prevent communication with sacrificed magic-users? the voice whispered inside me. A voice I no longer suppressed. I would know something shortly.

"Vivere!" I finished.

I watched Lazlo's body, a part of me hoping it would remain still, that the spell wouldn't take hold. I was violating a law of nature, which may have been the actual reason behind the Order's prohibition. But I steeled my mind, reminding myself that I was doing this for a magic-using community that could be in mortal danger. I doubted Lazlo would object. He—

I broke off mid-thought and stiffened. Had Lazlo's jaw just shifted?

I leaned nearer. His bared teeth parted, releasing two scratchy words. "I ... hurt."

"Lazlo?" I said, my own voice barely a whisper. "Lazlo, it's Everson."

His body remained still for so long, I thought I'd lost him again. But then his top arm trembled as though trying to lift his wasted hand. His jaw shifted again. "Everson?"

"Yes, Lazlo," I said, kneeling and placing my hand over his. I tried to ignore the wet feel of the fungi and tissue. It was like he was being slowly digested. "What happened?"

"Leave," he said.

"I need to know what happened to you."

"I'm in ... the pit."

"The pit?"

"In ... him."

"Who?"

"They'll ... take you ... too."

A shudder passed through me. "Who? Lich? The Front?"

His head shook, though whether in a tremor or to say he didn't know, I couldn't tell.

"My hair," he rasped. "Take it ... find me."

I nodded quickly, cut a wisp of his dark hair with the sword, and placed it in my pocket.

"Leave," he repeated in what sounded like a plea. I imagined his cloudy wolf-torn eye staring into mine, though on his corpse there was only the cluster of toadstools. "They ... they're coming."

"Is Lich alive?" I asked.

"Hurts," he mumbled. The trembling in his wet hand ceased.

"Lazlo?" I asked, giving him a light shake. But the resurrection spell was spent, the magic expired. My former mentor was a fungus-riddled corpse again, his soul returned to whatever plane it inhabited.

In the pit? I thought. *In him?*

Had Lazlo meant Lich? That would jibe with what Connell had told me—how Lich was sacrificing souls to feed his efforts as well as to sustain himself. But Lazlo could also have been cast into the pit by Marlow and consumed by Dhuul. Hence, "in the pit, in him."

They'll take you too, Lazlo had said.

Who were *they*?

Above me, the rain fell harder. Wind shrieked past the doorway to the cellar.

It was only when the wind died again that I realized the cellar stairs were creaking. Someone or something was descending. Above the creaks, a pair of low whispers sounded.

16

I rose from beside Lazlo's body, light radiating from my protective shield, and adjusted my grip on my sword. Shadows shifted on the wooden steps as the whispers grew. I remembered what Olga had said about no one coming here because of the ghosts. *You will know them by their whispers*, she'd said.

If Lazlo's soul had been sacrificed to the Whisperer, then a conduit now existed between his body and Dhuul's realm. Maybe no more than a seam, but enough for shadow entities to come and go, to feed on the lingering magic, of which there were still traces.

Those were the ghosts the villagers had seen. And now *I* was seeing them.

I shuffled back. Though immaterial, the man-sized beings were horrid. They descended on tentacled legs. More tentacles writhed from their shapeless bodies of matted hair and sharp beaks. They slowed as they neared the bottom of the steps, their whispers alien and wet. Multiple sets of pale eyes glowed into view, all of them watching me.

"Vigore!" I shouted.

In my fear, my force invocation lacked control. It rammed into the stairs, sending splintered timber ricocheting from the walls and off my shield. Shrieks sounded. I jumped back as something lashed out—a tentacle. It grazed my neck, suckers grasping for purchase, before recoiling back into the darkness behind the ruined staircase. The skin where it had touched me burned like fire.

My shield didn't stop that thing, I thought in horror.

I backed from the shadowy creatures as they crawled from the ruins, their whispers turning to low hisses.

"Illuminare!" I called, channeling power through my coin pendant.

The coin glowed, limning the creatures in blue light. They slowed, eyes squinting away. The coin held an enchantment to ward off shadow creatures, but these shadows were from much farther down. The enchantment seemed to have a stalling effect, but it wasn't stopping them.

Another tentacle lashed out. I grunted and brought my sword up in a parrying motion. The blade sliced harmlessly through the tentacle. The tip of the tentacle affixed to my chest, the contact like boiling acid. I screamed as I felt my soul lurch inside me, yanked toward the point of contact. I dug into my pockets, searching for *... there!*

I yanked out the glass vial Arianna had given me. Pulling the stopper free with my teeth, I splashed the creature with the clear liquid inside. The tentacle released me, the creature withdrawing with a screaming hiss. I advanced on the two of them, splashing more liquid. Steam spewed from their forms.

"Go!" I commanded, my voice trembling from the pain in my chest. "Go back to your cursed realm."

I splashed several more times. How much of this stuff would it take to banish them? The creatures had retreated, screaming, to the far corner of the cellar when I realized the vial was almost empty. *Need to make tracks,* I decided, easing back and recovering my sword.

The stairs were gone, but I could use a force invocation to launch myself like I'd done in the Refuge. I stood beneath the hole where the trap door had been, aimed my blade at the ground—and cried out as a tentacle whipped around my ankle. Fire enveloped my lower leg, and I could feel blood soaking into my sock.

A second tentacle seized my sword and wrenched it away. I heard it clatter off somewhere. Another tentacle wrapped around my staff. The light from the opal sputtered as the creature and I struggled for possession. Multiple pale eyes emerged from the shadows.

You're not thinking, I chided myself through the pain. *Don't have to banish them ... just have to close their portal.*

My gaze shifted to Lazlo's body. Burning it would shut the door on this end.

I plunged my free hand into another pocket and withdrew a vial of dragon sand. The tentacle around my ankle flexed. I landed prone with a grunt, out of range of Lazlo. Pain seared my stomach as a tentacle snaked underneath me. I could feel its suckers opening and closing.

Not suckers, I realized in horror. *Mouths.*

Each mouth had a ring of spiny teeth, and they were tearing at my soul, trying to suck it out. *They'll take you too*, Lazlo had warned. I clawed at the wooden floorboards, desperate not to meet my mentor's fate. I imagined my body buried in toadstools, my soul trapped in a pit, in endless pain.

I grunted as part of a fingernail tore off between the floorboards. The tentacles were winning. They flipped me onto my back and began dragging me toward the creatures' gaping beaks. As I passed beneath the cellar doorway, rain spattered over my face. I squinted against it. In the fog of pain, it took me a moment to realize someone's silhouette was framed in the doorway.

A deafening blast broke through the cellar. The creature holding me screamed. Its tentacles recoiled, releasing me. Another blast went off, but I was on hands and knees now, crawling toward Lazlo's body. I reached him and shook a dose of dragon sand over him.

"Fuoco!" I shouted.

I reared back, forearms to my face, as searing flames billowed from his body. The creatures' screams turned to piercing shrieks. I turned in time to see their shadow forms breaking apart as the fire from the dragon sand consumed Lazlo's body, slamming closed the portal.

I recovered my sword and looked up. A thick rope now dangled through the cellar doorway. Sheathing my sword and sliding the cane through my belt, I seized the end of the rope.

"Got it," I called.

In a jerky motion, I began to rise. After ten or so feet, I was able to reach up and grab the doorway frame. Grunting, I pulled myself through. Olga, who was larger than she had appeared in the truck was staring down at me, rain dripping from the bill of her newsboy hat.

"I heard screams. I thought you fell into ruins."

"Thanks." I gained my feet, the places where the tentacles had seized me still burning like a bitch. My soul didn't feel quite right, either. Like it had been gashed and torn. As I whispered a healing incantation, Olga slung the rope in manly loops around an arm. My gaze moved to the shotgun she had leaned against a charred length of timber.

"What was in that?" I asked.

"Rock salt," she answered.

I nodded. Sometimes the best deterrents against evil were the most basic.

When Olga finished gathering the rope, she stuck her arm through the coil, pushed it up to her shoulder, and grabbed her shotgun. In rubber boots similar to Lazlo's, she marched from the ruins. I took a final look around, my eyes falling at last to the cellar, where Lazlo's remains continued to flicker. Pain and rage stormed through me. Murdered.

But by whom? Lich or Marlow?

By the time I caught up to Olga, the rain was falling harder.

"Do you have place to stay?" she asked.

A pack of lean dogs ran up to the truck as we pulled into the yard in front of Olga's house. They began barking when they saw Olga had brought company, but when she shouted several harsh words in Romanian, they stopped and sniffed tentatively toward my crotch as I got out.

"I really appreciate this," I said.

"There is extra room," she replied.

Though it had stopped raining, water dripped from my pack as I grabbed it from the back of the truck, shouldered it, and followed her toward the one-story farmhouse. She lived on the outskirts of Bacau, not far from the train station. More important than a spare bed, she had a working phone.

Blocking the dogs with her body, she opened the door for me and then followed me inside, closing the door to their whines and whimpers.

"My father," Olga said, nodding into a living room where an older man in a stained T-shirt sat in a recliner in front of a television. When he squinted over at us, I raised a hand in greeting. He took a gulp from a mug and turned his face back to the glowing screen.

"Always drunk," Olga explained, not bothering to lower her voice. "Give me pack. Phone is in kitchen."

I did as she said and found the wall-mounted phone. Fortunately, it was a rotary dial, like my own. I pulled James's number from my wallet along with a phone card. After a minute of dialing, the line began to ring.

"Yeah," he answered.

"James, it's Everson."

"Dude," he said over the scratchy line. "Holy shit."

My heart thudded. "What's going on?"

"Alright, so I drove up to the Catskills yesterday, and the house is toast."

"Burned down?" I asked, already knowing.

"To the foundation. Neighbors said it happened a couple of years ago. They had no idea what 'came of Elsie. I went to the local police station and asked there, but they didn't know anything either. Not what started the fire or wherever Elsie might have gone. Her body wasn't found among the ruins. It's like she just dropped off the map."

I wondered if there was a clump of toadstools in Elsie's shape somewhere on the property, Elsie's soul in the pit with Lazlo.

"Did anyone talk about hauntings?" I asked.

"How did you know?"

"Just a hunch."

"Yeah, police said that not long after the fire, a couple kids drove up there to neck in a convertible. Bodies were found the next morning, both of 'em strangled, necks black and blue. Something similar happened to a hiker."

I rubbed the spot on my neck where the tentacle had lashed me.

"They never found the perp, so rumors about angry spirits started popping up," he continued. "When I was walking around that place, something felt off to me, foul. Couldn't nail it down, though."

I could hear my blood swishing in my ears. Two high-level members of the Order slain in the last few years, houses burned to the ground, murderous creatures set loose. But still the same question: Lich or Marlow?

"What did you find in Romania?" James asked.

"Same thing," I said hollowly. "Lazlo's house had been burned to the ground. His remains were in the cellar. Something used them as a portal to attack me, shadow creatures from Dhuul's realm. Probably the same things that killed those kids in the Catskills."

James was lucky they hadn't attacked *him*.

"What in the hell are we dealing with?" he asked.

"Whisperer shit," I said. "Nightmares from that realm are coming through. Right now the seams are few and far between, and the shadow creatures seem to be staying in proximity to the bodies, but if whoever's behind it completes the portal, it's going to get really ugly. "

"And you still don't know whether it's the bluff or the double bluff?"

The liquid in Arianna's vial *had* repelled the creatures. But was that all part of the setup to engender my trust?

"I don't," I admitted.

"And nothing from the Order?"

"Not a peep."

"Maybe that's your answer," he offered.

"Or maybe that's just the Order being the Order."

"So what do we do?" James asked. "Just wait around?"

"I'm going to make another call. I'll find you when I get back to the States."

"I can send an update to the Order," he offered.

"Yeah, please do." Though I wondered if there was any point.

We hung up and I dialed Detective Vega.

"Croft," she said. "I've been trying to reach you all day."

"I must be out of satellite range." I checked the pager—no signal—and put it away again. "Were you able to take a look at those files?"

"That's what I wanted to talk to you about. For most of them, the names weren't unique enough to be reliable identifiers. I couldn't pull up anything on those. But on the ones that were unique, there's nothing."

"Nothing?" I said. "What do you mean nothing?"

"They're not in the records databases. No addresses, phone numbers, voter registrations, utility bills, court records. There's nothing, Croft. That's what I'm telling you. It's like they don't exist."

"They're dead?"

"More like never born. Could this Chicory have, I don't know, made them up?"

I felt my face screwing up as I considered the question. I'd found my file, James's file. His wasn't made up ... or was it? "Hey, did the department do a background check on James before you contracted him?"

"Hold on." Through the buzzing line, I heard a keyboard clacking. I bit my lower lip. After another few minutes, she said, "Yeah, he's on here. And I just double-checked the public records. He's legit."

I released my lip. "Good. But the others...?"

"Nothing," she repeated.

I tried to think about it from two perspectives. In the Chicory as Lich case, he would have left the files out, knowing I would track down James—whom he had warned of my arrival in advance. The remaining files would be fakes, denying me access to the magic-using community. But in the Chicory as Chicory case, my mentor might have done the exact same thing, knowing that if I was captured by the Front, I'd be carrying Whisperer magic. Like someone infected with a virus, I would have to be quarantined, possibly even killed, so as not to infect other magic-users.

By winning over James, had I done just that?

"There's no info on Chicory's license plate either," Vega said. "It's a made-up number."

That didn't surprise me. Knowing Chicory, he'd probably enchanted it into inconspicuousness to avoid the hassle of registration. But *did* I know Chicory? I blew out my breath in frustration.

"Dare I ask how things are going?" Vega asked.

"Not good," I said, looking around the kitchen. Simple folk charms adorned several shelves, and I noticed someone had lined the window sills with salt. "How about there? I mean, apart from the files."

Vega gave a tired snort. "You'd think it's a full moon. Crimes are up across the city."

"Monsters?" I asked, thinking of the shadow beings.

"Nut cases," she replied. "All the perps have psych issues of one kind or another, and we're running out of places to stick them. The hospitals' lockdown wards are at full capacity. There was a riot over at Bellevue last night. The patients went full zombie, biting anything in sight. Not even sleeping gas could subdue them. The police ended up having to shackle them."

"Jeez," I said, imagining the scene. I remembered what I'd told James about things getting uglier if the main portal to Dhuul were to open. Were we witnessing the beginning?

"You might want to stay put," Vega said dryly.

"I'm actually flying back tomorrow morning. I'll let you know if I learn anything else about the case. Right now, we're still looking at Marlow or Chicory."

"Are you leaning more toward one or the other?" Vega asked.

I thought about it for a moment. Either Connell and Arianna had told me the truth or they had screwed with my head so badly that I didn't know which way was up. I wanted to tell Vega I was still leaning toward Marlow. Instead, I banged my forehead against the plaster wall twice.

"No," I said.

17

That night I had horrible, disjointed dreams of death and decay.

Lazlo's wolf-torn eye appeared from a mound of toadstools. *I hurt,* he repeated in a wet, whispering voice. *I hurt, Everson.* Shadowy tentacles lashed and grabbed me. I struggled to fight through them, to burn Lazlo's remains and close the portal.

And then the scene changed to a locked psych ward. Patients with blood-smeared faces and limp robes moaned and shrieked on all sides. I looked around for my cane, but I didn't have it. My coin pendant was gone from my chest. With insane eyes, the patients closed in. A stink of rot rose from them. I batted at their grasping hands, but there were too many of them.

Their eyes turned into fungus-filled sockets as they seized me and pulled me toward their gaping mouths. Mouths that became dark, fang-lined pits, plummeting to the very heart of madness.

I thrashed awake, blood roaring in my ears. I immediately sensed I wasn't alone in the guest bedroom. I turned my head. A white T-shirt with a swollen belly seemed to float in the center of the room. As my eyes adjusted, the rest of Olga's father emerged from the gloom.

He groaned as he hefted an axe overhead.

"Vigore!" I shouted, swinging my cane toward him.

The force blast caught Olga's father in the stomach and propelled him into the far wall. The axe fell, the blade burying itself in the middle of the wooden floor. Olga's father began to sob. A moment later, footsteps ran down the hallway, and the bedroom light flicked on. I looked from Olga's father to Olga, who stood in the doorway. I'd placed a locking spell over the door the night before, but it must have come apart during my nightmare.

Olga rushed to her father and helped him to his feet. *"Come, Papa,"* she said in scolding Romanian.

"Holy hell," I breathed, sitting up on the side of the bed, my heart still galloping at full tilt.

Olga walked her sobbing father from the room, bits of plaster falling from the back of his head. There was a bowl-shaped indentation in the wall where he'd impacted. Olga returned a minute later.

"I am sorry," she said. "The drinking has made him sick up here." She tapped her temple as she pried the axe from the floor.

"You think?" I asked, my voice hard and shaky.

"I fix your breakfast then take you to train."

I checked my watch and nodded. It wasn't like I was going to fall back to sleep anyway.

Thirty minutes later I sat across from Olga, bowls of porridge in front of us. We ate in silence for several minutes.

"So how long has he been like that?" I asked softly, feeling bad for having raised my voice at her in the bedroom. From the back of the house, I could hear her father snoring deeply.

"He has been drinking long time," she said. "But he turned sick a week ago."

"What do you mean 'turned sick'?"

"Getting up at night. Chasing dogs around yard. This was first time he carried axe."

Would have been nice if you'd shared the bit about his mental health before inviting me to stay the night, I thought, but didn't say it. I was lining up the info on her father with what Vega had told me about the sudden rise in crimes back in New York, the riot in the hospital's psych ward...

He turned sick a week ago.

That would have been about the same time I destroyed what I thought was Lich's book. The act should have deprived Marlow of his power. But if Connell was telling the truth, if I had instead destroyed an Elder book that had been jamming Lich's portal, then my act would have given the portal new life.

Allowing more Whisperer magic through, I thought.

But that was assuming the spike in insanity was a result of Whisperer magic. I could just as easily be seeing a connection where none existed. *Or being* made *to see one.* I thought.

"Why did you come?" Olga asked suddenly.

I looked up, only now realizing she had been watching me for the last minute. "I told you," I said, picking through my milky porridge with a spoon. "I wanted to check on an old friend."

"You needed his help," she stated.

I started to nod, then caught myself. "What makes you say that?"

"It is in your eyes."

Something in her forwardness made the skin over my chest prickle. I thought about how she had been waiting for me in the truck yesterday, how she had appeared with a shotgun armed with salt at Lazlo's house, how she just happened to have a spare room for me to stay in. Like James, had she been warned about my coming? Beneath the table, I gripped my cane.

"You knew I'd show up here," I said.

"Yes," she admitted, taking a large bite of porridge.

I scooted the chair out and stood, pulling my sword from my staff. "Who told you?"

She finished chewing, unconcerned by my weapon. "Bones."

"Bones? Who the hell is Bones?"

I flinched when she stood, but she walked the other direction into the kitchen, where she opened a cupboard. I watched her carefully. She returned with a small leather pouch, which she held out to me. No magic stirred around it. I hesitated before I moved my sword to my staff hand and opened the pouch with two fingers. It contained a pile of small animal bones.

"Oh," I said, feeling foolish.

She had been referring to cleromancy, or bone-reading, a folk practice as old as human settlement. One many people still dabbled in. For the reading to be accurate, though, the diviner or the divination object needed to possess magic, and I sensed none in either.

Olga sat again. "I can do reading if you want."

"What did you see?" I asked. "In your earlier reading?"

"I was told that a man of great power would come. That he was trying to know something."

"I don't know about the *great power* part," I mumbled.

"I saw what you did at the house," she said. "You made fire with voice."

She was talking about the *fuoco* invocation, when I'd cremated Lazlo's remains to close the vent to Dhuul's realm.

"The bones said I would help this man," Olga finished.

She had already pushed our bowls and coffee mugs to one side of the table. Now she opened the pouch and upended it. The assortment of bones from what looked like a large rodent spilled over the table. Olga's brown eyes seemed to darken a shade as she gazed down on them.

"I see confusion," she said, her fingers hovering over a configuration of rib bones.

You've got that right, I thought, though she could also have overheard my conversations with James and Vega last night. I'm sure I had sounded plenty confused then.

"You are torn between difficult choices." Her strong, country fingers moved back and forth between where the bones seemed to have landed in two roughly equal quantities. "Is it this one, or this one?"

Lich or Marlow? I thought.

"And here is your answer," she said.

I leaned forward despite that I still felt no magic around the ceremony. Olga was pointing at a small, solitary shoulder blade that had fallen in between the two groupings of bones.

"What does it say?" I asked.

"That when you understand what this single thing means"— she tapped the shoulder blade—"one choice will fall away." In demonstration, she swept the bones on the right side off the table into her waiting palm and returned them to the pouch. "It will no longer be both."

No more fifty-fifty, in other words.

I eyed the shoulder blade for another moment. The shape of it seemed to tug at something in my mind, but I couldn't say what. Anyway, what was the point? There was nothing mystical at work here.

"Great ... thanks," I said.

She nodded and swept the remaining bones into the pouch and tied it off. How desperate had I become that I was looking to a mortal with a bag of rat bones for answers?

I pulled the pager from my pocket to see if it was getting a signal. Still out of range. I pocketed it again, hoping it would pick something up at the train station. James had planned to contact the Order, and on the off chance they'd responded, I wanted to know as soon as possible. I started to imagine James waving his message over his flaming cup and then stiffened.

The cups.

I thought of my own silver cup. Narrower at the bottom, wider as you approached the rim. From the side, it looked roughly like...

"A shoulder blade," I said.

"You understand?" Olga asked.

I stared but without seeing her. I had been told that our cups gave us access to an administrative branch of the Order. An office where communications were prioritized and then sent up the appropriate channels for decisions to be made, which were sent back down and shot to us as responses. But if there was no Order, then those same communications were more than likely going to the one person most interested in keeping tabs on us.

I thought of the gold cup I'd found in Chicory's room.

When Olga's face reappeared beyond my thoughts, a small smile was wrinkling the beauty mark above her lips. "Your eyes have changed," she said. "You understand the meaning."

"I think so, yeah," I replied, my heart beating urgently. Like Olga's rock salt, sometimes the best magic was no magic. "How soon can we leave for the train station?"

"As soon as you are ready," she said.

I stood quickly. "Give me five minutes."

I've got a gold cup to hack.

18

Somewhere over Spain it occurred to me that I might not have to hack Chicory's cup. My own cup required an incantation to send messages, but not to receive them. As long as my cup was jetting a flame, the messages arrived on their own. Hopefully, Chicory's cup operated the same way—in which case, it would just be a matter of igniting the oil crystal.

By the time the plane touched down at Newark International, I was running on unhealthy levels of adrenaline and caffeine and little else. I shouldered my way through the crowds and stood in the taxi line outside.

"Where to?" a cabbie asked when my turn came.

I climbed into his backseat with my pack. "Gehr Place. Near 495."

He nodded and shifted his ample bulk as he put the cab in gear and reset the meter. "Where you coming in from?"

"Eastern Europe."

He snorted. "Surprised you were in a hurry to get back."

"What do you mean?"

"You haven't been following? The city's a flipping zoo. Last night, we had maniacs running around the streets, climbing buildings, breaking windows. A couple of 'em tried tipping over my taxi on East Fourteenth. Told dispatch I was done for the night. Screw that."

"Who were they?" I asked.

"From the looks of 'em? Vagrants and junkies. The police eventually rounded them up, but it took all night. Like some kind of frigging *Night of the Living Dead*. Cost a few officers their lives too." He shook his balding head. "Must be a nasty new drug on the streets."

Or a nasty new magic, I thought. *One I potentially let through.*

If Whisperer magic *was* coming through, it might not have been powerful enough to influence sound minds—yet—but it looked as if it was worming its way into those already afflicted, dragging them into deeper madness. I thought about the patients in the psych ward Vega had mentioned, Olga's alcoholic father, and now junkies.

"You're my last drop of the evening."

"Oh, yeah?" I said absently.

"Gonna return the cab and go straight home to the missus. Bar the doors. No way I'm gonna be out and about with crap like this going on. Not worth it for a few extra bucks, you know?"

I nodded as, with stinging, sleep-deprived eyes, I peered out the windows. We were climbing onto I-78, the setting sun throwing final, long shadows over the interstate. The west-bound lanes were clogged. It looked like the afternoon rush, but it was almost eight p.m.

The cabbie snapped on the radio.

"...mobs and mobs of them," a woman said in a breathless voice. It sounded as though she was speaking through a telephone. *"They're going block by block, setting fire to anything that'll light. We've got cars on fire, buildings on fire..."* She took a sobbing breath. *"...people on fire. Me and my husband barely got away. They're ... they're crazy."*

"Aw, Christ," the cabbie said. "You hearing this?"

"Are you somewhere safe now?" the male talk show host asked.

"Yeah, I think so," the woman replied, not sounding at all certain.

"If you're just joining us, ladies and gentlemen," the host said in a grave voice, *"the Bronx is burning. I repeat, the Bronx is burning. Roving gangs with no apparent affiliation began setting fire to the south Bronx about an hour ago, and their numbers have only grown despite the arrival of police on the scene. Something similar is happening in Staten Island and east Brooklyn, we're being told, but the details at this time are sketchy. The mayor has declared a state of emergency and is recommending that those who can safely evacuate the city do so at this time. Everyone else should remain inside with their doors and windows locked."*

I looked over at the lines of bumper-to-bumper cars in the opposite lanes. Even from my distance, I could see the fear and tension on the drivers' faces, several of them with children in the back seats. I squinted and craned my neck until I could make out a brown haze rising in the north.

"Evacuate the city?" the cabbie complained. "How am I gonna do that? My wife weighs five hundred plus. She's practically bedbound."

My pager began to go off. Its signal had come back on in the airport in Romania, but no one had sent any pages. I dug into my pocket, pushing past the Ziploc bag of Romanian salt Olga had given me for protection, and found the pager. I pulled it out and checked the number. Vega's.

"Hey," I said, "mind making a quick stop so I can make a call?"

"You're not carrying a phone?" he asked.

"No."

I thought he was going to offer me his, which I would have had to turn down or risk exploding it, but he sighed and said, "I should probably fill up anyway. Let's make it quick, though, huh?" He turned off the next exit ramp and pulled into a gas station with a payphone.

I ran up to the phone and called.

"Vega," she answered.

"Hey, it's Everson. What's going on?"

"That's what I'd like to know," she said. "You back in the States?"

"Yeah, just got in."

"The nuttiness I told you about yesterday? It's gone into overdrive. Mayor Lowder's been asking about you. He wants to know if there's something supernatural at work and, if so, what you can do about it."

"I'm hoping I'll have an answer shortly," I said.

"One that'll put an end to this?"

"Eventually." *I hope.*

Off to my left, stupid laughter filled the inside of a parked Plymouth station wagon, its windows cloudy with smoke. When the skunky smell of pot reached me, I turned the other way and blocked the fumes with my collar.

"Eventually?" The rawness in Detective Vega's voice told me she hadn't gotten much sleep either. "Croft, I'm not sure we have till eventually. The crazies are going after people now."

In her voice, I could also hear her fear for her son.

"Yeah, they were just talking about that on the radio," I said. "Look, I'll contact you as soon as I know something. In the meantime, tell Budge I'm working on it."

"How bad can we expect it to get tonight?" she asked.

I paused as I considered the question. Like black magic, Whisperer magic was probably more potent at night. And if today's craziness had started before sunset... "Bad," I said. "Probably the best you can do is get everyone vulnerable out of their path. I think Budge is on the right track with the evacuation order. I promise I'm doing everything I can."

We said goodbye, my hand trembling as I hung up.

Had I unleashed this? *Was* I responsible for the death and destruction?

"Hey!" the cabbie shouted. "The hell you think you're doin'?"

I turned to the island of gas station pumps, where the cabbie had pulled in to fill up. A man had been hanging around the pumps with a squeegee when we arrived, offering to wash car windows for a few bucks. Now he was wrestling my cabbie for the gasoline nozzle.

"Help!" the cabbie gasped.

I ran over as the cabbie sagged to the pavement, clutching his chest. Squeegee Man stepped on his stomach and wrested the nozzle the rest of the way from his grip. He stood back and aimed the nozzle at the cabbie like a gangster preparing an execution.

I fumbled for my cane and shouted. The cabbie threw his arms to his ducked head as gasoline jetted from the nozzle—and hit my shield invocation. The gas poured off both sides and splashed to the pavement.

At neighboring islands, people began to scream and back away. Squeegee man wheeled with the nozzle, jetting gallons of gasoline everywhere. Wild, red-rimmed eyes stared from a twitching face. The man was gone—but not far enough. His other hand was rooting inside a jacket pocket for what I rightly guessed was a lighter.

As I caught the flash of red plastic, I thrust my cane at him and shouted, *"Vigore!"*

The force blast caught him in the chest and shot him from the pumps. He dropped both lighter and nozzle en route to the side of a tractor trailer, where he slammed to a stop, then pancaked to the pavement.

Exhaling, I turned back to the cabbie, who was using the side of his cab to climb to his feet. A tide of gasoline rolled toward a metal grate, its fumes bending the air and making my eyes water. Those who had fled began to venture back. A woman in business attire stooped for the dropped lighter.

"Are you all right?" I asked my cabbie.

"Did you see that?" he wheezed, still clutching his chest. "You see that?"

Behind me, I heard the distinct *snikt* of a metal wheel. I turned to find the woman who had retrieved the plastic lighter holding it in front of her face, staring at the slender flame. She was an older woman, dressed in a pants suit and wearing expensive-looking jewelry, but like Squeegee Man, she didn't seem all there.

"Put that out!" I shouted.

Her staring eyes fell to the tide of gasoline, some of it running under cars. With a strange flattening of her pupils, she knelt as though to touch the flame to the gas.

"Protezione," I called, enclosing the lighter in a shield. Without air, the flame died. The woman released the lighter and stepped back. I shrunk the shield until the lighter detonated inside it.

The woman's eyes shifted toward me. Her face began to contort, red lips peeling back from her teeth. I glanced around. Everyone else seemed fine. Maybe this lady had a touch of age-related dementia, making her more susceptible to Whisperer magic. I readied my cane reluctantly, not wanting to hit her with an invocation, but not sure I would have a choice.

At that moment, two young men strolled into our midst, smoke wafting from their long hair and jackets. They were the ones who had been hot-boxing inside the Plymouth—and smelled the part.

For the love of God.

"Whoa, check it out," one of them said. "It's like a gasoline pond or something."

The other one gave a deep, throaty laugh of agreement. I watched in horror as a third member of their party slung his arm around the woman who had nearly finished Squeegee Man's job.

"What happened, lady?" he asked her.

"Get back!" I shouted.

The three potheads turned toward me. "Dude, what's your problem?" one of them asked.

"She's…" I almost said *dangerous*, but the woman was looking around now in uncertainty, eyes normal again. With a sound of disapproval, she drew the young man's arm from around her shoulder and marched to her car—a shiny white Bonneville—got in, and drove away.

"Can we get outta here already?" the cabbie asked me.

The lights over the pumping stations turned on, pushing back the dusk. Near the diesel pumps, Squeegee Man was still down, a gas station employee standing over him to ensure he stayed that way. How long before the magic became strong enough to overwhelm the rest of us? I wondered.

I turned back to the cabbie, who didn't appear to have seen my magical exhibition.

"Yeah," I said. "Good idea."

When we pulled up to the safe house at Gehr Place twenty minutes later, I paid the cabbie double the fare.

"You sure about this," he asked, counting through the bills.

"I feel responsible for what happened to you back there," I said.

"You weren't the one who went apey with the gas hose."

No, I thought, *but if I let that magic through, I might as well have been.*

"Stay safe," I told him, clapping his large shoulder.

"Thanks, you too."

The cab droned away as I climbed the front porch steps. At the threshold, I checked the house for wards or protective energy. Still down. Inside, I dropped my pack, then flicked on lights en route to Chicory's room. A quick look around showed it to be in the same state of general disorder as when I'd left it four days ago. His gold cup still sat on the corner of his lab table.

"Fuoco," I said.

From the bottom of the cup, a red flame jetted up and stood in a spire. I watched it for several minutes, waiting for messages to begin spouting forth. I had only been present a handful of times when messages arrived through my own flame—pieces of parchment paper that would unfold as they descended, coming to a neat rest in the center of my desk as though someone had set them there.

But Chicory's flame only hissed quietly.

What did that tell me? That Chicory had locked his own cup with an enchantment? Or that he wasn't Lich? Given the insanity unfolding outside, I was leaning more and more toward the first.

But was I certain enough to return to the Refuge?

The answer was not yet. *"Goddammit,"* I hissed at myself.

I was considering my options when the front door opened.

My chest locked around my slamming heart, and I froze.

The door closed. A stuffy silence followed, as though the person were standing in the foyer, studying my pack.

Cutting the light, I whispered, *"Spegnere."* But the flame from Chicory's cup continued to burn. I tiptoed over to it, removed the cup from the table top, and placed it behind a stack of books on the floor. The corner of the room glowed as if from a night light, but the flame was no longer in plain view. As I was creeping into a position behind the door, sword sliding from staff, a floorboard creaked under my foot. I stiffened, swearing at myself.

"Hello?" someone called.

Footsteps began to click down the hallway.

"Everson? Is that you?"

It was Chicory.

19

"Everson?" Chicory called again. "Are you in here?"

My throat tightened and I swallowed with a dry click. I couldn't have answered if I'd wanted to. His return on the fourth day meant he was Lich, didn't it? Or was there some other explanation for his return? As his footsteps drew nearer, a corkscrew of dizziness hit me. I risked another few steps to make my way to the wall beside the door, out of sight.

"Oscurare," I whispered, deepening the shadows in the room and drawing back my sword.

Chicory began muttering to himself in his curmudgeonly way. He sounded so familiar, so ... harmless. Was it all a guise? His footsteps stopped in the doorway. I could see his hand pawing the wall before it found the light switch. When he stepped in, his mop of gray hair gave a little hop.

"Everson!" he exclaimed, his lips breaking into a smile. "Goodness, I feared I'd lost you!"

He stepped forward as though to clap my shoulder, but I showed him the ends of my sword and staff. "Stay right there," I said, backing away, my voice low and husky. "Reach for your wand or utter the first foreign syllable, and I swear to God, I'll end you."

Chicory frowned sternly. "They got to you, didn't they?"

"It doesn't matter. I want to hear how you're alive."

"It *does* matter," Chicory countered. "Don't you remember what I told you before you left? How long did they hold you for?" When I didn't answer, he said, "Well, long enough to poison you thoroughly, I can see that much. Come, there's no time to waste. This is going to take Elder-level magic, but I can at least contain the poison, keep it from consuming the rest of your mind."

"How are you alive?" I repeated.

Ignoring my earlier warning, Chicory began bustling around the room plucking spell items from the mess. "I'll tell you everything after we've begun," he said. "No telling how much time you have left."

I pressed the tip of the blade to his back. "No," I said. "You'll tell me now."

The coldness in my voice seemed to get through. He stopped and let out a huff. "I never died, Everson."

"Bullshit. I saw you get run through down there."

"You saw a doppelganger get run through down there."

"Doppelganger? You better start making sense."

Chicory turned to face me. "When I received the message that you had destroyed the book, I tried to retrieve you, but the defensive magic around the realm was too strong. I then tried to go there myself, but the same magic repelled me. My only recourse was to send a doppelganger. A weaker version of myself that I managed to imbue with your father's essence. It got in but was slain before my doppelganger was able to kill Marlow and pull you out. An unfortunate turn of events, certainly. But that's what you saw. Not me."

"What happened to the real you?" I challenged. "Tabitha said you never came back."

"The death of one's doppelganger is like suffering a mini-death oneself. I transported myself to a healing plane where I went into a coma to speed my recovery. I would have been recuperating for months, otherwise."

Could the Front have known that?

"Then why didn't the Order come for me?" I asked.

"The Order didn't know you were there, and that's ... well, that's my fault, Everson." He gave an apologetic shrug. "In all the excitement, I neglected to tell them I was sending you in."

I shook my head. "Nice try, but I sent them a message when I was in the Refuge."

"I don't doubt you did, Everson—or at least tried. The message never would have gotten past their defenses."

I thought about Connell's lack of concern upon seeing the cup I'd manifested.

"What about the messages I sent when I got back?" I pressed. I was about to mention the messages James had sent as well but felt a sudden protective instinct for him and held back.

"Still going up the chain of command, no doubt," Chicory said. "Once we get you stabilized, I'll use my direct line to the Elders to update them and arrange to have you cleaned. Listen to me, Everson." Despite my aimed sword, he leaned nearer, eyes growing sterner. "Whatever they did to you down there, whatever they told you, it was with the aim of turning you against the Order. That's what Whisperer magic does. It takes any doubts you may have and bends them so that their version of the truth seems the only one that can be believed."

I wanted to trust him, but I steeled myself.

"If I destroyed Lich's book," I said, "then how come things are falling apart out there?"

"Falling apart?" He looked around in confusion. "I just came from the city. I got my coordinates mixed up when I returned from the healing plane and ended up on Roosevelt Island." He chuckled at his own carelessness. "In any case, I didn't notice anything amiss."

"So the fires didn't raise a red flag for you, or the riots, or the mass evacuation?"

"Everson," he said, pulling one side of his jacket slowly open until I could see his wand in the inside pocket. "I'm going to draw my wand and use it to cast a spell to stop the spreading magic."

"Try it, and I'll run you through for real."

"You're not making any *sense*," he insisted.

"Oh, so that's it? I'm crazy? Is that the game?"

"Not crazy," he said. "Under the influence of magic."

I stared at him, trying to arrange my thoughts into something coherent, but they were slamming around like bumper cars. Everything Connell had told me about my mother, my grandfather

... it had all fit. But if what Chicory was saying about Whisperer magic was true, of course it would all fit.

"Lazlo's dead," I said suddenly.

"What?" Chicory asked, looking genuinely surprised. "When did this happen?"

"Five years ago."

"And how do you know this?"

"I went to Romania. I saw his body."

"Went to Romania?" He looked at me askance.

"Here." I moved my sword to my staff hand, pulled my flight itinerary from my pocket, and handed it to him. "See for yourself."

I watched Chicory as he unfolded the piece of paper and moved his gaze down it. At last he nodded and handed it back. "I want you to take another look at this, Everson, and tell me exactly what you see."

"I already know what's on here," I said, snatching it back. "I've been carrying it for the last three—"

But when I looked down, it wasn't the printed flight itinerary from the airport. It was my packing list from when I was about to leave my apartment for the safe house a few weeks earlier. I rechecked my pockets before looking at the packing list again. "What did you do to it?" I demanded.

"Nothing," Chicory said quietly. "The protective energy around the house is charging up again. It must be clearing your mind."

It was a trick. It had to be. I wasn't crazy.

I dropped the list, pulled out my wallet, and tossed it to him. "Look inside and you'll find boarding passes, train tickets. Check out the bills while you're in there, too. Do you think I just walk around with Romanian currency?" My laugh verged on a mad giggle. I pressed a hand to my sweating upper lip as I watched him.

"The only thing resembling a boarding pass is this," he said, holding up my transit card. "And your currency is all in U.S. dollars."

"My passport, then," I said quickly. "It's in my pack in the front room. It'll be stamped." I started to push past Chicory, then stopped cold. Tabitha had just walked into the room.

"I see we're a happy household again," she said dryly.

"What are you doing here?" I demanded. "Why aren't you at the apartment?"

"That's what I'd like to know. We've been in this pit for almost a month. A month too long, if you ask me." She parked inside the doorway and combed a licked paw over her right ear.

"I took you back to the apartment four days ago."

She snorted. "Four days ago you were hardly in the land of the living."

"What the hell's that supposed to mean?" My temples were beginning to ache.

"Oh, come now, darling. Ever since you got back from that realm, you've been practically catatonic. I've been doing everything. Fixing our meals, feeding you." She made a face. "Helping you to the bathroom."

I shook my head. "No."

"Um, *yes*," Tabitha said.

I opened my mouth, then hesitated. Another thought occurred to me. "Detective Vega and I have been in contact. She even gave me back my pager." I pawed my front pockets, but the bulky device was nowhere to be felt. Impossible. It had been there not forty minutes earlier when she'd paged me. Had I left it in the cab?

"Everson," Chicory said sharply.

"No," I backed away from him. "I *know* what I experienced."

"Think for a moment," Chicory said. "Listen to me. This is exactly what Marlow wants—to bias you against us, to turn you against the Order, to harness your powers to his purposes. He had you down there for several days. He convinced you that what he'd told you could be verified up here, correct? He set you free for you to find out. But not before ensuring that the only journey you took would be in here." He tapped his temple. "A mind he poisoned with Whisperer magic."

"James," I nearly shouted. "James Wesson!"

Chicory shook his head. "That means nothing to me."

"He's a—a wizard—a member of the Order. Here in New York City. You left his file out so I'd find him, but not before you told him to expect me so that he could stop me from..."

From what, exactly?

"From finding the truth?" Chicory asked, raising a bushy eyebrow. "And if this James failed, and you learned the truth despite his efforts to stop you, the more convincing those truths would appear to you, no?"

I stammered for a moment, then looked over at Tabitha. She looked back at me as though I was suffering a nervous breakdown and couldn't decide whether that merited pity or scorn.

I sat down hard on the one chair in the room and dug a hand into my hair. Chicory was right. There were two versions of reality: the one before the Front had captured me, and the one after. I had been counting on my reason to determine which was the truth. Reason. The very thing Marlow would have corrupted.

I looked up at my mentor. "I need to talk to Detective Vega. If she says we never spoke, that will settle it. I'll go along with whatever needs doing, and we'll get back to the business of Marlow." That decided, the exhaustion I'd been holding back broke through me, and I slumped in the chair.

Chicory nodded. "Very good, Everson. Stay here and rest, lie down if you need to." He waved a hand toward the cluttered bed. "I'll bring the phone up."

When he left the room, Tabitha fell in behind him. My gaze moved from their departure to the flight itinerary—correction, packing list—I'd dropped on the floor. I thought back over my journey to Romania. The flights, the trains, the visit to Lazlo's farm, my stay with Olga and her father, the bones she had read. It had all felt so damned real!

I lifted up my shirt to check the place on my stomach where the shadow creature had lashed me. Last night an ugly blue-green mark had run from my left ribcage down to my right hip, complete with bite marks. Right now there was nothing save pale skin, the faintest suggestion of abdominal muscles, and a mole I'd had since birth. Was Whisperer magic really that powerful?

Apparently so, I thought with a stab of disgrace.

I patted my pockets again. No pager. I looked through my wallet. Nothing to suggest I'd been in Romania. I stepped out into the hallway. Back in the kitchen, Chicory had stopped to heat up some goat's milk for Tabitha. I went the other direction. My backpack wasn't in the foyer where I was sure I'd dropped it. In the bedroom where I'd stayed, I found my clothes, books, and duffel bag, never packed. I could feel the hum of protective energy that encircled the house. *Was* it helping me to perceive clearly again?

Or is it poisoning your thoughts once more, the insidious voice whispered. But the voice no longer held the same power.

I looked down at the bed, where I could see an imprint of my body. I imagined myself lying there in a catatonic state for the past four days, Whisperer lies twisting through my mind like black tentacles.

I returned to Chicory's room and walked along the lab table, absently touching the glass tubes and notebooks, telling myself there was no shame in succumbing to a magic that had nearly overwhelmed the Elders. Anyway, I had destroyed Lich's book, not an Elder book. Meaning no Whisperer magic was flowing into the world. That was a huge relief right there. And as Marlow's power dwindled, he and the Front would have nowhere to hide. The Elders would take care of them.

With that knowledge, I no longer cared to see the face behind the gold mask. Marlow was corrupt and evil, a vessel for the Whisperer. He wasn't my father. He was nothing to—

At the end of the table, I had arrived at the pile of newspaper clippings and begun poking through them: the article on the robe of John the Baptist as well as those concerning exhibits of other magic-sounding artifacts. But near the bottom of the pile, at a depth I hadn't ventured to the last time, I arrived at a glossy program for an opera. The program showed a black-robed figure standing center stage.

He was wearing a gold mask.

Heart thudding, I pulled the program all the way out.

The gold mask with its frowning mouth was identical to the one I'd seen on Marlow. I read the caption below:

"Radical! Violent!"

In this reimagining of Verdi's *Macbeth*, we go not to Scotland, but ancient Greece, where an ambitious young magician murders the King of Athens and embarks on a bloody rule.

My eyes skipped to the bottom:

Praise for *The Death Mage*, recent Opera Award nominee and...

"Here we are," Chicory said.

I jumped and shoved the program back into the stack. My mentor had returned with the phone, but he wasn't looking at me. In search of a jack, he was kicking through the clutter along the baseboards. I glanced back at the articles. In his carelessness, Chicory had neglected to conceal the most damning clue: his model for what would become my boogeyman.

There was no Death Mage. Chicory had invented him.

I turned from the table and eyed the chair where my cane was leaning. As Chicory continued to root around, I crept toward it.

"Could've sworn there was a place to plug in," he muttered.

I reached the chair and slowly grasped the cane's handle. But when I tried to unsheathe the sword that had slain Lich's form once before—the doppelganger story was BS too, I decided—it wouldn't come free. I rearranged my slick grip and tried again. Normally, it was an unconscious act, a smooth release, but now the wood around the blade seemed to clench.

As though magic were holding it closed.

"Ah, there it is," Chicory said, stooping down to snap the plastic head into the jack. He turned, a pair of fingers hooked under the phone's switch hook, and was in the act of extending the handset when he stopped and pulled it back. "Why, Everson, you're as pale as a ghost. Something the matter?"

"No," I replied, thinking about what James had said about bluffs and double bluffs. I watched Chicory for a tell. A subtle force wriggled through my mind, and Chicory glanced past me to his lab table.

And there it is, I thought numbly.

"Damned Whisperer magic," he said, setting the phone on the chair and bustling past me. "What's it making you see now?" He arrived at the stack of articles and began searching through them.

The odds had finally shifted decisively, away from Marlow as the culprit and toward Lich. If the magic around the house was clearing my mind, I shouldn't have been able to see the program. Not in a way that implicated Chicory and not in that much detail.

Praise for The Death Mage...

There was no time for second-guessing. I would only talk myself back into a fifty-fifty stalemate—or Chicory would do it for me.

I rushed forward.

With my cane locked, I wasn't sure I would be able to cast through it. Rather than risk it, I raised the cane overhead and, using all of my strength, brought it down on the back of Chicory's head.

20

The blow landed at the base of Chicory's skull with a dull thud, and he collapsed to the floor.

"Darling! Have you gone fucking mad?"

I spun to where Tabitha was entering the room, her eyes large with alarm. I stared back down at my mentor, terrified now that I'd been wrong and had killed or severely injured him. I backed from him, the cane limp in my suddenly-cold hands.

Blood spread through the back of Chicory's moppy gray hair in a bloom so dark it was nearly black. I imagined Marlow watching through Tabitha's eyes and congratulating the Front on their successful manipulation of me.

My gaze jerked to the opera announcement, still on the table, the cover featuring the robed figure in the gold mask. An illusion? But something was releasing in my mind, as though a hand that had been balling up the vessels was letting go. Familiar colors swirled around my vision. I'd last seen them in the Refuge, after I'd watched Chicory fall. They dissipated quickly this time, and I looked around until I spotted my dropped packing list. It was a flight itinerary again. I snatched it up and held it toward Tabitha.

"Can you read this? Tell me what it says."

But Tabitha was backing away, refusing to look.

I dropped the itinerary and lifted my shirt. The ugly blue-green lash across my stomach was back. "Or how about that? Can you see it?"

"Um, darling," she said, nodding past me.

I turned and almost lost my balance. Chicory was pushing himself up from the floor, but he wasn't Chicory anymore. He was changing, shifting. A red layered robe replaced his professorial attire while his mop of gray hair shed to reveal a bald, vein-mapped head. When he turned toward me, his eyes glowed the same yellow I'd glimpsed on the night Chicory had appeared in my apartment following Lady Bastet's murder. Violent power warped the air around him.

"No more artifice," he said, his voice deep and strange.

I was vaguely aware of things fluttering down around me. One landed next to my foot. I glanced down. It was a message from James Wesson, updating the Order on our situation. Other messages were spewing from the column of fire still hidden behind the table, landing around the room. I spotted the one I'd sent from the Refuge. No Order meant all of the messages had gone to the only Elder still alive. Murderer of his siblings. Pawn of Dhuul.

There was no longer any doubt.

"Lich," I said.

"I know what I penned in the archives," he said, "but I did not create the fissure to the Whisperer—I merely found it. Dhuul's coming is inevitable. That is what my brothers and sisters refused to accept. They wanted to expend all of our power and resources to stall Dhuul's arrival—for that is all we could have done, stalled it—while I proposed we align our purposes to the being's and become true immortals."

"At the expense of the world and every living thing in it," I said thinly.

As Lich's transformation finished, he loomed on the far side of the room, his wasted head nearly touching the ceiling. The gray skin around his starved mouth was so tight and sunken that I could see the outlines of his teeth. His lips peeled back into a gruesome simile of a grin. "The world and every living thing would have been pulled into chaos anyway."

"Is that why you've been sacrificing magic-users?" I asked, remembering Lazlo's fungus-riddled corpse.

"I am not sacrificing them, Everson," he replied, his teeth continuing to show. "I am taking them with me. When I attain immortality, so too will they." He stepped toward me. "So too will you."

I turned and lunged for the doorway but collided into an energy field. A mind-numbing charge ripped through me, dropping me to the floor. I looked around for Tabitha, but she had already fled.

"I have little more use for you," he said. "Your soul is too green to harvest. Ending you would be the most prudent action, but you did destroy the Elder book, and for that you've earned a place among the immortals. It's what you've longed for."

I *had* been fascinated by the idea of the Elders, of one day attaining that state, but not like this.

"You'd only be fighting the inevitable," Lich reminded me.

"Inevitable, my ass. You murdered the Elders because you knew they had the power to close the fissure and keep Dhuul from our world. Or maybe I should say Dhuul had you murder the Elders."

Lich's brow bunched together and his yellow eyes flared. He raised a hand of long fingers and stretched them toward me. I felt my mind begin to twist and bend.

"Vigore!" I shouted, thrusting my cane toward him.

But instead of a force blast, a torrent of nightmare bats spewed from the end of my cane. I covered my head as they flapped around the room on membranous wings the color of human flesh.

Beyond them, Lich said, "You are in my world now."

I peeked beneath a forearm, and discovered that I was no longer in Chicory's room, but standing at the edge of a monstrous hole that plunged into the earth. The bats I'd unleashed flapped around its opening, poisonous vapors drifting up from the roaring black depth. I peered over the precipice. A matrix of bile-green energy held the hole open. I understood these were the souls of those Lich had murdered and claimed over the centuries. I sensed they were still living, still conscious. *I hurt,* Lazlo's voice rasped in my mind.

My head pounded with the knowledge he was in that foul-smelling pit.

Around the pit's inside was a staircase that spiraled down. Creatures like the ones I'd encountered in Romania, all tentacles and shaggy bodies, trundled up and down in a nightmare procession. But most disturbing to me was the hole itself, a growing portal to Dhuul.

I could hear the being's wet, horrid whispers now, issuing from the depths. The sound pulled and dug at my mind from all sides, like something chewing on rotten meat. Hands clamping my temples, I backed away, squishing through the toadstools that swelled and stretched toward a forest like the one I'd seen in my nightmares. Across the pit stood a forbidding stone fortress, from where I guessed Lich oversaw his excavation project.

"Are you ready for immortality?" he asked.

The mage was looming over me, an astral projection—like myself, I realized. Our bodies were still in the safe house. Lich's long-fingered hand writhed toward my head like tentacles. He began to chant, his voice aligning with the whispers climbing from the pit until they were one.

I struggled to wrench myself away, but a force pierced my soul like the hooks in the mouths of the shadow creatures I'd faced in Lazlo's cellar. Only these hurt worse. Much worse. I squirmed, teeth gnashing, half insane from the pain. The hooks began to jerk and pull. I tried to draw back, but they had my soul. I could feel them drawing it out of me.

"Are you ready to become a god?" he pressed.

"No..." The word squeezed from my throat, a strangled cry.

The tugging stopped. I squinted my eyes open to find that Lich was no longer chanting. His head was tilted to one side as though listening. In the next instant, the world seemed to rip open. Wind roared around me as a pair of silver bolts slammed into Lich's head.

The hooks released my soul, and I crashed back into Chicory's bedroom, back into my body. More wind cycloned around as I pushed myself into a sitting position. An entire side of the house had torn away, as if by a storm. The neighbor's bug lights glowed yellow in the dark. Beside the toppled lab table, Lich was on his knees, clasping his smoking head.

"C'mon!" someone shouted.

James was standing in the yard, energy crackling from his wand, waving for me to follow him out. *You'll have no defenses against his magic out there,* Connell had said. I found my cane and staggered to my feet. The staff still refused to release the sword, but the shield Lich had erected over the doorway had fallen.

"This way!" I shouted back at James.

A hand on the top of his cowboy hat, James climbed inside, shot a worried glance at Lich as he crossed the room, and followed me down the hallway. I threw open the doorway under the staircase. *"Illuminare!"* I shouted. Light swelled from the orb as James and I raced down the staircase and across the basement's earthen floor. At the basement's far end, the casting circle was still intact.

"Inside the circle," I panted.

James followed me into the etched circle, and we turned toward the staircase. "So, double bluff?" he asked.

"Double bluff," I confirmed.

From the stairs, a pair of glowing eyes approached. I aimed my trembling cane at it. "Is someone going to tell me what in Lucifer's name is going on?" Tabitha asked, her orange coat emerging into my light.

"Quick," I said, waving to her, "get inside!"

To Tabitha's credit, she picked up her pace to a heavy trot and even jumped over the edge of the circle so as not to disrupt it. "Ooh, who's this?" she asked, blinking up at James.

"James Wesson," he said, affecting a slight drawl. "Pleased to meet you, ma'am."

"Believe me, the pleasure's entirely mine," Tabitha replied.

"How did you know where to find me?" I asked.

"Your pager," James said, gesturing to my pocket. Sure enough, there was a heavy lump there again. "When I asked to hold it back at the bar, I slipped a hair of dog ear between the device and case. Gave me something to eavesdrop through for the last few days, make sure you were shooting straight. When I heard Chicory denying all the things you'd done, I knew the fix was in. I tracked the hair here before the magic over the house had ramped up to full strength." He looked around. "But now what are we doing?"

Arianna had said I was to return to the portal on my side and they would transport me back to the Refuge. I was about to tell James as much, when the house began to shake. Debris rained from the rafters overhead. At the far end of the basement, a green glow descended the stairs.

"*Cerrare,*" I shouted, snapping the circle closed.

But had I just protected us, I wondered, or trapped us?

Lich appeared at the center of the sickly orb of energy, the outstretched fingers of one hand writhing toward us. I felt the magic penetrate the circle, penetrate our minds. Tabitha's hair puffed out, and she let out a low yowl. Even James looked uneasy as he edged back a step.

C'mon, already, I thought desperately toward Connell and Arianna.

"You're only fleeing the inevitable," Lich said. "If not here, then there…"

With the next blink of my eyes, we were in the forest in the Refuge. Connell, Arianna, and a small army of magic-users surrounded the clearing, wands aimed toward us. James adjusted his cowboy hat as he turned in a circle.

"Well, I'll be damned," he said.

"Stand clear!" Connell shouted.

I became aware of a ripping sound above me. Tabitha bolted from the clearing first. James and I followed, taking up positions behind the ring of magic-users. Above the spot where we had been standing, reality itself was tearing open onto a growing black portal.

Calling power to my prism, I readied my cane.

Lich was coming through.

21

Lich's eyes burned yellow, his red robes flapping around him in the widening portal between our worlds. In one hand he held a wand while with his other, he fashioned a warding sign. His lips moved in a chant, but above the tearing noise, I couldn't hear what he was saying.

"Respingere!" Connell cried. A current of blinding white energy ripped from his wand and exploded into Lich.

The other magic-users began to cast as well, streams colliding into the portal like ribbons of lightning. Within seconds a harsh scent of ozone filled the air—and no wonder. These were centuries-old practitioners unleashing some of the most powerful magic I'd ever witnessed. Any contribution I made would be puny in comparison.

I readied my cane anyway, squinting at the flashing impact site where Lich had been emerging. How much more magic could his defenses withstand? They surely had to be faltering, I thought, though with more hope than conviction. Lich was a first-generation magic-user and drawing power from a being more ancient than the oldest saints, a being that hungered for chaos.

A black tentacle shot from the exploding light and wrapped around a female practitioner's throat. She dropped her wand as the tentacle hoisted her into the air. Another tentacle twisted itself into a man's long blond hair and jerked him from his feet. He shouted above the noise.

I sprinted toward the woman, who was closer. I instinctively pulled on my sword handle, forgetting that Lich's magic had entrapped the blade inside the staff. It refused to release.

Switching my grip, I aimed the cane at the tentacle and shouted, *"Vigore!"*

Much like what had happened in Lazlo's cellar, the power that emanated from the cane passed through the tentacle as though it wasn't there. More tentacles shot by me. Shouts and choked screams punctuated the riot of noise. As magic-users flailed, the streams of energy from their wands dwindled until I could see Lich again.

He was larger now, closer. His wand and hand were maintaining a protective field while writhing tentacles sprouted from his back. Without the Elder book to staunch the flow of Dhuul's influence, Lich was stronger than the last time he had come through, as Chicory.

He might actually overpower them this time, I thought.

Savage barking sounded, and several of the Refuge's mastiffs broke past me. Connell tried to shout them back, but they took no heed. They changed as they sprinted, white flames enveloping their muscular forms, making them appear larger, more mythic. One by one, they leaped at the portal, at Lich, only to burst apart. White flames rained around the clearing.

"Submit to the power of Dhuul!" Lich called, his molars bulging through the skin of his jaw. "Submit and all will be forgiven! I will take you with me! I will make you all immortals!"

The tentacles extending from his back gave a hard wrench. A pair of sick crunches sounded, and the woman and blond-haired man he had first seized plummeted to the ground.

"The alternative is death," he finished.

Anger exploded through me and emerged from my lungs as a *"Forza dura!"*

I thrust the cane toward Lich. Somewhere beneath my storm of emotions, I knew it was a futile act. But this was the mage who had murdered my mother, who had watched her burn, and who continued to flaunt his disregard for life. My invocation was as spontaneous as it would no doubt prove ineffective.

But the force that burst from my cane staggered the mage. I blinked for a second. I hadn't imagined it. Lich had taken a step back, tentacles recoiling. And the look on his face... What remained of Grandpa's enchantment had hurt the son of a bitch.

I gathered my breath for another blast, but before I could release the Word, a tentacle lashed toward me. I swung the cane into its path. The tentacle caught it, wrapping the opal end.

"Respingere!" I cried, struggling to hold on.

Light and force pulsed from the opal, but the tentacle

smothered both. I leaned from its muscular pull, the heels of my shoes digging into the ground. As the tentacle writhed toward my white-knuckled grip, I began to feel Lich's warping power, began to feel my thoughts pulling at the seams, threatening to burst into violence and disorder. A straining whine emerged from between my clenched teeth as I fought to hold onto the cane as well as my sanity.

No matter what, something was telling me, *you cannot lose your sword and staff.*

Lich was staring down at me, the vessels throbbing over his head. A grim determination creased his face, even as more magic-users arrived and fresh energy collided into his shield. I was practically sitting now, like the anchor in a game of tug-of-war, my palms on fire. The tentacle wound toward my cramping hands. My grip slipped to the end of the cane handle.

And the blade slid free.

I fell onto my back. The tentacle whipped back toward the portal, clutching my staff. I heard magic-users thud down around me as the remaining tentacles released them. The tentacles disappeared into the portal along with Lich as the final emanations from the magic-users closed the opening.

Smoke drifted through the silent clearing.

Someone coughed. I looked from my naked blade toward the sound to find one of the magic-users who had been hoisted up writhing on the ground, clutching her throat. A green-black bruising stained the skin around her neck. Her eyes bugged madly from her face.

Arianna rushed to her and spoke a healing incantation. Moments later, light from her wand enveloped the woman. When the light receded, the woman was gone, transported to the palace to be purged of Whisperer magic. Several others who had been injured were treated similarly by other magic-users.

"That was some crazy-ass shit," James said, coming up beside me, smoke curling from the end of his wand.

I nodded numbly as we watched the two who had been killed being covered with manifested sheets. Beyond them, a graying magic-user stooped to recover his wand. I watched him closely, wondering if he was Marlow, my father.

"Are you two all right?" Connell asked.

"I'm fine," I said, turning to face him. James grunted a similar sentiment. I looked up at the space where the portal had stood moments before. "Is it closed? Can he come back through?"

"It's sealed tight," Connell assured me.

A horrible thought hit me. "By coming back here, did I let him through?"

"Any passage creates a temporary soft spot in the membrane between our worlds, but that's not your fault, Everson. Lich's power is growing such that he'll soon be able to come and go at will."

Well, that part is definitely *my fault,* I thought sickly, remembering the triumph I'd felt when I destroyed what I'd thought was Lich's book. Connell gripped my shoulder and lowered his gaze to mine. A layer of perspiration made the faint scars stand out from his face.

"We're at war, Everson. The most important one we'll ever wage. We can't agonize over every battle. That may sound heartless, but it's the reality. What matters is that you know the truth and that you're here." He clapped my shoulders firmly. "And you've brought reinforcements."

I nodded, still not convinced I hadn't screwed everything up. "This is James Wesson," I said. "James, Connell."

As they shook hands, Connell said, "We followed you some years ago."

James gave him a suspicious look while my own brow creased in question. Then I remembered the Front's ability to tap into the demonic realm. Like with Tabitha, they must have had a line to the demon who had taken possession of James when he was a teenager.

"And you already know this one," I said, cocking my head toward Tabitha, who had just descended from a tree. She stalked toward us, a "what the fuck have you gotten me into?" look souring her face.

"Tabitha," he said, "I'm Connell. Welcome."

She muttered something about not having eaten a decent meal in days.

"Come," Connell said, already striding from the clearing. "Let's return to the palace. There's much to do and not much time."

I started to sheath my sword before remembering my staff had disappeared into the portal with Lich. *Damn.* I slid the blade through my belt instead and hurried to catch up to Connell and the others.

While James was taken to a dining room for a late dinner, Connell escorted me back to the infirmary. "You're tainted with Whisperer magic," he explained. "Not to the extent as before, but it's in you."

"Probably during my exchange with Chicory—I mean, Lich," I said, remembering how, among other things, he'd made me see my flight itinerary as a packing list.

Connell nodded. "There's no shame. It's powerful magic."

"How about James?" I asked.

"He's fine, but your cat was infected. Her cleaning will be quick."

Lich must have retrieved Tabitha from my apartment on his way back to the safe house and used magic to convince her she'd never left, that she'd tended to me in my catatonic state. I removed my shirt and lay in my former bed. Arianna entered with a steaming basin of healing water.

"Welcome back," she said with the warmth of a mother. I noticed a thin tension around her eyes, though. Connell wore the same tension, but it was in the lines of his jaw.

"The situation with Lich," I said. "It's bad, isn't it?"

"It's urgent," Connell said. "Once Arianna finishes, we're going to hold council to discuss the situation. In the meantime, I'd like to hear what happened out there, from your departure to your return."

I started telling them. When I got to my trip in Romania, I described the condition in which I'd found Lazlo's body. I told them what Lazlo had said, including his request that I take his hair.

"That may help us find Lich's glass pendant," Connell said, then frowned. "Lazlo fought in the war against the Inquisition, but he wasn't a member of the Front. Your grandfather was very careful about who he selected. There were undoubtedly many good and powerful magic-users who never knew the true nature of the Order until it was too late. Your grandfather felt awful about that, but he feared that the larger the resistance, the greater the chance someone would undermine it from within. With so much at stake, he kept the resistance small."

"Makes sense," I said.

"What happened then?" Arianna asked.

I described the attack by the shadow creatures as well as by Olga's father later that night, drawing comparisons to the attacks James told me had happened near Elsie's former home.

"You're right," she said as she set damp towels over my injuries, the towels' warm, healing water drawing the Whisperer magic from my system. "The shadow creatures use the portals between the fallen magic-users and the domain of Dhuul to spread fear and madness. The effects are local, but that will change when the portal to Dhuul is complete."

"It's already changing," I said, telling them about the situation in the city.

"Then he may be closer to completing the portal than we feared," Connell said.

As Arianna incanted softly over me, I finished the account with my confrontation with Chicory at the safe house and why I'd become convinced he was Lich. The room wavered over their nodding heads. My eyelids grew heavy. As Connell's and Arianna's forms began to blur, I saw something I had received subtle hints of but never put together.

I'll be damned, I thought blearily.

Following our confrontation with Lich, I had watched the other men of the Front, especially the older ones. I had sized them up, studied their eyes, the angles of their faces, all the time ignoring the man beside me. Now, I could see it clearly in his fading stance, so similar to my own.

Connell is Marlow, I thought as I drifted off.
Connell is my father.

22

I was awakened by an automaton removing the towels from my body. The room was dark save for the two moons glowing through an open window. I sat up on the edge of the bed and inhaled through my nose. I had been cleansed, the Whisperer magic purged from my system.

The male automaton handed me my shirt.

"Thanks," I said before I could catch myself. I was talking to a magic-imbued machine. *And thank God*, I thought, thinking of the automatons I'd decapitated and gutted on my first visit to the Refuge, believing them the enemy. Those could have been members of the Front. Or my father.

"I'm to take you to the council meeting," the automaton said.

"Okay."

I finished dressing and followed the automaton from the infirmary room. We walked down handsome stone corridors and climbed several stairways. As the automaton's gears whirred quietly, the revelation I'd had before falling asleep spun through my thoughts. I felt both a short-breathed excitement to see Connell and a deepening anxiety. What did you say to a father you'd never met? *Hey, Pops, how's it going? We should, you know, go fishing sometime?*

Before long we arrived in the altar room on the top level, the same room where I'd seized what I'd believed was Lich's book. Whisperer magic polluting my senses, the room had appeared evil then, with its gunked-up statue pillars and foul pool. Now, it appeared grand.

Around the room, the massive statues of the nine First Saints gleamed marble-white, their hewn forms and faces speaking to power and wisdom. The raised pool at the room's center was still long and rectangular, but its water was deep blue and lined in handsome stones. More than twenty magic-users sat around the pool, including James, who was easy to pick out with his cowboy hat.

Connell and Arianna sat on the pool's far side in robes. My heart gave a hard double thud when Connell raised his eyes to mine. "Have a seat, Everson," he said, indicating a place across from him.

I settled in beside James.

"Too bad you missed dinner," James whispered. "They had a killer spread."

"Tabitha must have been in seventh heaven," I muttered, imagining her in a food coma on a plush bed somewhere.

"She could barely walk afterwards," James affirmed.

I peered around. The other members of the Front were men and women of varying ages and races, some recruited by my grandfather, no doubt, others born and trained within the Refuge. I considered how remote the highest echelons of the Order had always felt to me. Now, for all intents and purposes, I was sitting among them.

Connell stood. "The situation is more dire than we feared," he said. "Though our efforts slow Lich's progress, they cannot staunch the outflow of Whisperer magic. That magic is pouring into the world, beginning the dissolution, a process that will gain momentum as it deepens and spreads. Lich has only to bide his time, but he appears intent on hastening that process."

"How so?" a woman asked.

"When Lich was forced from the Refuge earlier tonight, he took Everson's staff with him," Connell said. "I believe that was intentional. The staff's magic acts as a beacon. He's taken the staff to where he's building his portal to Dhuul, a parallel realm, not unlike the Refuge."

"I've been there," I blurted out. "Lich transported me there earlier tonight, or at least my astral form. He was preparing to claim my soul." For the benefit of the other magic-users, I described what I had seen.

Connell nodded gravely. "It is Lich's home. It's where he's most potent. And he plans to lure us there to destroy us and complete his work. Perhaps it is his way of getting the last laugh—using the souls of those who resisted him to finish the portal to his master."

I considered how the power possessed by those in this room would be greater than the remaining magic-users in the world.

It wasn't a stretch to think their souls could accomplish Lich's objective the instant he claimed them.

"So what do we do?" a young-looking man to my right asked.

"What we must," Connell said. "We fight him there."

My body broke out in a sweat as I recalled the nightmare realm. The creatures going up and down the stairway that spiraled into the pit had seemed endless. And the whispers... If we didn't fall to Lich or the creatures, we'd be seduced by Dhuul's magic.

"He's confident," Connell went on. "Perhaps overconfident. Not only does the staff enable us to track him, he has lowered the defenses to his realm, where he likely keeps his glass pendant. Nothing prevents our passage. This is the first time he's given us this kind of access. It's a trap, yes. But we must use that to our advantage somehow. With time running out, we have no other choice."

I watched Connell as he spoke, the way his hands clasped behind his low back, the fingers of his right hand hooking his left thumb. The same gesture had bothered me days earlier because it was how I clasped my own hands when I lectured.

"But we've still no weapon," an older man said.

Weapon? I thought.

Connell turned to James and me. "Though it may sound like a contradiction, Dhuul requires an organizing force to reduce our world to chaos. Someone to build the portal, harvest the souls, execute certain rites and magic. Lich is the key to Dhuul's designs, even in these last stages."

I nodded, understanding he was filling us in on something the others already knew.

"In Lich's hunger for supremacy, he made a deal with Dhuul and became an undead being. The power that sustains him lives inside a pendant protected by a rare and indestructible enchantment. Your grandfather divined as much. But through his research, he also discovered that the Elders designed a weapon to pierce any magic, no matter how powerful. The Banebrand. It was a fail-safe so that a single magic-user couldn't become invincible. Your grandfather believed Lich stole the Banebrand and then lost it, which was part of the weapon's magic: to not end up in the hands of the one wielding the abusive power."

"That's why my grandfather was collecting magical artifacts during the war," I said, remembering what the vampire Arnaud had told me. He claimed that Grandpa had used the Brasov Pact to steal from his fellow magic-users. "He wasn't stealing. He was searching for the Banebrand."

"Yes, during the war and for long after," Connell said. "That was why, while we used Elder magic from here to push back against Lich's efforts, your grandfather remained in the world. He devoted his life to finding the artifact that would destroy Lich's glass pendant and deny Dhuul access to the world."

I thought about the business trips Grandpa would frequently take, allegedly for purposes of insurance.

"I assume he never found it?" I said.

"That's what we'd like to ask you," Connell replied.

"Me?"

"There was no description of the Banebrand in the archives," Arianna said. "Only what it was designed to do. Your grandfather was able to detect and retrieve many artifacts over the centuries, but discovering their true purposes was another challenge. He spent his final years going over and over what he'd amassed. But after Lich sealed us in the Refuge, we lost contact with your grandfather. Though he had taken possession of a familiar, our contact to that creature's realm became hazy and indistinct. Not like the line we later established to Tabitha."

I thought about the chilling voice I'd heard in Grandpa's trunk the time I'd snuck into his study.

"Did he ever say anything to you?" Connell asked.

"Say anything?" I let out an involuntary laugh. "I can probably count the number of actual conversations we had on two hands, and they had nothing to do with magic or magical artifacts." Looking back, I got the impression he'd wanted to steer me as far from the subject of magic as possible. Probably to keep me off Lich's radar. "And then he died unexpectedly," I finished.

Something flickered in Connell's eyes.

I stiffened. "Wait, it *was* unexpected, right?"

"We believe it was premeditated," Connell said.

A chill crawled down my spine. "You mean someone killed him too?" How hard would it have been to manifest a bee in the face of an oncoming driver at the moment Grandpa stepped into the street? Not hard at all. It was something even a junior magic-user could have managed.

"We believe your grandfather killed himself."

"What? Why?"

"Probably because Lich was closing in," Arianna said. "For centuries your grandfather's advantage was Lich's single-minded obsession with bringing Dhuul into the world and growing his own power. When your grandfather convinced him he could no longer contribute to the Order, Lich's interest in him faded. It was how your grandfather was able to work unnoticed for so long. It was also how he kept your mother's presence a secret. He waited until she was much older to train her to control her magic, just as he had planned to do with you. Eve was the one who insisted on acting as the courier between our realms so your grandfather could concentrate on locating the artifact. Not long after, and unbeknownst to us, Lich deduced the source of the magic that was frustrating his efforts to open the portal. He waited for the next passage into the Refuge, when the membrane would be weakest. That happened to be your mother's. He entered behind her, killing her and several magic-users before we were able to destroy his form. Once reconstituted, Lich set his power obsession aside long enough to look around. He discovered someone had been gathering magical artifacts in secret."

"And Lich started searching for him," I said, remembering the visitor Arnaud had spoken of, the man who had come asking about artifacts stolen during the war against the Inquisition.

"Your grandfather persisted in his work for as long as he could," Connell said, "but when Lich got too close... You see, Lich would have performed a mind flaying, something your grandfather couldn't have resisted. Any and all information would have passed to Lich. That your grandfather ended his life before that could happen suggests he *was* protecting something."

"Maybe just me," I offered.

"Maybe," Connell agreed. "But he might also have found the artifact and begun his search for Lich's glass pendant. Did he say anything to you, anything at all. Think hard now."

"No," I replied, "but I do know where he was storing the artifacts." I told them what Arnaud had shared about Grandpa making periodic visits to Port Gurney and about the basement-level vault in the bar.

Connell nodded. "He moved the artifacts several times during his time in New York. After Lich sealed us in, your grandfather tried to tell us of a new location through his familiar, but as Arianna said, the connection was poor. And the communication only operated in one direction, so we had no way to tell him we never received the information. Very good, Everson."

"Well, before we get ahead of ourselves, Arnaud's blood slaves broke into the vault and cleaned it out. Arnaud had a few magical items in his armory, but I turned those all over to Chicory." Which probably explained Lich's present confidence, I thought, wanting to kick myself.

"It's worth investigating, anyway," Connell said.

"But … can't you just manifest this Banebrand weapon?" I asked. "You know, think it into being."

"We can manifest objects," Arianna explained, "but we must supply the magic. And the kind of magic of which we're speaking came about through a collective effort by the Elders. It is beyond us."

I glanced around the table of magic-users. Expecting to be met by the stern, judgmental faces I had long associated with the Order—I had destroyed the Elder book and allowed Lich into their realm twice, after all—I was surprised to find expressions of acceptance.

You're one of us, they seemed to be saying. *Our struggle is mutual.*

My gaze returned to Arianna and Connell. "If there's a way to keep my return to the world from allowing Lich back in," I said,

"I'll go to the vault and see what I can find. There were some items at the safe house, too. I can bring everything back here for you to examine."

Arianna looked at Connell, who nodded. "Lich is waiting for us at the pit to Dhuul," he said. "The passage back should be safe, but you'll still need to be careful. The world is fast disintegrating."

James stood and adjusted his hat. "Then what are we waiting for?"

"You're in?" I asked in surprise.

"Hey, this is exactly the kind of gig I signed up for."

I nodded, grateful for the company. When I turned back to Connell, something like pride shone in his eyes. "Excellent," he said. "Before you depart, would you mind if I used your memory of Lich's realm for a rendering?"

"A rendering?"

As Connell walked around the table, the water began to shift as though trying to assume shape. And then I understood. Connell wanted to create a likeness of the realm for their planning.

"Oh, yeah, yeah, of course," I said.

I started to stand, but he gestured for me to remain sitting and placed a hand over my brow. His palm was warm with magic. I helped him by remembering the experience, the nightmare pit, the hills of fungal growth, the building opposite me. He extracted the information gently, his other hand extending toward the pool, where a three-dimensional likeness was beginning to take shape.

You know, he said in my thoughts.

Marlow, right? I answered.

That is my birth name, yes. I assumed the name Connell upon coming to the Refuge. I didn't want to deceive you, but neither could I tell you in those first days. It would have been too much.

Probably a good thing, I agreed.

We'll talk upon your return, he said, his voice gentle in my thoughts.

I thought about Arianna's carefully crafted words before my first departure from the Refuge. *I'm sure you've been wondering about your father,* she'd said. *He visited your bedside while you slept. He is anxious to meet you and for you to meet him, but only when that is what you desire.*

Meet one another as father and son, she'd meant. Well played.

By the time Marlow removed his hand from my brow, the scene in the pool was fully rendered, the pit plunging deep into the water. While the other magic-users leaned toward it, I grasped my father's retreating hand, a lump growing in my throat. It was all I could do to keep from bawling.

Without realizing I was going to, I said, "I missed you."

He gave my hand a firm squeeze.

"I missed you, too, Everson."

23

James and I arrived back in the basement we had fled only hours before. A miasma of death and magic clung to the darkness: the remnants of Lich's presence. James beat me to a light invocation.

"Illuminare."

Silver light swelled from his wand and reflected from the sunglasses he'd slipped on. I reached out with my wizard's senses, scanning the basement and house. "I'm not picking up anything," I said, "but he's cloaked his magic before. Every inch of this place could be booby trapped."

I cast through a wand Marlow had given me as a replacement for my staff and watched the light it emitted harden into a protective shield. From inside his own shield, James shook his head in disbelief.

"Goddamned Chicory," he muttered.

"Yeah, I'm still getting used to the idea too."

I held out my sword as we made our way across the littered basement. I was especially wary of the mounds from which Lich-as-Chicory had summoned elementals during my training, ready for them to lumber to life again. James loped past them, apparently unconcerned.

"Hey, mind slowing it down," I whispered.

"Place is clean."

"How do you know?"

"Cause it's not his play."

"What do you mean, 'not his play'?"

James trotted up the stairs, his boots clunking loudly on the wooden steps. "You were at the meeting. Lich wins either way, he's just aiming to win big. He knows we've got no choice but to go to him. That's his play. What we do up here doesn't mean crap to the man."

"It will if we find the weapon."

James turned enough to make a skeptical face. "Really think that's gonna happen, chief?"

Hot anger flushed over my own face, but I didn't say anything. James was only voicing the obvious. Lich was acting too damned confident for there to be a weapon out there that could kill him. Meaning he had either destroyed the weapon or made it impossible to find. But what if Grandpa's suicide had been about more than protecting me? What if he *had* wanted to hide something?

"Where to?" James asked.

We'd arrived in the main hallway, and I stood in our shifting lights for a moment. The safe house felt anything but. "There's a trunk in the attic where he stashed some wands and weapons. I can take care of those if you wouldn't mind searching the other rooms again."

James nodded and headed off while I climbed the stairs. I readied my sword upon entering the attic, but nothing jumped out at me. My locking spell still held the trunk closed. I dispelled it and lifted the creaking lid. The items remained where and—as far as I could tell—how I had left them. From one of my coat pockets, I drew out an enchanted sack Marlow had given me. One by one, I set the items inside, including the maces I'd used in the battle against the werewolves. If they carried any magic, even the Whisperer variety, the bag would suppress it until the items could be examined in the Refuge.

"Yo, Everson!" James called. "You might want to take a look at this."

I hurried downstairs and turned down the hallway to find the front door open. James was standing outside, arms leaning on the railing of the small front porch. Beyond him, in the direction of New York City, the sky was an evil-looking brown and orange. The fires that had sprung up in pockets around the city were spreading, just like the influence of the Whisperer.

We were running out of time.

"Did you find anything?" I asked him.

"Nothing interesting," he said in a way that made me wonder how thoroughly he'd searched. "Guess it's on to … where, exactly?"

"Port Gurney," I muttered. "Other side of the city."

James spun a set of keys around his finger. "Good thing I brought my ride, then."

James's ride was a black Trans-Am parked curbside, the firebird emblem spreading its golden wings across the hood. The inside smelled of oil. James barely waited for me to buckle in before gunning the engine and performing a squalling U. Though the car slewed sideways, I sensed he was in control. He threw it into second as the car straightened.

"Port Gurney," he said, tapping a finger against the steering wheel as though consulting a mental map. "North central Long Island? We could take the interstate up through the Bronx, avoid the city."

"Yeah, except that the rioting and fires started in the Bronx. There's no telling what kind of shape the interstate's in now." I imagined lanes clogged with piles of burning vehicles and debris. "I think our best bet is to take the Lincoln Tunnel and go straight across to the Queens-Midtown Tunnel, hope the chaos hasn't reached the center of the city yet."

James chuckled. "Rolling the dice. I like it."

The car engine rose an octave as he shifted again. Houses blurred past on the empty streets. People had either evacuated the area or locked themselves inside for the night. Before long, we were dropping into the Lincoln Tunnel and then cresting again, emerging into Midtown. Black smoke billowed past the Firebird's headlights, and I could hear sirens in the distance.

I was in the middle of wondering how Vega was faring when she paged me.

"Hey, would you mind pulling over up there," I said, pointing out a payphone. "It's Detective Vega. Probably wants an update, but she can also advise us on the best route through the city."

"Vega?" James said, easing up to the curb. "You mean that

Puerto Rican mamma? Talk about a hot ticket." He grinned at me in a way that made me wonder whether Vega's eye roll from earlier had meant more than just James being an arrogant ass. Had he tried to hit on her?

"Hey, let's keep it professional," I said, a knot twisting in my gut.

He showed his hands. "I just call 'em like I see 'em."

"Well, she's a friend, all right? A ... good friend."

His grin broadened. "How good?"

"Just..." I felt my face warming over. "Just drop it." Flustered, I got out of the car. Breathing through my shirt collar to filter the acrid smoke, I made my way to the payphone, pushed in two quarters, and punched Vega's number as a pair of helicopters batted past.

"It's Everson," I said when she answered.

"What do you have?"

"The perp is Chicory," I said. "Not Marlow. Not my father."

The relief at being able to say that washed through me like a strong surf. I was still adjusting to the idea that Marlow—a good and powerful wizard—was my father. If only the timing had been better.

"Where are you?" she asked.

"West Midtown, south of Forty-second." I filled her in on where we were going and why. "Are we okay driving straight to the Queens-Midtown Tunnel, or should we try another route?"

"You should be all right if you hurry," she said. "There are rioters all along Forty-second Street, and they're moving south. Another group is coming up from Gramercy." I could actually hear them: shouts and screams punctured by the sounds of things breaking. I could also hear the strain in Vega's voice.

"How's the NYPD holding up?" I asked.

"We don't have enough officers to contain them. The rioters are charging the cordons and breaking through. We've tried gas, rubber bullets, real bullets. Nothing's deterring them. And the one's we've hauled in are going absolutely nuts. Budge is asking the president for National Guard troops, but I'm starting to wonder if *that* will be enough. Croft ... whatever's happening out there, it's starting to affect normal people."

I remembered the aging woman in the pants suit at the gas station, the way her pupils had seemed to flatten as she lowered the lighter toward the pool of gasoline...

"Once we find the Banebrand weapon, we're going to the source," I promised her.

"And that will end this?"

I considered the odds: venturing into Lich's turf, where he was expecting us, surviving long enough to find his glass pendant and destroy it—all assuming, of course, we obtained the Banebrand weapon first. So, a thousand to one? Ten thousand to one?

"Only if we succeed," I answered honestly.

I waited for Vega to ask me the likelihood of that success, but she only blew out her breath. I glanced back at the car and caught James puffing a joint. I turned up a hand and mouthed, *The hell are you doing?* He smirked and shot me with a finger pistol.

"I should let you go then," Vega said.

"Is your son someplace safe?"

"He's at the apartment with Camilla."

She hadn't really answered my question, but I picked up the undercurrent of worry. Her apartment was too close to the city, the chaos.

"We'll swing by on our way back," I said. "Check in on them."

"No, Croft, that's not—"

"I'm not asking," I interrupted.

Behind me, James laid on the horn. When I looked, he was stubbing out the joint in the ashtray and jabbing a finger past me. I craned my neck around the phone stand. "Crap," I said. Then to Vega, "I'll call you later."

I hung up and backed away from the mob running toward us, their screams an insane squall. Windows broke in their wake; awnings burst into flames. Men and women shimmied light poles, rocking them until they crashed over the street. A hydrant burst, jetting water twenty feet into the air.

I climbed into the car and slammed and locked the door. *"Protezione,"* I called.

A glimmering shield grew around the Firebird, which James had already thrown into gear. He sped toward the mob, a hailstorm of bottles, concrete chunks, and other thrown objects breaking around us. A blue USPS mailbox landed on the shielded hood and tumbled over the roof. Within seconds we were close enough that I could pick out the crazed faces.

James wasn't slowing.

"Hey, wh-what are you doing?" I shouted, throwing my forearms to my face.

But instead of clunking through bodies, the car took a hard right, rear wheels screaming, and then a just as sudden left that fishtailed us the other direction. I lowered my arms to find us on a parallel street. Straggling members of the northbound mob armed with pipes wheeled toward us.

James let out a "Yee-haw!"

Without slowing, he cut around them as they tried to dart in front of the car. Pipes banged off the windows and clunked under the tires. Gunfire erupted, flashing from the shield. Twice James had to drive up onto the sidewalk to avoid hitting someone, but within another few seconds we were past the mob, their mindless screams trailing in our wake. In my rearview mirror, I watched them turn and resume their assault on the street and buildings.

"Good God," I muttered. "It's like Zombieville out there."

"So seriously, man," James said, shifting into a higher gear. "What's up with you and Vega?"

I looked over at him. "Me and Vega?"

"You know what I'm talking about."

"I have an idea, but is now really the time?" I flinched as James squealed onto a street with a new wave of rioters, slammed the brakes, threw the car in reverse, and accessed the next block.

"There's no shame in it, man," he said, not missing a beat.

I relaxed my grip on the armrest. "We work together, that's all."

"But you feel something for her."

"I feel what I'd feel for anyone I worked closely with. I might even develop feelings for you some d—look out!"

More bullets flashed off the shield. James swerved to avoid a group spilling from a Thirty-fourth street subway entrance, then down-shifted and turned north.

"Naw, man, this runs deeper than that," he said. "Every time you say her name, your eyes do this thing."

"What thing?"

"This tiny shift. It's your tell. Saw it when you first brought her up at the pool hall. Didn't think much about it till a few minutes ago when you wanted to rip me a new one. And bam, there it was again."

"Whatever," I said, my face growing warm.

He turned toward me. "Say her name."

"What?"

"Just say it, man."

"Hey, would you watch the road?" I cried.

James swerved at the last moment, avoiding a toppled light pole, then turned back to me. He made small steering adjustments without looking, his tires clunking over debris and glass. "C'mon, man, I want to see."

"Vega," I said quickly, for no other reason than to get us across Midtown in one piece.

James leaned back and laughed. "I knew it. You've totally got a thing for her."

"If my eyes did anything, it was only because you made it awkward," I stammered.

"What's the big deal? You like her. You've got good taste."

I grumbled. My eyes did a lot of things without my knowledge, apparently. *Was* I developing feelings for Vega? It had only been a month since Caroline had had her feelings for me wiped clean. I hadn't gotten over that, not yet. So how could I have a thing for Vega? And yet ... I did care about her. And yeah, I looked forward to seeing her now.

"I respect her," I allowed at last.

"Respect her," James echoed. "Have you told her?"

"Told her what?"

"About your, cough, *respect* for her."

"For God's sake. Has it occurred to you that the city is literally falling apart?" As if on cue, James turned a corner and sped past a blazing building. Bricks landed on the shielded roof.

"I'm just trying to help a wizard out," he said, switching the vent setting to Recirculate as the smoke outside thickened. "You're not the smoothest number. You know that, right?"

"Yeah, I'm an academic. I know that."

"My advice, then? Start simple. A casual dinner, maybe. Or drinks. See what kind of chemistry you two have outside work."

"Getting a little ahead of ourselves, aren't we?"

"You talking about finding the Banebrand weapon?"

"Yeah, the small matter of finding the Banebrand weapon, something even you're skeptical about. Oh, and then there's the whole destroying Lich's pendant and closing the portal to Dhuul. Otherwise, yeah, we're golden. I'll go ahead and make that dinner reservation."

James shrugged. "You were the one who brought it up. I was just trying to help."

I stared at him in disbelief, but we were arriving at the Queens-Midtown Tunnel, which had to have been a record for an west-east traverse of Manhattan. Once through, we had the highways to ourselves. James shut up, thankfully, and urged the Firebird past one hundred. Other than distant pockets of fire, the destruction was nothing like what was happening in Manhattan, but that would change as the disorder spread. I imagined the world and everyone I cared for, Vega included, reduced to a mindless soup for the Whisperer to feed on.

Please let the Banebrand be in the vault, I thought.

24

James steered through the empty streets of Port Gurney, the Firebird's beams sweeping past boarded-up buildings and weedy lots. A pack of feral dogs scattered ahead of us, their backward-peering faces lean and fearful.

"Sure this is the place?" he asked.

"The town took a hit when the shipping industry crashed. It's been a downhill ride ever since. There," I said, pointing out a leaning strip of buildings that made up the town's waterfront. "The name of the bar was the Rhein House." As James turned, I rolled down the window and squinted in search of a sign. A smell of seawater and sewage wafted into the car.

"I see it," James said, and took a sharp turn in front of a building on the end of the strip. The front window had been smashed, but the hand-painted letters "RH" still showed in the upper left corner of the glass.

I got out of the car and, wand and sword readied, listened a moment. Except for the wind and the slapping of the sea, the town was quiet. But something was telling me to be wary.

"Door's unlocked."

I jerked at James's voice and found him already stepping into the bar. I hurried to catch up. Glass crunched underfoot as I stepped into the orb of silver light growing from his wand. The establishment was a leaf-blown space where I imagined tables had once stood, photos from the old country adorning the sooty brick walls. A U-shaped bar took up the far side of the room, ringed by stools bolted into the wooden floor, though several were missing. I imagined Grandpa sitting on one of the stools, ordering a stein of beer, then using illusory magic to go down to the vault to add to his collection or perhaps examine the magical artifacts already there. My gaze shifted to a corridor to the left of the bar.

"Access to the basement is probably back here," I said.

James followed me into the bar's former kitchen. The stairs down were beside a cleaned-out pantry. I took a tremulous breath—why did everything important have to be in basements?—and led the way down. The basement was a dank, concrete space. Rats skittered from the expanding glow of my wand, taking refuge among heaps of trash and old furniture. James sent a bolt after one and chuckled when it zapped the rat's hindquarters.

"I'm sorry," I said, "is this boring you?"

"Hey, just trying to keep my skills honed."

"Well, how about looking for the vault?" I snapped. The uneasiness I'd felt outside was still swimming through my system like a harsh stimulant. I was in no mood to play babysitter. I moved from James and began scanning the walls. He took the hint and began doing the same, moving in the other direction. When we met on the far wall, he shook his head.

"Nothing," he said.

When Arnaud had told me about the vault, I'd pictured it in a wall. Maybe that was the wrong assumption.

"*Vigore!*" I shouted, sweeping my sword in an arc. James jumped out of the way as the heaps of refuse blew toward the staircase. Clusters of squealing rats spilled out and scattered, chasing down their former refuge. A moment later I spotted the vault door in the floor where one of the piles had been sitting. The door was made of cast iron with a lever handle.

"Looks like someone's already been in there," James remarked.

"Blood slaves," I said, sensing the residue of the old locking spell. "They must have overpowered the spell." Which had no doubt weakened with Grandpa's death, I thought. He'd probably saved his most powerful locking enchantments for the items themselves—like the vampires' Scaig Box that had held a shadow fiend. And hopefully whatever held the Banebrand.

I double-checked the door for traps before gripping the lever and giving it a hard yank. The door clunked loose and opened onto a cylinder with a metal ladder leading down.

"Hold on," James said. He cast a silver ball of light and, with a small flick, sent it down the cylinder ahead of us. A skill he must have learned during the five years of training I'd never received. About fifteen feet below, the light spread into a room of which I could only see a small section.

I climbed down the ladder first, the skin across my chest stretching tight, breaths thinning, and ducked into a bunker-like room. I turned toward the hovering ball of light, and my heart sank. Against the far wall lay a scatter of metal boxes inside which the magical artifacts had no doubt been stored. The open boxes had been picked through, if not by the blood slaves then by whomever had come after them. Gone were the wands I'd imagined, the amulets and charms and enchanted blades. All I could find among the boxes was a dagger the size of a letter-opener.

"Think that's the weapon?" James asked.

I turned the rusty dagger around in my hand. I sensed no magic or enchantment in it. The blade's tip had bent, and the blade was dull. Was that the point? I wondered. For the weapon to appear ordinary to anyone who found it? Was the magic hidden deep inside it? I looked over the dagger once more, made a dubious face, and placed it in the sack.

"Probably not," I said.

"There's still this."

I turned to where James's ball of light was hovering above a trunk set in a corner. With its black wood and battered metal, I recognized it immediately as the steamer trunk that had once sat in Grandpa's attic study. I'd always wondered what had become of it. But as I looked at it now, I had no hope it would contain anything. The central lock was busted and both hasps open. James lifted the lid and then jumped back with a sharp holler.

"What is it?" I asked, remembering the sniveling voice I'd heard in the same trunk years earlier. But the bone-white creature that sprang out was no familiar. He perched on the edge of the trunk, bloodshot eyes flicking between us. When his pale lips began to bulge, I saw what we were dealing with.

"Vampire!" I shouted at James.

The creature sprang and rammed face-first into James's shield. He hissed and scratched at it, a ragged business shirt and slacks covering his emaciated body. And now I recognized him. The vampire was a former CEO of one of the financial firms in downtown Manhattan. I'd sat with him in Arnaud's conference room, fought alongside him against the wolves.

Grandpa's ring pulsed around my finger. I aimed it at the vampire and shouted, *"Balaur!"*

The force from the ring nailed him and, in a burst of fire, slung him into the far wall. The vampire lay writhing, his face torn as though by dragon talons, smoke billowing from his body.

James and I stood over him. "So this is where you've been hiding out," I said.

"A drop," the creature groveled. "A single, blessed drop. Please. Your blood is potent, and I am so hungry."

He gripped my pant leg, but I kicked his hand away. He was one of the two former CEOs who had escaped following the battle against the city and, by the looks of it, had planned to remain in hibernation until the threat passed, maybe even for several years. He'd probably learned about the vault from Arnaud when the vampire had reclaimed the Scaig Box.

"So hungry," he moaned.

The thing about hibernation was that the vampire emerged weak. If we had been mortals, no problem. He would have devoured our blood to the last drop and gone back to sleep. Unfortunately for him, he'd awakened to a pair of magic slingers.

"Tell you what," I said. "You help us, and maybe we'll help you."

James shot me a consternated look, but I shook my head, letting him in on the bluff.

"What do you want?" the vampire moaned. The wounds across his face were puckering grotesquely along the edges. He was trying to heal them, but he lacked the regenerative power.

"Information," I said. "You've been down here, what, a month? In that time, has anyone else been down here?"

"No, now feed me."

His hand crawled toward my leg. I stepped on it. "Think harder," I said, his fingers crunching beneath my shoe. It was cruel, but this creature had done far, far worse in his lifetime.

His scream was thin and piercing.

"One person," he said when he'd caught his breath.

A charge went through me. "Who?"

"I didn't see them, I was sleeping. Now let me feed, curse you."

"But you sensed this person. What did you sense?"

I kept my ring trained on the vampire as his mouth opened and closed, fangs thirsting for blood. "Death and decay," he panted. "Ruination. Now let me feed!"

James raised his eyebrows. "Lich?"

I'd never told Chicory about this place, but he could have picked it up from my thoughts. Either that or one of the magical items Arnaud had taken—and that I'd subsequently given to Chicory—had left a trail of some kind, one the mage was able to trace back here. Either way, Lich had beaten us to whatever had remained of the magical stash, maybe even found the weapon in question. That would certainly explain his confidence.

"Crap," I spat.

"You promised you'd help me," the vampire hissed. "You *promised.*"

"You're right," I said tersely. *"Vigore."* The force from my blade lifted the vampire and dropped him back into the trunk. I tossed in some dragon sand after him, shut the lid with another force invocation, bound it with a locking spell, and shouted, *"Fuoco!"* The vampire unleashed a withering scream as flames burst through the seams in the trunk.

"That's helping him?" James asked.

"Putting him out of his misery, anyway," I muttered. "Not to mention his blood slaves." I imagined the mortals whom the vampire had hollowed out either dying at last or regaining their humanity in the steel shipping container that held them in the city. With the way things were going, though, it felt like pulling them out of a frying pan and into the fire.

James turned from the burning trunk and peered around. "So, that's it, I guess. No magical weapon." He paused, head cocked as though trying to sense something. "But there *is* magic kicking around down here."

And now I picked it up too, a shallow pulse. We followed the pulse to its source—three symbols on the back wall. The symbols had been drawn in dark red ink, and the faint magic was emanating from their lines. James parked his shades atop his head and leaned in.

"Looks like a sigil," he said.

"It does, but I don't think that's what it is," I said. "I mean, there's magic, but it's not coming from the symbols. It's *maintaining* the symbols, making sure they can't be washed away."

"Yeah?"

And now I sensed something else. "My grandfather drew them," I said. "It's hard to explain, but there's a familiarity to the magic, something I've felt with other items he enchanted."

"What do the symbols mean?"

"It's Akkadian cuneiform," I said as I studied them more closely. "Phonograms."

"And for us non-PhD types, Prof?"

"Sorry, they're sounds."

"What do they mean?"

"That's the thing, they don't mean anything. They're just random syllables. *Gug-lugal-i*," I whispered, careful not to push any power through them. "It would be like saying la-de-da in English."

"I don't remember anything like that from my training," James said.

"And I don't recognize it from my spell books." Still, something about the symbols resonated. Not on a magical level this time, but from a more intellectual space, as though I should have known what they meant.

"We could always test them," James said. Before I could stop him, he was repeating the sounds, releasing them as an invocation. I flinched back, hardening my light into a shield.

But after several seconds, nothing happened.

"It was worth a shot," James said with a shrug.

"What? A shot at getting us both killed?"

"Dude, you need to relax."

"Relax?" I could feel a vein throbbing in my right temple. "You don't go around channeling random sounds. You had no idea what might have been stored inside those symbols."

"Maybe something good," he said.

"And maybe something that would have cooked us like McCrispy over there," I said, jerking a thumb at the smoking trunk.

"Let me know when you're done lecturing." James wheeled toward the ladder.

"Hey!" I grabbed his shoulder. It was as much my anger at his cavalier attitude as the hopelessness of our mission. When he spun on me, I was surprised by the intensity in his blue eyes.

"Listen, man," he said, leveling a finger at me. "We didn't find the weapon, and you know it. Not here, not at the house. The outing's been a bust. Which means it's time to start rolling the dice, hoping to hell we get lucky. And if that involves testing out random sounds, then yeah, that's what I'm gonna do. I'm not gonna sit around, waiting to be eaten by what's-his-name."

"Dhuul," I said.

"Whatever. We done here?"

I stayed glaring at him, but he had a point. "Just give me a head's up next time, all right?" I said with a sigh.

James dropped his shades over his eyes and climbed the ladder, his orb floating up above him. I turned back toward the small room to glance it over and read the symbols a final time. Why had Grandpa written them? Why would he have wanted them to endure? And where had I seen them before?

Gug-lugal-i.

Repeating the syllables silently, I followed James up the ladder.

25

By the time we reached Brooklyn, the fires had spread. We'd had to detour twice thanks to roving mobs and entire sections of highway in flames. Our argument back in the vault felt petty now, a sentiment James seemed to share. He didn't make a fuss when I mentioned needing to stop at Vega's to check on her son and sitter. I directed him through the streets of Williamsburg until he was pulling up in front of her apartment building.

I stepped from the car and squinted into the blowing smoke. The street was quiet, but I could hear the chaos mere blocks away. Vega's son and sitter wouldn't be safe here much longer.

"C'mon," I said to James.

He finished casting a shield spell around his car and caught up to me at the building's front steps. I looked up and down the steel monster of a front door. "Damn, forgot about that," I muttered.

When James started to raise his wand, I stopped him. "Breaking the lock will get us inside, but it will also make the residents more vulnerable."

I was considering what to do when I heard the bolts turning. A lucky break. I stepped back as the door opened and a woman wearing a crooked headscarf slipped out. I caught the door before it closed behind her.

"You should go back in," James said to the woman. "It's too dangerous out here."

When the woman turned toward us, I recognized her as Tony's sitter. "Camilla?" I said. "Where are you going?"

She gestured absently. "I go ... I go..."

"Camilla," I said, taking her by the shoulders. "Where's Tony?"

"Tony?" Her expression was vacant, her pupils flattening like I'd seen in the eyes of the woman at the gas station. Shit. Camilla was falling under the influence of Whisperer magic.

I pulled her back into the building, shorted the magnetic lock on the glass door inside, and with James following, climbed the steps to Vega's floor. Camilla complied, occasionally mumbling something in Spanish. At least she hadn't turned violent yet ... I hoped. When we reached Vega's apartment, the door was open. I handed Camilla off to James.

"Tony!" I called, making a quick circuit of the apartment. The boy was nowhere in sight. Panic pumped through me. Though I'd only met Tony twice, I felt a responsibility toward him. In part because I'd imperiled him, but largely because he was the most important thing in Vega's world.

"Tony!" I called again.

From back in the kitchen, I could hear James trying to coax the boy's whereabouts from Camilla, but her responses weren't even in Spanish anymore. She was just babbling. Not good.

"Tony, it's Everson Croft. I'm a friend of your mother's."

I heard a spring squeak in Vega's bedroom and returned to find Tony's curly head peering from underneath the bed. "Mr. Croft?" he asked. When he squirmed all the way free, I was there to lift him up.

I looked him over to make sure he was all right. "What happened?" I asked.

He cinched my neck with both arms. "She stopped making sense," Tony whispered. "Started picking at her arms and saying strange things, screaming at nothing." At that moment, Camilla screamed from the kitchen. Tony flinched and squeezed me tighter. "Like that," he said.

I held him another moment before setting him on the edge of the bed. "I want you to stay here, okay?"

He nodded uncertainly. "You gonna help her, Mr. Croft?"

"I'm going to try."

I entered the kitchen to find Camilla sitting in a chair, bound by silver cords of energy. A muzzle of energy covered her mouth, silencing her screams. "She started flipping out," James said, "scratching herself."

I looked at the bloody jags down both her arms. Her pupils were nearly flat lines now. I thought of the woman at the gas station again. Her eyes had looked exactly the same, but when that pothead had slung his arm around her, she'd seemed to snap out of it, her pupils dilating again. I hesitated on that image, remembering the smoke drifting from the guy's long hair and jacket.

I suddenly remembered something James had told me.

"When Chicory last visited you," I said to him now, "you told me he mashed his thumb between your eyes."

"Yeah?"

"But nothing happened," I said.

"Nothing I could feel."

"Do you have any more of that stuff you were smoking earlier?"

"Yeah, but ... you really think now's the time?"

"Go ahead, light it up. You said you were high when Chicory stamped you, right? I think there's something in cannabis that throws off Whisperer magic. That's why you were never affected." James was patting his pockets now, and I gestured for him to hurry. At last he found the half-smoked joint, lit it with his wand, and took a few uncertain puffs.

"Blow it on her," I said.

James leaned down and released a stream of smoke that broke against Camilla's muzzled face. We both stood back and watched. After several seconds, her face relaxed, pupils returning to their spheroid shapes. She blinked several times and looked around in confusion.

"Release her," I said.

James flicked his wand, and the muzzle and bindings dissolved.

"Mr. Croft?" she said, rubbing a wrist. "What are you doing here?"

"What happened, Camilla?" I asked.

"I ... I don't know. I watching T.V. with Tony and then ... I must fall asleep. I wake up here."

"But you feel all right?"

"Sleepy. But yes, I feel all right."

"Keep an eye on her," I said to James, and picked up Vega's phone and dialed her cell.

"Camilla?" she asked when she answered.

"No, it's Everson," I said. "I'm at the apartment. Tony's fine."

"Thank God," she breathed. "No one was answering the phone."

"Listen, I think we've found a way to control the mobs."

"Really? How?"

"Has the Narcotics Division made any marijuana busts lately?"

"Marijuana busts?"

"And I mean big, as in bales of the stuff. You're going to need as much as you can get your hands on."

"What are you talking about?"

"Listen, I only have a few case studies to go on, but I believe there's something in cannabis that alters brain chemistry, changes it in a way that doesn't let the bad magic take hold. Makes the insanity go away. If you can get it in the air, light it, and drop it over the city..."

"You're asking me to fumigate New York City with pot smoke?"

"It's a temporary solution until we can tackle the problem at the source."

"Hold on," Vega said. I heard her shout something into the mass of voices around her. When she came back on, she said, "I got some funny looks, but the wheels are in motion. They're desperate."

"Good."

"How's it look around there?" she asked.

I peered down through the security bars of the nearest window. The mobs were arriving on the block. Several floors down, a window shattered. Fires blazed from parked cars. James's car was surrounded, the mob trying to bang their way through the glimmering shield.

"Could be worse," I said, which was never a lie. "But listen, I'm going to have James stay here to look after Tony and Camilla. Problem is, that leaves me without a ride. Any chance the NYPD could send a chopper?" There was no chance of driving back through the city now.

"Consider it sent," Vega said, no hesitation. "They'll pick you up on the roof."

"Thanks." I almost ended the call there. "Hey, listen. If for some reason I don't, you know, make it back, I just wanted—"

"Shut up, Croft. I'll see you soon."

Despite everything, I smiled.

"Sounds good," I said.

With a relentless blast of air, the chopper set down on the apartment roof, landing lights glaring. James had agreed to stay behind, as much to keep Tony and Camilla safe as to give the city a wizard presence, someone Vega could call if new issues arose. James's ready acceptance of the role suggested he didn't think he would have been much help in the fight against Lich. I knew the feeling because I was thinking the same thing about myself.

I climbed into the back of the chopper and strapped myself in.

The woman pilot turned to face me. "Where to?" she shouted.

"Gehr Place in New Jersey," I shouted back. "You can set me down in the cemetery across the street."

She nodded, replaced the cup over her ear, and lifted off. When the helicopter cleared the surrounding rooftops, it batted west, through smoke and toward the apocalyptic scene that was Manhattan.

Welcome to the End of the World Tour, I thought. *Sponsored in part by Everson Croft.*

It still killed me that I had been manipulated into destroying the Elder book. As I looked over the spreading flames, I struggled for how I might have seen through the artifice, done something different. My hands balled into helpless fists. The copilot, a young man, turned around. "You the one who said we should dust the city with pot smoke?"

I nodded tiredly and awaited the inevitable deriding.

"Department thought it was crazy," he shouted. "So they tested it out on a group they'd arrested earlier. Filled their holding cell with smoke. Know something? It calmed them right down." He smiled wide enough to reveal his crooked lower teeth. "I believe you're onto something."

I nodded back, but the drug wasn't a permanent fix. Something told me that as the Whisperer magic strengthened, it would overpower whatever blunting effect the cannabis was having—no pun intended. Which meant we couldn't fail. Despite what James had said in the vault, I'd managed to hold on to the remote hope that Lich had overlooked something, that one of the items I'd dropped in the magic sack was the weapon that would destroy his pendant.

The key was in the syllables Grandpa had left behind: *Gug-lugal-i.*

Minutes later, the helicopter set down in the cemetery, both officers wishing me luck. I waved as they lifted off again, and I ran down the street to the safe house. From overhead, I had marked the mobs' progress by the fires. They hadn't pushed this far into Jersey yet, but they'd be here soon enough.

At the front door of the safe house, I stopped to make sure Lich hadn't returned. I sensed nothing. That disturbed more than relieved me. He had made no effort to stop us, which suggested he hadn't needed to.

I made my way down to the basement and stood in the casting circle.

Within moments, the wooden rafters and earthen floor disappeared, and I was standing in the moonlit clearing in the Refuge. "How did it go?" Marlow asked. He was alone this time.

"We took what we could find," I said, holding up the sack. "A few items at the house, and one at the vault in Port Gurney. An old dagger. Unfortunately, the vault had been raided. And it sounds like Lich went down there as well. But there were some Akkadian syllables my grandfather had drawn on a wall: *Gug-lugal-i.* Does that mean anything to you?"

Marlow repeated the syllables as though testing their power. "It's not a sound I'm familiar with, no."

My heart sank. If one of the most powerful magic-users didn't know what it meant, who would?

Marlow accepted the sack and beckoned for me to walk with him.

"And James?" he asked.

"He stayed behind to help out in the city. That was sort of an executive decision on my part. I hope that was all right."

"A good decision," Marlow said.

I looked over at him. I'd become so conditioned to being berated by the magical society to which I thought I'd belonged that being commended was almost jarring. And coming from my father...

"How does it look up there?" he asked.

"Honestly? Bad and getting worse." I described the scene going and returning. "But through a series of, um, happenstances, James and I discovered that cannabis frustrates the effect of Whisperer magic."

"Cannabis," Marlow repeated reflectively. "We've been working on various spells and potions as a prophylactic against Dhuul's influence, but that's not an ingredient we'd considered."

"Its effect may only be temporary."

"That may be all we need," Marlow said.

He closed his eyes and a vibratory energy moved around him. We were emerging from the forest and entering the plain. The rocky hill and palace rose out ahead of us, backlit by the twin moons. The serenity was as much a shock to my system as the chaos had been only minutes before. To fill the silence, I asked, "Are you going to miss this place?"

Marlow opened his eyes again and smiled faintly. "A part of me will, yes. It's been my home for centuries now. But the point of coming here was never to stay. It was to defeat Lich so we could return to the world and resume the important work of the Order."

His robe whispered as he walked. Something told me he could have transported us to the palace—we were in a thought realm, after all—but that he had wanted to steal a few minutes alone with me.

"How old was I when I left here?" I asked.

"Barely one. In fact, your grandfather spirited you out right before Lich sealed us from the world. This was shortly after Lich's attack. Your mother and I had discussed what we'd do if he ever found our refuge while you were still young. We decided you would be placed in your grandparents' care. Your grandfather was very powerful, and your grandmother, though not a full-blooded magic-user, had some veiling spells in her repertoire. With Lich's focus largely in parallel realms, we felt you'd be safest with them."

"Wait, my *grandmother* was a magic-user?" I rifled through my memories. She had never demonstrated any magical abilities— none that I could remember. But veiling spells were often subtle.

"And a wonderful cook, too," Marlow said. "I'll never forget her blueberry cobbler topped with homemade ice cream."

I smiled. That had been one of my favorites, too. But I caught a note of loneliness in Marlow's voice.

"You still miss her," I said. "My mother."

"Every day, Everson."

I wanted to ask him what she was like, but the question felt strangely personal. Like I'd be prying, even though he was my father. *My father.* I still couldn't get my head around the idea that this man strolling beside me was him. No longer an idea, no longer a lie, but a living, breathing presence.

"How did you meet?" I asked.

"Your grandfather introduced us on Eve's first visit to the Refuge. She was preparing to take over his role. He asked me to give her a tour of our realm, explain what we were doing, that sort of thing. I was exhausted that day. I'd been up late the night before doing spell work and frankly wasn't in much of a mood to play guide. But your mother had this effect on me—call it magic," he said with a laugh, "as though our auras were in constant resonance. By the end of her visit, I felt more ... *alive* than I had in a long time. My efforts here, which had taken on the dull weight of drudgery, assumed fresh purpose. You have to remember, we'd been working against Lich for hundreds of years and couldn't claim much more than a stalemate. But with your mother's arrival, the work felt brand new. She restored me."

We'd come to the staircase leading to the palace, and now he stopped. "That went double when you arrived, Everson. A new life is a growing system of order. In your case, one that was very precious to me. In your eyes—eyes already showing the first glimmers of insight and intelligence—I beheld the true horror of what Lich could do. Or more aptly, what he could undo. All so Dhuul could feed on the dissolution and Lich could know immortality."

I nodded, not sure what to say.

"I wanted to be there with you, Everson. Through your questions, your struggles, through the lies and distortions that followed. But know that all this time, you've been with me. In my thoughts, my work."

Tears stood in Marlow's eyes. For the first time since realizing he was my father, it felt natural to hug him. We embraced solidly, every so often clapping the other's back. I didn't want to be anywhere else. When at last we separated, moisture stood in my eyes as well. I blinked it back.

"So is it time to save the world?" I asked.

"We'll need to depart for Lich's realm shortly," he said.

"I'm coming, you know."

For the first time it occurred to me that I might not be included in the plans, that I would be considered too junior. But I was the one who had destroyed the Elder book. I was the one who had allowed Lich into the Refuge—twice. Besides that, I was Eve and Marlow's son. I was a member of the Front. I was about to say as much, but my father was already nodding.

"Yes," he said, "we'll need you too."

26

When Marlow and I arrived in the altar room, Arianna and the rest of the Front were already there. The model of Lich's realm remained in the water, the pit dropping like a narrow whirlpool. The members of the Front stood around it, eyes closed. I sensed a unifying force moving among them, conjoining them.

"A guiding principle of the Order," Marlow said to me, "is that the whole is greater than the sum of its parts."

I thought about the old Order and its practice of keeping us segregated.

At the sound of Marlow's voice, several members of the Front separated and made room for us. As we took our place at the pool's edge, the strange force seemed to invite me to become a part of the magical collective. I flashed back to my nightmare of a gold-faced mage urging me to join the cluster, to become one. *Ever*son, he'd whispered, emphasizing the *son*. But this wasn't the same feeling. I wasn't being compelled or even coaxed. I had a choice.

I looked around at the statues of the great Saints. Four men and five women, rock-solid purpose in their frames and steady gazes. Beyond the head of the pool stood the statue of Saint Michael, the line to which all magic-users belonged. As I studied the image of my ancestor, I couldn't help but feel he was looking back, asking me if I was ready.

When I nodded, I imagined him returning the gesture.

In a dizzying flash, my mind opened. The lone planet I had been zoomed out to become part of a revolving galaxy. Power hummed around my prism in a giant corona, but it didn't overwhelm me. That power was being contained by the collective and the specters of those who had come before.

"The world is fast succumbing," Marlow announced, "meaning Lich's thousand-year project is almost complete. By the First Saints, we unite in a common purpose. To destroy Lich, close the portal to Dhuul, and restore the Order to the purpose for which it was originally created."

No one spoke, but I felt the collective power deepen and move through me.

"Lich has placed Everson's staff here," Marlow said, pointing his wand. In the pool, a light glimmered on the side of the pit opposite the fortress. It was the same spot Lich had taken me to. "Nothing stands between us and it," he continued. "Lich's plan, no doubt, is to bait us in and set the spawn of Dhuul upon us. There are many, yes, and Lich is counting on them to overwhelm us so he may claim our souls and complete his portal." My gaze shifted to the horrid creatures climbing from the pit. "But thanks to a discovery by Everson, we've concocted a potion that will resist their influence, hold them off longer."

Hold them off? I thought to myself. *That doesn't sound like a plan for victory.*

"While we are thus engaged, Everson will steal into the keep, find the glass pendant, and destroy it."

"Me?" I stammered in alarm.

"Lich's attention will be on us," Marlow explained. "Indeed, he will be salivating at the prospect of claiming the collective soul of the resistance and turning it to his own purposes. You haven't enough power to interest him. You're beyond his care. You'll also have this." An automaton entered, holding the robe of John the Baptist. It had been repaired, its cloaking energy coursing through the fibers once more. The automaton held the robe toward me.

"The Banebrand," I said, accepting the robe, "are you telling me I found it?"

"I've inspected the collected items for Whisperer magic. They're clean, but there isn't time to examine them more thoroughly," Marlow said. "The only way to know whether one is the Banebrand will be to try them all."

I thought of the collection of items in the sack: wands, amulets, the sorry-looking dagger. "If we don't have the weapon, we can withdraw through the portal to regroup, right?" I asked.

Marlow shook his head. "Lich won't allow it. This will be our one chance."

I looked around at the other members of the Front, men and women who would be sacrificing themselves so that I might accomplish the impossible. Like the statue of Michael, though, their gazes were steady, resolved. They frigging believed in me. I fought the urge to look away from them. Instead, I centered myself in the collective until its resolve became mine.

"What happens after I destroy the glass pendant?" I asked.

"That will depend on Dhuul," Marlow said. "Should he emerge before the portal fails, we will need to act. Part of our work here has been to cultivate a Word. A single, powerful note similar to that which brought the universe into being, that delivered order from chaos. Speaking the Word will drive Dhuul back. And without Lich to hold open the portal, it will collapse in Dhuul's wake."

I sensed a thought move through the collective.

"It will destroy us as well," I said, voicing the thought. But of course it would. No one could survive the power of creation, not even through a collective. The Word would blow us apart.

Are you still willing? my father asked in my head.

The chances of returning alive had already been slim, but if we reached a point where the Word needed to be spoken, it would at least mean we had succeeded. I wouldn't be alone in my sacrifice, either. I would be with my father and the highest echelon of magic-users.

I am, I answered.

He nodded. "Arianna will remain here," he announced. "Should we succeed in our mission, but fail to return, it will become her duty to locate the remaining magic-users of the world and reestablish the Order. She'll look after Tabitha as well," he said with a wink that made me smile despite the terror pounding through me.

A pair of automatons entered the room, each carrying a large goblet.

"The time is upon us," my father said. "We will drink and prepare to depart."

The automatons handed the goblets off at the end of the pool. The goblets made their way down, each member of the Front taking a sip, as though the potion was a kind of communion wine. When my turn came, I did the same. The potion was plain-tasting, but I felt its magic immediately, enveloping my mind in a protective field. I understood now that when my father had closed his eyes on our walk here, he had instructed the automatons to add an essence of cannabis to the potion.

"Don your robe," he said to me.

As I pulled the robe of John the Baptist over my head, I noted how everything had come full circle. I'd first donned the robe on my journey here, in search of my mother's killer and the book I'd been told sustained him. Both lies. Instead, I found the truth, a community, and a father. Now I would use the same robe to find and destroy the liar and help cast Dhuul from our world.

My father handed me the sack of artifacts. I took it and secured it in my belt.

"Wait a full minute after we've entered," he said. "We'll push the fight to the edge of the pit. That will give you ample space when you come through. But you must make your way to the fortress quickly."

"I understand," I said.

He squeezed my shoulder, gray eyes peering into mine. "I'll see you there."

He stepped onto the edge of the pool with the others. Power

emanated from the ends of their wands. As though by unspoken agreement, they dropped in at the same time, the pool swallowing them without a splash. Light flashed from the water, and then only Arianna and I remained.

"Do you have anything to give me this time?" I asked with a shaky laugh.

I was cloaked now, and it seemed to take her eyes a moment to focus on mine. "Not this time, no," she said. "The only way, Everson, is to trust you have everything you need."

I could feel my analytical mind wanting to discount the words as meaningless, but she was right. At this point, that was the only way. I tightened my belt and adjusted my grip on my sword. Then I climbed onto the edge of the pool, my heart booming like a base drum.

I could feel Arianna behind me, watching.

"Thank you," I said, and dropped into the water.

I experienced a stomach-dipping feeling of falling. Something rammed into my side—the ground, I realized—and I began to roll, black toadstools breaking around me. I finally came to a stop at the bottom of a hill. As my vision steadied, I stood and got my bearings.

Away to my left, the pit to Dhuul belched bile-green fumes. Marlow and the other magic-users advanced on it, bright energy flashing from their wands. Shadow creatures were emerging from the pit to meet them, inky energy spewing from their tentacled forms.

Take your staff, a voice sounded in my head—my father's. *It's clean.*

I looked around and spotted the slender wood staff several feet ahead of me. I retrieved it and then cleared an area in the toadstools. In the spongy earth, I etched a casting circle and filled it with copper filings. In the center of the circle, I placed the strands of Lazlo's hair, aimed my staff at them, and incanted. Light swelled from the opal as it absorbed the hair's essence.

Seconds later, the staff kicked in my hands and pulled me toward the pit, which made sense. The lion's share of Lazlo's soul was somewhere inside the portal, maintaining it. But by concentrating into the spell, I could feel another force splicing from the main pull. And that force was directing me to the keep on the opposite side of the pit, directing me to the glass pendant where the rest of Lazlo's soul was being held to give Lich life. It was here.

I glanced over at the battle. The shadow creatures had surrounded the magic-users but were keeping their distance as white magic burst from wands. Flesh-colored bats shrieked and circled above. In the collective mind, I could feel the magic-users' straining efforts. I had to hurry.

Eyeing the plain around the pit, I chose my route. With the creatures' attention on the magic-users, and the robe of John the Baptist to hide me, I set off, staying well away from the action. I checked myself as I went. The small sack of magical artifacts swung from my belt while my coin pendant did the same over my chest. I had my staff back, my sword now sheathed inside it.

The only way, Everson, is to trust you have everything you need.

Holding to Arianna's words, I rounded the pit, jumping oozing rivulets that coursed from the hills and flowed toward the abyss. The battle raged like a growing storm behind me, while across the pit, the keep loomed larger and larger. It was square-shaped and forbidding, walls black with mold. A large door stood in the front, its portcullis raised like an upper set of fanged teeth.

Okay, he's left the front door open. Overconfidence or an obvious trap?

Certainly he had to have something defending his keep. No sooner than I'd begun considering what that could be, my right leg plunged through the toadstools. I tried to throw myself backward, but my forward momentum was too strong, and I plunged the rest of the way into water.

Wonderful.

I resurfaced with a sputter and splashed for solid ground. When the toadstools rippled in a spreading wave, I realized they hid a large pool, one surrounding the keep like a moat. I struggled harder, but it was like trying to climb out of a break in the ice. More and more of the surface kept coming apart in chunks of toadstools. As the water dragged on my clothes and robe, I felt my magic fizzling. I kicked furiously to keep my head above the surface, but the water was different here, heavier. Desperate, I aimed my cane downward.

"Vigore," I whispered, hoping for a force to propel me from the water. But my magic was waterlogged.

I stopped scrabbling and forced a pair of calming breaths. My only option was to swim for the keep. I turned and began to breaststroke, arms breaking through the floating toadstools. The pond was deep—my feet had never touched bottom—and I didn't want to think about what might be lurking beneath me. *Just have to hope the robe is keeping me veiled.*

I was halfway to the keep when the water bulged ahead of me. My gut clenched. Something large had just passed beneath the surface. I slowed and peered around. The toadstools were rippling on all sides. *Keep going,* I counseled myself. *Have to keep going.* I resumed swimming, eyes fixed on the front of the keep. Something brushed my leg. *Keep going.* What felt like a hand wrapped my left ankle. I kicked it away. *Keep going.*

When my knee sank into something, I nearly shouted before realizing I'd encountered semi-solid ground. I clawed my way up the pool's far shore, the foul water running off me. I peeked over a shoulder and wished I hadn't. My passage had stirred the bottom of the pond, and now leeches the size of small boats were flapping to the surface, their black bodies writhing over one another.

I scrambled to higher ground, water streaming from my hair and splattering onto the back of my hand.

But this water was bright red.

I raised the hand to my head and felt the slick skin of a leech. The creature, whose weight I had mistaken for water, extended down my back, its tail ending below my waist. Its mouth was attached to the crown of my head, sucking the life from me. I tried to peel the creature away, but it held fast. Panicked, I balled my hand into a fist and began hammering its head. It wouldn't let go. I could feel its body warming and swelling against mine, bulging with blood. White spots danced around my vision.

Not thinking, Everson, I scolded myself.

I stopped punching and dug into my pocket until I encountered the bag of salt Olga had given me. Tearing it open, I grabbed a handful of the salt and threw it over my back. The creature slapped against me. I took a second handful and ground it against the leech's head. The leech released me, landing with a heavy thud. I staggered the rest of the way to the keep, stopping outside the portcullis. I felt faint and my legs were trembling. I'd lost a lot of blood.

I turned toward the battle that continued to flash and rage on the far side of the pit. They were counting on me. And I'd be damned if I was going to let a leech doom the mission.

I recited my centering mantra. My prism came back quickly, perhaps for the power of the collective, and fresh power crackled through me. With a whispered *"Respingere,"* I blew the excess water from me and then sized up the entrance. No wards from what I could detect. Lich must have limited his defenses to the barrier to his realm, counting on Dhuul's shadow creatures to intercept anyone who made it through. Anyway, without the Banebrand weapon, what could anyone who entered actually do?

I tested the threshold with my cane. The opal end passed cleanly through.

I reactivated the hunting spell, waited for the cane to kick in my grasp, and entered Lich's keep.

27

I hadn't gone far when I began to encounter guards. The fish creatures appeared first, the same ones I'd been made to see in the Refuge when Whisperer magic had superimposed nightmares over my senses. Their large, incandescent eyes shifted wetly as they passed, their pupils flat lines.

I kept to the shadows, counting on the robe to hide me. When the creatures had gone, I moved on, the hunting spell tugging me deeper into the keep. One level up, I encountered a new variety of creature that oozed along on slug-like appendages. Blank eyes stared from gray heads without mouths.

I felt like I was walking backward along an evolutionary line. But that was Dhuul's objective, after all. To devolve everything, return it to chaos. These creatures may well have been human once.

Where are you? came my father's voice in my head.

Inside, I replied. *The pull of the hunting spell is getting stronger.*

Good, he said. *Use the power of the collective as you need to.*

I didn't like the pain in his voice. *How are you doing?*

Don't think about us, he said. *Your focus is the glass pendant.*

Before he could break away, I felt a member of the Front get buried beneath an assault of shadow tentacles. The Front was beginning to falter. I swallowed hard and broke into a run: down a corridor, up another flight of steps, the cane and the desperateness of the situation urging me on. Creatures stopped and turned, sensing my movement.

Screw 'em, I thought.

At what felt like the top level of the keep, I arrived in a room. I stopped and peered around. The space was crammed with bookcases heaped with old tomes and folios, papers spilling from them. Various writing implements, scrying devices, and spell items were scattered across tables. Chairs for writing and reading sat here and there. I picked my way further inside, half stunned.

I was in Lich's library/lab, yes, but I was also in the de facto headquarters of the Order of Magi and Magical Beings. And it wasn't the huge celestial hall I'd imagined, but a bachelor pad in need of housekeeping. My eyes fell to a half-finished letter to a magic-user regarding some request or other she'd made. Many of my own messages would have been sent to and from this same room. I felt like I was peering behind the curtain in Oz.

My cane tugged and pointed at the far side of the room. On a corner of one of the tables, a necklace with a lamp-shaped pendant hung from a small stand. A sickly orange light glowed through the pendant's sides. *The glass pendant,* I thought in disbelief. *I've found the glass pendant.*

I glanced around. *And still no sign of Lich.*

I pulled the sack from my belt as I sped across the room. I set the sack on the table but hesitated as I reached for the glass pendant. Strong magic stirred inside it. *Of course there's strong magic*, I thought, trying to talk down my wariness. *It's sustaining Lich's life force.*

I nodded to myself and lifted it from the stand.

The pendant began to scream.

I cupped a hand over it as though it were a mouth, but the screaming persisted. "Shut up," I hissed, encasing the pendant in a shield, hoping that would mute the sound. But no luck. The alarm was magical.

I looked around wildly as footsteps slapped up the steps. The fish and slug creatures were emerging from the stairwell and entering the room, scimitars drawn. They advanced on the glass pendant, which was pulsing brightly enough to throw my shadow against the back wall.

"Vigore!" I cried, sweeping the cane toward the creatures. As the force toppled bookcases and shoved the creatures back, I reached into a pocket for the dragon sand. I scattered it in an arc and shouted, *"Fuoco!"* Flames exploded from the sand, engulfing tomes and creatures before settling into a high wall between us.

I really had to hurry now.

I dug into the sack, pulled out a wand, and aimed it at the glass pendant.

"Disfare!" I shouted. A burst of bright red energy emerged, enveloping the pendant. But when the energy dissipated, the glass faces remained intact. The pendant continued to pulse and scream.

I exhausted the wands and moved on to the maces and amulets, repeating the invocation. But though the magic in each enchanted item was powerful, none seemed to have any effect on the glass pendant.

C'mon, dammit, I thought, digging in the sack. *It has to be one of you.*

I squinted back at the flames. The fire was keeping the creatures at bay, but it would only be a matter of time before the commotion attracted Lich—unless, of course, he was already on the battlefield, claiming souls. I was tempted to tap into the collective, to check on them, but my father was right. My focus needed to be here. I reached into the sack again.

Only one item remained: the rusty dagger.

"Please, let it be you," I whispered, and plunged the blunt blade against a glass face.

Something broke. The screaming stopped. *Holy crap—it worked,* I thought, my ears ringing in the sudden silence. But when I looked down, the pendant was intact, the glass not even scratched. It was the dagger that was in pieces.

"How unfortunate," someone said.

I wheeled to find Lich standing on the far side of the room, his back to me. The flames had been extinguished. Several of the fish and slug creatures were on the ground, burnt to a smoking crisp. The rest were arrayed on either side of Lich in a defensive formation.

"Your collaborators were counting on you," Lich said. "Now half of them are fallen while the rest hardly have strength enough to stand, including your father." A cold wind blew through the narrow window he was peering out of, ruffling his robe and shuddering my sweat-soaked body. "I'll harvest their souls in a moment, but first I want to make you an offer."

I spiked the glass pendant against the floor and tried to smash it with my heel. I grunted with the effort, but it was like trying to crush a block of granite. The magic that protected it was too strong. I called up the syllables my grandfather had left on the vault wall.

"Gug-lugal-i!" But though I drove power through them, they did nothing.

"Come now," Lich said, turning to face me. "There's no point in carrying on like that."

I looked up at him, my legs trembling with exhaustion and fear. As a last resort, I unsheathed my sword and stabbed the pendant. Lich watched me patiently, his gray, vein-mapped head canting to one side as though in pity. He signaled to his creatures to move away as he stepped between them.

"I understand your fear," he said. "When I discovered the fissure to Dhuul, when I understood his desires, I was just as revolted as you are now. He whispered of returning the world to a primordial state, of feeding on the dissolution. Horrible, horrible images, Everson."

"Yeah, so horrible that you're helping them come true," I said, giving the pendant another vain jab.

"Like I told you, his arrival was inevitable. One could either ignore that or come to the best terms possible. My siblings chose the former, leaving me to act as Dhuul's lone diplomat. Not at all what I wanted."

"Sure."

"It was a Faustian bargain, Everson, I agree. I would help deliver Dhuul into the world in exchange for the Order being spared. Understand this, though. Once Dhuul feeds on the enormous release of energy, he will leave in search of other worlds. He will leave us to rebuild *this* world, to construct new order from the chaos. Don't you see? The Order of Magi and Magical Beings will become a godhood, Everson. We will be the Creators, the life-givers."

With Lich's mind warped by centuries of Dhuul's influence, I could only imagine the nightmare world he would bring about. I peered at the horrid creatures on either side of him.

"The souls you believe I've sacrificed," he said, gesturing toward the window, "they suffer now, yes, but they will soon know power they never thought possible. And all because I was willing to look on the horrible being Dhuul, and where others saw dissolution and death, I saw opportunity."

"Opportunity for yourself."

"For the *Order*," he insisted. "The only entity I have ever truly served."

"Bullshit." I aimed the sword at him.

"I understand the enmity you feel toward me," he said, taking another step forward. "I did take your mother's life. Nothing I say can, or should, lessen that in your mind. But do know that when I entered the Refuge, it was to make the same appeal to them as I'm making to you now. They were only stalling the inevitable and, in doing so, prolonging the agony of the souls toiling below. The members of the Front attacked me, and I fought back."

"And lives were lost, yeah, yeah, yeah," I interrupted, anger spiking through me. "Do you want to know what really happened? You were the runt of Saint Michael's children. You didn't get the powers you thought you deserved, and so you went looking for them. You found the fissure to Dhuul, a being that could only emerge into our world if someone helped him. He promised you power. You jumped at it. Period. End of story. All this talk of making the tough choice for the Order is horseshit. Dhuul probably didn't have to convince you of anything, either. Didn't even have to use Whisperer magic. He simply made the offer and then let your power-hungry little mind come up with the rationalizations all on its own. You killed your brothers and sisters. *Murdered* them. Let that sink in for a second."

Lich's brows crushed downward. "I could destroy you now, is that what you want? Your power is undeveloped, your soul of no use to the effort, and yet I'm offering to safeguard it, to make you a god."

"Why?" I challenged.

"Because it's my role, Everson. I may appear different, but in many ways, I am still Chicory. I am still the one who looks after you. The only reason I kept you in the dark—*all of you* in the dark—is because I didn't want to see you destroyed. As head of the Order, I'm responsible for you."

Something like pleading took hold in his hideous eyes, and I hesitated. Lich actually saw himself as a parental figure.

"It offended me to learn that your mother and grandfather cloaked their powers from me," he continued, "that others faked their deaths and went into hiding. It offended me deeply. If only they'd listened." His voice faltered, as though threatening to regress to the little brother he'd once been. "If only they'd *trusted* me."

I saw an opening, however slim, and lowered my sword slightly. "I know you believe Dhuul's arrival is inevitable," I said. "I know you believe the bargain you made is the only way to spare the Order, but it's not." I thought about the Word my father and the others had spent centuries cultivating. I thought about them battling Dhuul's creatures below. "Please. Release the souls from the portal, and help us cast Dhuul out. It *can* be done."

"And what would become of us?" Lich challenged.

"There's a chance we won't make it," I admitted. "But the magic-users you've watched over these years will survive. The Order will survive. Isn't that what you want?"

I was trying to appeal to his paternal instincts, and for an instant, I believed he might relent. But his jaw clenched suddenly, molars bulging through the skin of his cheeks. Dark energy stormed around him as tentacles sprang from his back. "Die then!" he shouted.

The creatures, which had been shifting and murmuring while Lich and I talked, rushed forward, scimitars flashing. I battered the monstrosities with force blasts and slashed my blade at those who came too close. I didn't hold back. If this was to be my final fight, there was no sense in conserving energy. But as a second wave of attacks commenced, my vision began to waver. I was still suffering from the blood loss. How much longer before Thelonious came swooping in?

"The Banebrand was meant to prevent the ruination of the Order," Lich said from behind his horde. "It's ironic, then, that you and the others intended to use the weapon to bring that ruination about. To destroy the only member of the original Order strong enough to still be standing." He was no longer the father figure, but the gloating youngest child.

I grunted as I swung my sword through a fish-man's neck.

"Your grandfather found the Banebrand, yes. But he did a poor job concealing it. The weapon remained in the vault after his death. I acquired it—a handsome stiletto, I'm sure you've been wondering—and cast it into the pit. The Banebrand is no more. I cannot be destroyed."

I refused to let his words bury my will.

Flinging the last of the dragon sand at him, I used what strength remained in me to ignite it. Red-orange fire swallowed him, but Lich stepped through the burst a moment later, unscathed. He strode from the flames and his army of creatures. I backed from his glowing eyes and writhing tentacles. Tripping over the glass pendant, I fell against the back wall.

"I cannot be killed," Lich said, "As far as you are concerned, *I* am the Death Mage."

The tentacles seized me and wrapped me around. A smell of rot and death came off them. When Lich's withered face clenched, muscles inside the black appendages bulged. I grunted as my ribs crushed around my heart and lungs. With the pain, red lights slashed over my vision.

A blast from the sword repelled him once, I thought weakly. *If I can just summon enough power...*

My sword arm was pinned to my side, but my hand and wrist were free. I cocked them up until the blade was aimed at Lich. With the breath of air I had left, I prepared to utter the invocation ... and then stopped.

The stiletto Lich had recovered in the vault.

The symbols Grandpa had written on the wall and made permanent through magic.

A gift he had left me long ago.

In an instant of insight, the pieces snapped together. I wanted to laugh at the obviousness of it. Instead, I grunted as the ribs down my right side cracked in a goring line.

I know what they mean, I thought through the pain. *I know what the symbols mean.*

And with that knowledge, my sword stiffened in my grasp and began to sing in a high and powerful note. Lich's eyes canted downward. His tentacles softened and writhed, as though in distress.

I drew a choked breath and uttered, *"Vigore."*

Rose-colored fire exploded from the blade and plumed against Lich's chest. He screamed as the force sent him into a backward roll, tar-black blood spilling in his wake. I fell to the floor at the same moment he landed against the far wall. The tentacles that had been torn from his body twitched and slapped over the burning floor between us. The sword was still in my grasp, still glowing.

The creatures fled, while Lich moaned and tried to push himself upright.

"There's an ancient Hittite story," I grunted through my jagged breaths. I staggered in a circle in search of the glass pendant I'd kicked with my heel moments before. "Known mostly to scholars … mythologists. Goes like this. Poor farmer raises prize ram. Greedy king wants ram for himself. Farmer coats prize ram in mud, then cleans and festoons common ram from his stock. King's soldiers come and take common ram. Farmer gives prize ram to son."

Lich sat against the far wall, a tarry pool spreading around him. I spotted the glass pendant behind a table and used a foot to drag it out by its chain.

"King never knows the difference," I finished.

I'd been wrong in the vault. The symbols Grandpa had etched were Akkadian syllables, yes, but when that script had been adopted by the Hittites, the symbols became logograms: entire words. In this case, *gug lugal-i* meant "ram to king." Grandpa had encoded his actions in the Hittite story. A story that, as scholars of mythology, we both knew.

I held the sword up. Fresh rose-colored light bloomed along the blade's glinting edge. It had taken a few moments, but across the room, understanding finally dawned in Lich's eyes. The king in this case was him; the prize ram was the Banebrand weapon. Which meant the stiletto in the vault had been a fake. The blade Grandpa had passed to me was the real item.

"N-no," Lich stammered. "No!"

He threw his hands forward, fingers writhing. Inky black magic spewed from them and coursed across the room. But upon reaching me, the magic broke apart, killed by the Banebrand.

I positioned the glass pendant between my feet and, gripping my sword in both hands, squared my body to Lich's. "For your crimes against the Order of Magi and Magical Beings, including the murder of my mother, Eve Croft, I sentence you to the ultimate penalty."

"I can give you eternal life, infinite power," he babbled. "Anything and everything you've ever—"

"Disfare!" I shouted and drove the blade down. The tip crunched through the glass face, and, in a blinding flash, the glass pendant blew apart. I fell against the back wall and landed hard.

I looked up in a daze as slivers of light streamed from the glass pendant in a celestial show. They were the souls Lich had entrapped. Their beauty stole my breath. In them, I saw the wrongness—the absolute wrongness—of what Lich had done. Such things were never meant to be imprisoned.

The souls encircled me on their way from the keep, healing me. And in them I felt the wisdom and power of those who had come before, all the way to Lich's siblings: the original Order.

One soul lingered.

"Lazlo," I whispered.

You found me, he said. *Now see that it is ended.*

The final light, Lazlo's light, streamed off, and the ruined room dimmed. The glass pendant lay in pieces beyond my outstretched legs. Beyond it, against the far wall, slumped a rotting corpse, black toadstools and mold already growing over it, consuming it. The only thing streaming from Lich's body was a dark, putrid liquid. He had no soul of his own, after all. He'd pledged it to Dhuul long ago.

The earth shook.

I pushed myself to my feet and made my way to the narrow window beside Lich's body. The pit yawned in the middle of the nightmare landscape below, but the matrix of souls that had held it open was no more. The sides were shuddering and sliding down, taking the shadow creatures with them. What remained of the Front backed from the far side of the pit, carrying the fallen.

The magic-users were too far away for me to distinguish the living from the dead.

Marlow? I called into the collective. *Father?*

28

Father? I tried again, but something seemed to have disrupted my connection to the collective. The keep shuddered and rumbled around me. I spun to find cracks spreading in the walls, chunks of stone falling from the ceiling. Without Lich to sustain them, his creations were falling apart.

I fled down the stairs as a wall collapsed behind me.

"Protezione!" I called. More stones broke over the spherical shield that took shape around me. I darted and leapt my way down, bursting from the keep moments before the entire structure collapsed.

Without breaking stride, I aimed my sword behind me and shouted, *"Forza dura!"*

The force launched me like a cannon ball. I cleared the leech-infested moat, landing in the toadstools beyond. I rolled for several yards, sprang up, and stumbled into a fresh run. By the time I reached the other magic-users, I was out of breath, heart hammering. I removed the robe of John the Baptist.

Only half of those I'd arrived with remained. The others lay in a solemn line.

"What happened to—?" I started to say, but several of the magic-users silenced me with fingers to their lips. They stepped apart, and I saw Marlow kneeling, facing the pit, power warping the air around him.

Joy and relief flooded through me.

"He's forming the Word," a woman whispered to me.

It took a moment for the message to register. "But I destroyed the glass pendant," I insisted. "The pit is collapsing." I looked beyond my father to where the hole in the earth rumbled and coughed.

"Dhuul is emerging faster than the pit is failing," she said.

I stopped to listen. I could hear him, the ancient being's whispers climbing like an ungodly force of nature, growing louder, more terrible. We had no choice now but to speak the Word, to repel Dhuul and collapse the hole to his realm. My father, the rest of the magic-users, me...

We would all perish.

But the world will be spared, I reminded myself. *That's what matters.*

I thought about Vega and her son and all of the good and decent people I had known. Then I thought about my mother, who had died in service to them. I thought about my grandfather, who had sacrificed himself so Lich wouldn't find the Banebrand. I watched my father, the vast pit rumbling and fuming before him, and the love I felt for him became enormous.

At last Marlow stood and walked over to us. "The Word is ready." His eyes glowed with magic. When our gazes met, he smiled and nodded. *Well done*, he was saying. *I'm proud of you.*

I nodded back, fighting to contain my emotions.

"You'll only have a brief moment," he said to us. "When you feel the membrane failing, Arianna will pull from the other side, but you must push. With everything you have. Do you understand?"

I looked around as the others voiced their understanding.

"Are you saying we can destroy the pit *and* return?" I asked.

"You will return," my father answered.

"You're not coming?"

His sober look told me everything. As the most powerful magic-user, he alone would speak the Word. He would unleash the impossible force that would repel Dhuul. The hope that had been swelling inside me ruptured and deflated. He held up a hand before I could say anything.

"It's the only way, Everson."

"Let me help," I said. "Maybe together we can channel the force, contain it..."

But he was already shaking his head. The hand he had raised came to a rest behind my neck. He pulled me against him. "I feel your willingness, Everson," he whispered, "but you wouldn't survive, and the sacrifice would be pointless. Arianna and the new Order will need you."

I squeezed him back, a huge knot of grief closing my throat.

After another moment he stood back, held me by the shoulders, and looked intently into my eyes. "I have to go. But I go with the joy that I finally got to see you, to know you."

His imaged blurred as I blinked back tears.

He smiled, then peered past me. "Be ready, everyone." Then to me, "Be ready."

"I ... I love you," I said.

"I love you too, Everson."

With a final squeeze, he turned and strode toward the pit. It was spouting up giant gouts of green bile now. The horrible whisper continued to climb as Dhuul stormed toward the surface to claim our world. My father stopped at the pit's edge and peered down. He looked back at us, nodded once, and before I could raise a hand in farewell, dropped from sight.

I stood stunned, then ran toward the pit. I couldn't bear the thought of him descending alone, no one to watch him. The magic-users shouted behind me. I arrived at the edge of the pit in time to see my father's flapping robes consumed by the vast darkness. The horrid whispers continued to swell, but now something was meeting it: a Word, more potent and resonant than anything I had ever heard.

Far below, a light flashed like an exploding star and Dhuul's whisper became a scream.

A blinding force rushed up and threw me back. In the next moment, the scream was buried by a roar. The pit was imploding. A new force pulled me from the pit's edge. I was back among the magic-users. They were leaning toward me, trying to tell me something, but I couldn't hear them. As the roaring grew, they began to disappear, popping from existence. I looked around. The entire realm was sliding toward the pit. Even the nightmare sky stretched and tore.

When you feel the membrane failing, Arianna will pull from the other side, my father had said, *but you must push. With everything you have.*

I glanced back at the pit where the Word continued to echo in my father's voice.

And I pushed.

29

Two weeks later

"**Y**our grandfather hid the blade's power well," Arianna said, looking up and down the length of my sword. "But it's just as you say. He removed the blade from the Banebrand, smelted it, and from the metal fashioned this."

"And set up his own double bluff," I said.

"I'm sorry, a double what?"

I had spent two days in the Refuge before returning home to grieve my father's death. I lived and relived our scant time together: his revelation about Lich, our walk together across the plain, our final embrace beside the pit. I was fortunate to have had those fleeting moments, I decided. But the fact was hard to

BRAD MAGNARELLA

reconcile with the pain of *only* having had those moments. Of never really having gotten to know the man behind the figurative mask. I spent the two weeks in a tearful fugue of thankfulness and regret until, at last, I woke up one morning—this morning, in fact—and decided to recommit myself to magic-using.

Naturally, Arianna knocked on my door shortly after.

Now sunlight streamed through her white hair as she turned from a bay window in my apartment. Though she'd adapted her attire to blend in with the modern world—a long skirt and peasant blouse with a plum-colored shawl—she still looked strange to me outside the Refuge. A place the Front no longer had to hide inside. The Front was no longer a resistance group, after all. They were no longer even "the Front." They were the Order.

"A double bluff," I repeated. "It's a concept I learned from James. My grandfather hid an enchantment inside the blade, one that cleaves magic, but beneath *that* enchantment he'd hidden the true design of the blade."

"Which could only be released by the story he'd bound it to," Arianna said.

I nodded, thinking about my staff and sword in pieces across the table at the safe house. I suspected now that Lich had disassembled it to make extra certain there was nothing inside that could harm him. All he'd found was the magic-cleaving enchantment—one he tried to warp to his own purposes, using me as his unwitting agent.

"I didn't know my grandfather was a mythologist until Marlow told me," I said. "Grandpa passed the sword on to me after I'd begun my own studies in mythology. Bound it to me." I remembered how, during our final conversation, he'd asked me to unsheathe the sword. I hadn't been watching his face, but he'd no doubt been incanting to ensure that, if lost, the blade would find me again. It had already tasted my blood. "I must have been his fail-safe."

"Your grandfather bound the blade to you, yes," Arianna said. "But through you, it was also bound to Marlow. That was how you were able to reunite and end Lich's reign."

I nodded in growing understanding: my father and I had shared the same blood. And then something even more startling occurred to me. "So ... *Lich* was the unwitting agent?"

Arianna smiled. "Even though he believed he had all the contingencies covered, Lich took a great risk in sending you to the Refuge alone. He should never have done so. But the bond between you, the Banebrand, and your father was too strong. It compelled him. And in the end, it improved the likelihood of his demise. Just as the weapon was designed to do."

I marveled at the power of the blade, but something continued to bother me. "I hate to second-guess my grandfather, but it seems like he took a huge risk, too. I mean, counting on me to find the symbols he'd left?"

"You have to remember, he was dealing with incomplete information. He assumed we were receiving his messages through his familiar, such as the location of the vault in which he'd stored the artifacts. Once he had determined which artifact was the Banebrand and made the switch, he wouldn't have told anyone, the information being far too sensitive. His focus turned to finding the glass pendant. Clearly, he never did or he would have destroyed it himself. When he felt Lich was too close, your grandfather left the clue in the vault, passed the blade to you, and ended his life. He trusted that, with the power of the blade, and enough time, you would connect with the Front and correctly interpret his message."

"Still," I said, "there were no guarantees."

"There were never any guarantees," she agreed. "Just better chances."

"I mean, I *barely* made the connection between the words and the myth before it was too late," I went on, remembering the pain of Lich's crushing tentacles, his eyes burning inches from mine.

"Your grandfather saw something else in you besides your schooling."

I pushed away the memory. "What was that?"

"Your luck quotient."

"Luck quotient?" I repeated. "I thought there was no such thing. I thought all those last-second solutions were the result of Whisperer magic."

"We told you that because a luck quotient is not a thing you want to count on. Experience is more important. However, in this situation, it was something Marlow and I and the rest of the Front were very much counting on. With time running out, it was all we had."

That explained why they had sent me into the keep alone despite my relative inexperience.

"So ... it's rare?" I asked.

"To the extent it exists in you, it is. But like I said, it can't be counted on. I'd prefer you—and us, for that matter—never to have to resort to it again. We'll start you on a new course of training once we're able to locate the remaining magic-users. That may take some time, however. Lich's segregation of the community was thorough, and he covered his tracks. Not everyone has a demonic companion." She cut her eyes to where Tabitha was snoring on her favorite divan.

That reminded me of a question I'd been pondering. "The night I faced Lich, I was blood-drained, low on power, nearly passed out from pain and exhaustion. But Thelonious never came. Is he still ... with me?"

"He remains bound to you, yes," she said, "but he shrinks from the power of the collective. With enough exposure he may decide to terminate the contract on his end and leave you for good."

"That would be nice," I said. "So I can call on the collective when I feel him near?"

"Always. But it's something else you shouldn't count on, at least not in the near term. The portal to Dhuul's realm was so deep that when it collapsed, it sent shockwaves through many realms, including this one. Small tears formed in the fabric that separates them. The more experienced of the Order have already begun repairing them, but it will take time."

"Are you saying our world is *more* porous now?"

I thought about my father's sacrifice, worried now that it had been for nothing.

"None of the tears extend to Dhuul's realm, or even close," she reassured me. "The portal is sealed. But yes, our world will be more porous for a time. Creatures who yearn to enter our world will do so more easily, and sorcerers who command such creatures will become more powerful, especially where there are potent currents of ley energy. We've restored the wards in the city for you to monitor. Your work here will become more important than ever."

Her words felt daunting. "I'll have help from others in the Order, though ... right?"

"When it can be spared, yes. Like I said, the most experienced will be addressing the problem at the source while others will be tracking down the Diaspora of magic-users. That's what is most urgent right now. In the meantime, you're to form a team."

"A team? Of magic-users?"

"Of anyone committed to protecting our world from the darkness and the creatures that darkness spawns. That was the original mandate of the Order. Our numbers are down, however. Lich murdered many, including our most powerful. We must solicit help where we can."

"I suppose I can start with James," I said, not entirely enthused at the prospect. Though he'd been a big help against Lich, our styles weren't exactly complementary.

"We're sending James out west," she said.

"What's out west?" I asked, feeling disappointment now.

"An area better suited to his particular energies. And it's what he wanted."

I thought of his cowboy hat and battered leather boots. Made sense, I guessed.

"We'll introduce you to his replacement when we have one. You'll be able to collaborate as needed."

"No more compartmentalization then, huh?" I said with a smile. "So, where do I find this team?"

Arianna looked at me as though reading an invisible cast of bones. "They will find *you*, Everson. One at a time."

I was preparing to ask what she meant, but she held up the sword. "We'll have to keep this, of course."

"Of course," I agreed.

"But know that for twelve years you wielded the mightiest weapon the Order had ever forged. Not many can say that." She smiled and disappeared the sword into a fold in her skirt and then produced a new sword. "Your father made this for you. It will fit inside your staff."

My heart cramped as I accepted the sword from her and looked up and down its length. The handsome steel blade was beveled, its edge lined with silver. Runes ran down one side. Something about the grip reminded me of our final embrace, which made sense. My father would have willed the blade into being, then imbued it with his own magic. I was, in essence, carrying a part of him.

"He designed it to better channel your specific energies. As your power grows, it will unlock certain enchantments."

"Thank you," I whispered.

"I have something else for you," she said, reaching a strong, vein-lined hand into a skirt pocket. I imagined that same hand helping deliver me from my mother's womb more than thirty years before—much as she'd helped deliver me from Lich's imploding realm, her powers pulling me back into the Refuge. I was the last to arrive, and though Arianna hadn't said so, I sensed it had been close. When her hand emerged now, it was holding a misty orb the size of a tennis ball.

"Your mother wanted you to have this," she said, handing it to me.

The mist stirred as the orb settled inside my cupped palm. A feeling of profound warmth and what I could only describe as love overcame me. I hadn't felt anything quite like it since Nana's death.

"What is it?"

"It's an emo ball," Arianna explained. "After you were born, your mother invested it with her feelings for you. She knew well the danger of her work, and if something were to happen, she didn't want you to grow up without knowing the love of a mother for her child, for you. After Lich sealed us in the Refuge, we had no way to get it to you. But the feelings of an emo ball do not fade. They are as authentic as the day your mother put them inside."

I caressed the orb. As the mist stirred again, I felt another rush of warmth and love.

"This is incredible," I said, my voice beginning to tremble. The feeling of my mother's presence was a lot how I'd imagined it would be, but also wonderfully different. Deeper. "Thanks for safeguarding it all these years." I looked from the orb to the sword and back.

"I'll leave you now," Arianna said, "but we'll be in contact."

"And if I need to reach you...?" I asked. My mind was already going to cups and flames and special parchment paper and strange formalities, wondering how that was going to work now.

"Give us a call," she said.

"A call? You mean, like, on a phone?"

"I've left a number on your counter."

I turned to where she nodded. A rectangular business card sat on the kitchen counter beside the telephone. "Oh," I said. "Okay."

"And remember," she said as she strode toward the door, "until we repair the fissures, the world will be a little stranger."

At that moment, my fog-horn alarm sounded and the hologram upstairs began to flash red.

"Good luck," she said.

30

"What in the hell happened to you?" Vega asked.

"Oh." I touched the bandages on my forehead. "A group of teens thought it would be cute to call up their recently-deceased friend. An acid-flinging bug showed up instead. I ... was flung at."

She smirked. "In that case, you're forgiven for being late."

I started to tell her that the encounter had happened before I'd called to invite her and Tony to dinner, then decided against it. I'd take the mulligan. I slid onto the bench beside her. The venue was a popular restaurant in Brooklyn, its interior set up to look like a Latin American plaza: picnic tables arranged around a stone fountain, trikes and Big Wheels strewn about for kids to ride and fight over. "Mr. Croft!" Tony shouted as he flashed past, pumping one of the trikes like it was a scooter. He was gone by the time I waved back.

I smiled. I figured he'd enjoy it here.

"I went ahead and ordered," Vega said. "Hope you like street tacos."

"Delicioso," I said.

"In the meantime..." She lifted a sweating margarita pitcher and poured me and her a salt-rimmed glass apiece. "I think we've earned it."

The collapse of the portal had pulled with it the Whisperer magic that had begun flowing into the world. Those who had lost their minds regained their baseline sanity—or baseline insanity, in some cases. In the hours prior, the NYPD had followed through and fumigated the city with cannabis smoke. The smoke stopped the rioting in its tracks and spared large swaths of the city. The cleanup and rebuilding were another story, but it could have been a lot worse.

"No kidding," I said wearily as we clinked glasses.

I took a large swallow, glad to be out in the world again, glad to be drinking margaritas with a ... friend? Remembering my conversation with James, I snuck a sidelong look at Vega. Her midnight hair was down, spilling over the shoulders of a simple V-neck shirt that she managed to make look amazing.

Yeah, I liked her.

"Hey, slow it down," she called to her son as he zoomed past on another circuit. But Tony was too absorbed in his laughing, hair-whipping fun to hear. She frowned and shook her head.

"How's his sitter?" I asked.

"Camilla? Aside from the two pounds she gained binge-eating, she's fine."

"Caught the munchies, huh?"

"Yeah, I don't think she's ever smoked before."

That made me laugh hard enough to get Vega laughing too. As our chuckles wound down, a small fold appeared between her dark eyes and she peered around. "I'm almost afraid to ask, but what did you mean on the phone when you said New York might get stranger?"

I shared what Arianna had told me about the collapsing portal creating tears in the boundaries between worlds. The alarm that morning seemed to lend proof to that. I doubted the teens would have been able to call up a nether creature that large or mean even a month ago.

"Great, just what the city needs," Vega muttered. "What will *you* need?"

"Cooperation with the NYPD, for starters."

"Well, you have a lot of goodwill there after coming up with the cannabis idea. I don't know that there's enough money in the budget right now to pay you, though. Not after all the costs—"

"No, no, that's not necessary," I interrupted. Though Arianna hadn't explained how, the Order had funding resources going back to antiquity—resources Lich had been tapping. I used to think the grants that kept me afloat at Midtown College were reflections of the Order's relative pleasure with my work. Turned out it was just Lich dispersing the funds erratically. Remind me never to scoff at primitive beliefs in weather gods. In any case, the Order would be paying us monthly now. Even so, I planned to keep my newly-tenured position at the college, though the change meant I was going to have to start earning grants by my own sweat now.

"This is less about me working as a consultant," I continued, "which I'm still happy to do, and more about making sure we're not working at cross purposes."

"Cross purposes? You mean like the NYPD arresting you for suspected murder?"

I gave a dry laugh, reflecting back on Vega's and my first encounter more than two years ago. And now here we were, swilling margaritas like old chums. Talk about cosmic humor. "Well, yeah, that," I said, "but also getting info without going through a lot of red tape."

"Croft, the NYPD is one of the city's largest bureaucracies. There's always going to be red tape." She took another sip and licked her upper lip. "But you've got my number. If you need something, let me know. I'll do whatever I can to get it for you."

"Just like that, huh?"

"Only because it's you."

Wow, we really *had* come a long way. "Thanks," I said. "I mean that."

She nodded, and in one of the few times since I'd known her, I didn't see her as a ball-breaking detective. She was simply Vega. She seemed to shift a little nearer as she studied my eyes. "What you told me about your dad on the phone. I know that's gotta be hard."

"It's a process," I said, trying not to look away. "I'll be all right."

A silence followed where the chatter and gleeful cries around us seemed to pull back. Our gazes drifted after Tony as he went around again.

"When we moved from Ferguson Towers to the South Bronx," Vega said, "my dad got a job as a youth counselor. He was this big, imposing guy, but he was good with kids. Knew how to talk to them. He'd been doing that for a few years when a gang war threatened to break out in a park down the block from us. My dad had worked with some of the kids on both sides, so he went down to talk some sense into them, keep them from killing each other, you know? Fighting broke out anyway, and he was shot in the chest. They say he died before he hit the ground."

"I am so sorry," I said.

"I was seventeen at the time. Had sort of been at a loss as far as what I was going to do. My dad had wanted me to go to college. But at the service for him, the entire 43rd Precinct showed up, hats off, like he was one of theirs. That got me. I decided then and there to become a cop." When she looked up at me, her eyes were dry but strangely exposed. "I guess what I'm trying to say, Croft, is that the more I get to know you, the more of myself I see." She snorted and shook her head. "Probably doesn't make a lot of sense."

"It does, actually."

"The point is, I'm not going to make it harder for you to do what's in your blood, what you're clearly committed to. And if I can make it easier, I will. Consider me a part of your team."

She raised her glass as though for another toast. Instead, I leaned down and kissed her. Her mouth tensed, and I was sure she was going to draw away. But then her lips softened against mine, and I tasted the salty sweetness over them. When we separated, I felt like I was awakening from a long, pleasant dream, even though the kiss had lasted two seconds, tops.

She squinted at me. "Okay, what was that?"

My head still felt gauzy, and I had to blink her into focus. "Me saying 'thank you'?"

"I'm flattered, Croft. I am. But I've got a lot going on in my life right now. There's my work, there's Tony. I don't know if this is such a good…" At that moment, her son ditched his trike and ran up to the table. Red cheeked and panting, he clambered onto my lap.

"…idea," Vega finished.

"Did you bring your cane?" Tony asked.

"It's right here." I reached under the bench and handed it to him, my father's blade locked safely inside.

"Coool," he said, looking it up and down. "When are you coming to visit the apartment again?"

"Well, that's really up to your mom."

"Mom, when can Mr. Croft come over?" he asked.

When I looked at Vega, her head was tilted to one side, lids half cocked as though to say, *Sure, use my kid against me.* But her lips were turning up at the corners. "Is Mr. Croft free next Sunday for lunch?" she asked.

Tony trained his large, expectant eyes on mine.

"Barring any emergencies," I said. "He is. Absolutely."

"Yay!" Tony said.

"Yay," Vega echoed in deadpan, but still smiling.

Our tacos arrived, and Tony scrambled under the table and took his place opposite us. He babbled as we ate, the sound a pleasant backdrop to my thoughts about the strangeness Arianna had mentioned, the team who would find me "one by one," and the future of the Order. But mostly I thought about Ricki Vega and the beginnings, maybe, of something special.

"Who's ready for more tacos?" I asked.

THE SERIES CONTINUES...

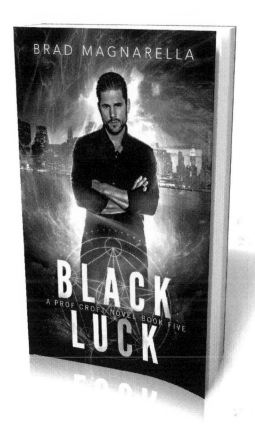

BLACK LUCK (PROF CROFT, BOOK 5)

On sale now!

About the Author

Brad Magnarella is an author of good-guy urban fantasy. His books include the popular Prof Croft novels and his newest series, Blue Wolf. Raised in Gainesville, Florida, he now calls various cities home. He currently lives and writes abroad.

www.bradmagnarella.com

BOOKS IN THE CROFTVERSE

THE PROF CROFT SERIES
Book of Souls

Demon Moon

Blood Deal

Purge City

Death Mage

Black Luck

Power Game

Druid Bond

THE BLUE WOLF SERIES
Blue Curse

Blue Shadow

Blue Howl

Blue Venom

MORE COMING!